Blood Horizon

Mark Dewar

For Jo and Betty

Table of Contents

PART 1

I shall pluck stars from the sky and place them on the sea to light a
path from
Al Andalus to Latakia

Ahmed bin Saeed the Navigator
884-952

Chapter 1

Kurtuba, 29th of Rajab in the year 338 in the Dar al Islam.
Cordoba 22nd of January in the year 950 in the Christian era.

The dead of night.

The cockroaches, gilded by the light of the pitch pine torch, looked for all the world like a rippling chain-mail collar as they gorged themselves at the mangled throat of the body. A feral cat sat in a corner of the yard carefully grooming human blood and brain from its whiskers. It had been the first on the scene after the man was dumped among the empty wine casks and baskets of rotting vegetables in the small, tight space behind the stairs that led away from the courtyard.

'So why have you got me here at this time of night?' asked General Ghalib. 'Don't you think I've seen enough bodies in my time? And another thing, why have you not pulled his robe down? No-one should be left to lie like that with everything on show. Cover him up.'

'Yes sir. Sorry sir,' said the corporal of the night guard as he bowed to the General. 'It's just that I thought you'd want to know.' He pointed to the other side of the courtyard where an oil lamp shone in a window on the first floor. 'The owner said it was important and when I got here I realised why.' The corporal tugged at the dead man's robe. It was difficult to get it down below the waist over the stiff, grotesquely twisted legs. 'I thought...'

'You thought!' said the General. 'That'll be a change. You thought that Omar Jaziri knows who's important. All he does is rent out rooms to merchants, feed them and make sure there are enough whores to go round.'

General Ghalib, the officer commanding the Alcazar guard, pulled his winter cloak close about his chest and grunted with pain as he hunkered down to have a closer look at the body.

He wasn't in the best of moods. He had been kept awake half the night by the sound of children screaming in delight and careering round the streets with their lanterns, blowing their reed flutes and banging drums.

11

They had been celebrating the Night Journey of Mohammed, the Lailat al Miraj. Some of the parents were just as bad. The crowded streets had been full of the smoke from kebab grills and mint and hyssop tea stands and the cries of hawkers selling their toys and paper birds on sticks.

The General couldn't for the life of him see why the authorities in Al Andalus allowed this festival to be celebrated in this way. The anniversary of the Night Journey should be a time of quiet reflection not this festival of noise and light and eating too much and buying toys for children that it had become here in Cordoba. It was mayhem in the city with crowds of families going to the mosques to hear again the story of the Journey then spilling into the streets to celebrate in the company of friends with spicy food and tea and lights and music and noise. Thank God it was over for another year.

The General's breath hung over the corpse in the pale, chill moonlight. It wasn't just the man's throat that had been cut. The side of his head had been opened up from crown to ear with a single blow from some kind of heavy sword or axe. Under the shimmering crust of cockroaches Ghalib could see the yellow bone of the skull which had been sliced open like a melon. He could see into the cavity where the cat had had its meal. The General reached out, grabbed the man's chin and rolled the grey-blue, lifeless face towards him. As the cockroaches scuttled he gasped in horror and looked up at the corporal who nodded in confirmation.

'Here,' he said to the corporal. 'I've seen enough, help me up. This cold has made my knee lock completely.'

He motioned to one of the guardsmen who was gawking at the body.

'You! Get rid of that bloody cat.'

The General stared again at the dead man's face.

'Let's go and see the owner then shall we?'

'He's in his office on the other side of the courtyard,' said the Corporal pointing at the narrow entrance to the yard. 'It's through here.'

'I know where Omar Jaziri's office is,' said Ghalib. Turning back to address the corporal he lowered his voice. 'You said Omar told you it was important. Did anybody else realise who this is?' The corporal shook his head.

'I don't think so sir, but from his robes I would guess a few people would have thought he was no ordinary sailor. I think that's what Omar meant.'

12

'Make sure you keep this quiet,' said Ghalib. 'I don't want people knowing who this is until I've had a chance to investigate. Get a message to the Vizier in the Alcazar. Tell him I need to brief him about something very important. Say that I would be grateful if he would wait in his office until I get there. Also, find Lieutenant Tariq Haytham and tell him to come here straight away. And if anyone asks, we've found the body of a sailor... that's it. Do not tell anyone who this is. If you do I'll have your guts. Do you understand?'

'Yes sir,' said the corporal who turned and was gone.

Chapter 2

Lieutenant Haytham lay in the shallow hot water pool of the old Yemeni's bathhouse which was tucked into a narrow alleyway in the oldest part of the city not far from the Great Mosque. Old Yousef had run the bathhouse here for as long as anyone could remember.

The place was empty save for Haytham who until now had had the three pools, cold, warm and hot, to himself. The hot water pool was in the smallest of the three rooms and the heady scent of sandalwood-perfumed massage oil warmed by candle burners filled the air. The oil lamps picked out the shimmering tiles of the mosaic walls. Haytham floated in the centre of the pool as the piping hot water steamed gently around his glistening body.

This ancient bathhouse could provide a sanctuary from the hot weather of the summer but now, in the middle of winter, the hot water pool could thaw tired, cold limbs.

High above the room several small, round windows were cut into the rock ceiling and cold moonlight shafted through whenever the cloud cover moved across the sky. As the moonlight penetrated the room it turned the rising steam into a silver mist and glittered on the surface of the water casting Haytham's shadow on the bottom of the pool.

The only sound inside the room came from the rats which chattered and shrieked as they lapped at the blood which had flowed from Haytham's lifeless body. His skin had turned purple from the heat of the water and his head, almost completely severed, hinged backwards taking his face under the surface of the water where his eyes gaped like duck eggs in the gentle ebb and flow of his long black hair. Several of the rats which had swum out to the body were busy clambering over Haytham's torso which bobbed up and down as they closed in on the massive wound at his neck. At the bottom of the pool, glinting in the moonlight which pierced the blood-stained water, lay the dagger that had ended his life.

Chapter 3

As the General walked slowly across the cobbled courtyard he clenched his teeth and pulled himself up to his full height. He was determined to fight his limp. He wasn't about to let Omar Jaziri see that he was in pain... or for that matter any of the rabble of mule-drivers who were huddled at the softly glowing braziers around the edges of the courtyard.

In the light of the pitch pine torches Ghalib could make out the funduq's central fountain with its horse trough and the solidly built, galleried booths which looked into the courtyard from three sides. He could see the stout wooden doors in an impressive arched gateway in the centre of the fourth wall.

This funduq was one of the main centres of commerce in Al Andalus. Here in the booths directly facing the gates, merchants could hire spaces to receive their customers. Some very wealthy traders even had private counters with their names on boards on the pillars. To the right and left were secure warehouses, strong rooms and stables. The upper two floors were bedrooms and suites opening to small balconies which also overlooked the courtyard. The place reeked of pack-animals, wood smoke and money.

The funduq stood just inside the city wall at the Bab al-Jadid in the south east of Cordoba. This gate to the city was the terminus of one of the most important caravan routes in the Caliphate of Al Andalus, the main thoroughfare from Caliph Abd al-Rahman III's capital to Jayyen and from there to his naval port of Almeria on the Mediterranean coast. Scores of merchants plied this route from the seaboard to the capital and they all needed a place to stay and do business in Cordoba. With his funduq Jaziri had built up one of the most important of all the merchants' inns and dealing houses in the Caliphate.

General Ghalib pulled himself up to his full height, reached inside his cloak to pull his leather jerkin down over his paunch, pushed open the door and stepped into the office. Omar, a tall, angular man whose bird-like movements were too quick for his own good, rose hurriedly, almost toppling the oil lamp which illuminated the piles of documents that covered his desk and every shelf in the room.

How can anyone work in this chaos? thought Ghalib.

Try as he might, Omar couldn't disguise the look of fear which swept across his thin face at the imposing sight of the General framed in the doorway standing with his left hand on the hilt of his short Frankish sword. The rich silver embroidery on Ghalib's cloak twinkled in the lamplight, as did the silver brooch which attached the short peacock plume to his jet black bearskin hat. Ghalib's luxurious moustache glistened as black as his hat as he curled his lip at the sight of Omar who, having steadied the lamp, stood nervously cracking his knuckles.

'*A salaam u aleikum,*' said Ghalib.

It was all Omar could do to blurt out the answer. '*Wa aleikum a salaam.*'

'So,' said Ghalib. 'Perhaps you can tell me what's going on and why you had me called out in the middle of the night to see a body in your stinking back yard.'

Omar couldn't look the General in the eye as he spoke. 'I hope this won't take long General,' he said, fighting to control his voice in his scrawny neck. 'The man was not staying here at the funduq. He was visiting one of the guests. I think you should be able to…'

'Oh you think do you? You're the second thinker I've met tonight. You think he was a navigator, but how do you know? You seem to think a lot. And, who exactly do you think you are, telling me what to do? Do you think I have nothing better to do than be involved in the death of every whoring visitor who gets his throat cut just because you *think* I should?'

Omar looked at the floor.

'We know exactly what goes on here,' said Ghalib, 'so you'd better be careful… very careful. Do you understand me? One word from the Vizier to the Suq Inspector and your premises are closed. Then you'll have something to think about.'

As General Ghalib watched the colour drain from Omar's pinched face the call of the muezzin to the dawn prayer cut through the cold air to start the new day. Ghalib turned on his heel. He had wanted to pray at the Great Mosque of Cordoba by the Alcazar this morning but that would have to wait.

He looked at Omar. 'Before everyone disappears to the mosque get anyone who spent time with this "navigator", as you call him, here in your office. I shall want to talk to them all. I have a guard on your gate. No-one is to leave here until I say so.' Omar swallowed again, nodded and took his leave. As Ghalib watched him walk across the courtyard from the office window he wondered what on earth Suhail bin Ahmad, the Admiral of the Caliph's Royal Fleet, had done to end up lying in the back yard of this merchants' inn with his throat cut and one side of his head hanging off.

Chapter 4

Day 2

It was just before dawn and Yunus ibn Firnas pulled his woollen cloak about him as he stepped out of his courtyard into the quiet street. He felt good. He was to see his daughter Miryam later that morning at the university but for now his thoughts were taken up by the young navigators he would meet soon in the Al Bisharah teahouse. It was invigorating working in the university with these naval officers and now they had invited him to take breakfast with them after their prayers in the Great Mosque before the start of their day's training. Hot mint tea and fresh buns would banish the morning chill. There would be banter too no doubt. These men knew how to laugh. It was almost like being a student again, he thought.

As he turned to the south-east into the Clothsellers' Row the old man looked up into the gradually lightening sky and saw the fabulous trio of the moon in the first quarter with Kaiwan, which the Christians call Saturn, and Al Simak al A'zal, which they call Spica. *What better time is there than this to be an astronomer?* thought Yunus. *So many new discoveries and people who want to apply this science. We are living in such interesting times.*

He chuckled to himself as he thought of Miryam telling him he had to slow down a bit because he wasn't a young man any more. How could he slow down when there was so much to be done? Here they were in Cordoba at the cutting edge of modern astronomy. Why should he slow down?

When he arrived at the Al Bisharah he was met by Simon the proprietor who opened his massive arms to welcome his friend. 'Yunus! *A salaam u aleikum!* How are you? Welcome my friend. Your naval officers are not here yet. Come! Come in!' He took him through between the early customers to the back of the teahouse. 'Sit here. This is their table, big enough for them and their guards. I'll get another stool.'

'*Wa aleikum a salaam!*' said Yunus as he took off his cloak and hung it on a peg in the wall. He shuddered and rubbed his hands and said, 'It's good to get into the warm.' He breathed in the scent of freshly baked pastries and mint tea as he looked around in the hubbub. 'You're quite busy for this time in the morning.'

'Yes, thank god,' said Simon wiping his hands on a cloth that hung from his belt. 'I can't complain, the suq porters come in early and the place will fill up soon when people get here from the mosque.'

Yunus nodded to a small table just inside the entrance to the teashop where a man sat alone. 'He's a strange looking one isn't he?'

The man was wearing a thick hooded burnus of black wool and had the hood pulled down over his eyes. He had heavy beard which made his face disappear in the dark of his headgear.

'Oh him,' said Simon. 'Yes. He comes in most mornings. He hardly speaks to anyone and spends ages over one cup of hyssop tea. One of the beggar children comes to him every day and gets a couple of coppers from him so he can't be all bad. They say he works at Camp Maaqul. He leaves every morning at the same time and takes a basket of barad with him to the camp. So he's not a bad customer. But never mind him, here are your navigators. Listen to them laughing!'

The four navigators and their three guards came bustling in the door. '*A salaam u aleikum*, Simon!' they cried then they spotted Yunus at their table. '*Shaikh Yunus!*' shouted one of them, Siraj. 'Welcome shaikh. You must eat and drink with us.' Simon returned their greetings and went to bring them mint tea and pastries. 'Simon, bring barad too,' Siraj shouted, 'We know Shaikh Yunus has an appetite for your barad. Here Bandar, you sit here next to the wall so no-one will bump your injured arm. Shaikh Yunus ask Bandar what happened!'

While Bandar looked sheepish the rest of them laughed uproariously and even the three guards joined in. Yunus saw that Bandar was cradling his right arm and that his sleeve was wet from where he had washed himself before going in to the mosque but now blood was beginning to seep again through the stained sleeve of his robe.

'So what happened then?' asked Yunus.

'He got savaged by a tiger,' said Siraj and the others started to laugh again.

'Be quiet,' said Bandar who was obviously not enjoying this joke as much as the others. 'I tried to stroke a cat early this morning and I got clawed for my trouble. It's actually really painful.'

'Aren't you going to see the Vizier this morning before you go to the university?' asked Yunus just as Simon arrived at the table with a tray of mint tea and pastries.

'Barad for you Yunus,' said Simon

'Yes,' said Bandar, 'Vizier Hasdai has asked to see Siraj and me.'

'Thank you Simon,' said Yunus and turned to Bandar. 'The chances are he will treat your arm for you. He is an accomplished doctor. Do you know how long you will be with the Vizier?'

'I am sorry,' said Bandar, 'I don't, in fact I have no idea what he wants to see us about.'

'I hope it doesn't take too long,' said Yunus. 'We have a good deal to do at the university today. I suppose the Admiral of the Fleet will join us there.'

'We don't want to be with the Vizier for very long,' said Siraj with a grin, 'when we could be spending the time with your charming daughter.'

Yunus didn't quite know how to take this quip from the man from Qartajana. 'Well,' he said, 'be that as it may we had better get on now. Finish your breakfast and we can go to the university while you two go and see Vizier Hasdai.'

Chapter 5

The pine log fire crackled in the fireplace bathing the room in warmth and keeping at bay the chill of the pale morning light which streamed in at the window. The three men were in the Vizier's office a short distance from the Crown Prince's private wing in the Alcazar, the royal palace in Cordoba.

'Now this may sting a little,' said Hasdai ben Shaprut.

'Your Excellency, they told me that you were a diplomat not a doctor,' said Bandar bin Sadiq, the Vice-Admiral.

The giggle of his colleague Siraj bin Bahram soon stopped under a glare from the Vizier.

Bandar winced as the Vizier and chief diplomatic advisor to the Caliph of Cordoba rubbed his arm with a damp cotton cloth.

'I am,' said Hasdai his brow furrowed in concentration. 'This is more of a hobby.'

'Look,' said Bandar quickly, 'it's really nothing. It's just a scratch.'

'Then why are you pulling your arm away?' said the Vizier. 'Try and keep still. And why do you think this is so amusing Siraj?'

'I am sorry Your Excellency. It's just that I am not used to seeing Bandar like this.'

'I think if you laughed less and observed more you might learn something of the benefit of hygiene in medicine.'

'Yes sir. I'm sorry sir.'

'What is this stuff?' said Bandar as Hasdai dabbed at the wound.

'Hmm? Lavender and thyme with a little chamomile. It is supposed to help to clean it.'

'Supposed to? How long have you had this hobby? Please tell me that you do know what you are doing.'

'How did you say it happened?' said Hasdai.

'I got scratched by a cat,' he said through gritted teeth.

'It looks like you've been wrestling with one of the animals from the Caliph's zoo,' said Siraj.

'We can do without your flippant comments Vice Admiral,' said Hasdai to Siraj as he patted the bandage he had applied to Bandar's arm.

'There…that's it. Just keep this bandage on and try and keep the wound clean.' He set the bowl aside, ran his fingers through his thinning hair then smoothed his square-cut beard.

'Thank you, Your Excellency,' said Bandar as he rolled down the sleeve of his robe. It was his turn now to glare at Siraj.

'Right, there are a few things we need to talk about before we go in and see the Crown Prince. Sit there,' said Hasdai. He nodded to a stool next to Siraj then reached over to his desk to pick up a string of exquisite amber prayer beads on a silver chain which lay beside the inkwell.

The Vizier saw the look of confusion which flickered rapidly across Bandar's eyes as the two Vice Admirals looked at each other.

'Yes Bandar bin Sadiq,' he said. 'I *am* Jewish. But these were a gift from the Caliph himself. He thought they might make me more patient. Let's hope he was right eh, Siraj?'

'Yes Your Excellency,' the young man muttered and cast his eyes down at the table which was covered with maps and star charts.

'Why is the Crown Prince still here?' Bandar asked quietly.

'What do you mean?'

'I thought the court had moved to the new palace at Madinat al-Zahra.'

'It has. At least the Caliph has. But the Crown Prince prefers it here. He wants to keep his office in Cordoba; especially during the winter. He thinks it's warmer. I have to say I agree with him about that.'

'So you have to go backwards and forwards between the two. That must be difficult,' said Siraj.

'It's not *that* far,' said Hasdai, 'for a patient man.' He looked at Siraj for a long moment then pointed at the documents on the table. 'Now, tell me what's happening.'

Siraj smoothed one of the charts and turned it round to face the Vizier. He pointed to the southern coastline of Al Andalus.

'Well, as you know in order to support the main military campaign it has been necessary to ensure there are four hundred horses ready for the cavalry regiment. So we've sent four boats as an advance party.' He pointed at the map again. 'The boats set off thirty days ago from Almeria, here, for Malta, where they'll regroup before sailing on.'

'Did all four ships set sail at the same time?'

'Yes Your Excellency,' said Bandar, 'both troop carriers and the two ships carrying the horses. I must say I am slightly envious of their voyage to Malta.'

'Why's that?' asked Hasdai.

'That was my first command. I captained an escort for some traders to Malta. I stayed there for three months.'

'Let's keep to the business in hand,' said Hasdai and clicked his beads along their chain. He looked up at the Vice-Admirals. 'I don't know why the Khazars couldn't supply all the horses.'

'Well, they could have done, sir, but our officers in the advanced guard wanted their own mounts,' said Siraj. 'They wanted Barbary horses.'

'They would, wouldn't they,' said the Vizier. 'So how many men have we altogether?'

'Well, not counting the four hundred oarsmen we have six hundred men in total,' said Bandar.

'Where are they now?'

'Well sir they should only be a few days away from Malta. With good winds they may even be there already although we haven't had any birds back yet. The flotilla sailed from Almeria to Ténès on the Barbary Coast. From there it will have sailed past Algiers, round the cape at Tunis to Pantelleria and then on to Malta. As soon as they arrive in Malta they'll send messages to both Cordoba and Almeria. We've made sure they've got enough sets of carrier pigeons with them.'

Hasdai peered at the chart then put a finger on it. 'That's Malta there isn't it?'

'Yes sir,' said Siraj. 'Once we get their message it will take us six days to get from here to Almeria and then another ten days to get the main fleet under way.'

Bandar rubbed his bandaged arm. It was beginning to itch. 'You know Your Excellency, it really is rather inconvenient for us to be here right now. This is taking up valuable time that could be better used preparing the fleet.'

Hasdai sighed and looked up from the charts. He looked from one of the navy officers to the other as he clicked his beads quickly along their chain. 'We are not really interested in your convenience Vice-Admiral,' said Hasdai in a voice which chilled them both. 'You have no choice in the matter. The Crown Prince wants to brief the Admiral of the Fleet personally on the latest intelligence from Baghdad. The Caliph is returning to Cordoba to host a reception in your honour before you depart for Almeria.'

'I'm sorry Your Excellency, it's just getting on my nerves being under guard all the time. The only place we are allowed to go is the Al Bisharah teahouse and even there our escort comes with us. We are spending most of our time stuck at the University being taught astronomy by a woman and her elderly father,' said Siraj.

'Tell me Siraj bin Bahram, are all the navy officers from Qartajana al Halfa as careless with their words as you are?' said the Vizier trying to contain his anger. 'That "elderly father" as you call him, is the Astronomer Royal,' said Hasdai, 'and "that woman" has developed something that just might win this campaign for us. The least you can do is listen to what she says.'

'I'm sorry,' said Siraj. 'But to be honest it is a little difficult concentrating on what she's saying...if you know what I mean, Your Excellency.'

Hasdai knew exactly what he meant and bristled as he thought of this man fawning all over Miryam. It had been weeks since the Vizier had had any time alone with her.

'Look, the Crown Prince and I appreciate you are keen to set sail,' said Hasdai, 'but the work Miryam and her father have being doing to develop their new navigation instruments might well be critical to the success of your mission.'

Bandar stepped in to stop his colleague from talking. 'We've been extremely impressed with their work. They teach well.'

'Indeed,' said Hasdai. 'How have your men been getting on with the training?'

'They are good men, sir, but it is frustrating for all of us. Navigators want to navigate, not be stuck here miles from the sea.'

Siraj checked himself as he sensed Hasdai's impatience in the rapid clicking of the beads. 'To answer your question Vizier, the training is going well,' said Bandar.

'Good. And I trust they are keeping out of sight and behaving themselves?'

'I've told them that they are to remain in their rooms after evening prayers.'

Hasdai nodded. 'It is very important they continue to do so. We don't want any more people than necessary to know they are here, and we especially don't want people knowing what they are being trained on.'

'I've been meaning to ask, Your Excellency,' said Siraj, 'why is there so much secrecy about this astrolabe? I mean I hardly think Miryam and her father are working for the Baghdadis.'

Hasdai breathed deeply. 'Let's just say we've learnt to be cautious. The Crown Prince is keen to restrict awareness of the astrolabe. Just in case Baghdad is a little closer than we think.'

'Ah,' said Bandar, 'I see. But help me understand something else Vizier. You're a diplomat. I'm surprised you are supporting this mission.'

'What do you mean?' said Hasdai.

'Well, if this campaign is a success it will mean hundreds if not thousands of Baghdadi troops will be killed.'

Hasdai sighed. 'Vice-Admiral, you help *me* understand something. Why do all military men judge success in terms of the scale of death and numbers of bodies?'

Bandar shrugged and looked at Siraj who had the sense now to say nothing.

'The reason I support it,' said Hasdai, 'is because I truly believe this astrolabe is so advanced that it may give our fleet such an advantage that we can declare victory without the loss of life you seem so keen to inflict.'

'How can that be?' asked Siraj.

It was Hasdai's turn to organize the maps on the table.

'As you know about eighteen months ago we signed a treaty with the Kingdom of Khazaria,' he said spreading out the maps. 'It has taken until now for both our kingdoms to be ready, from a military perspective, to act on that treaty. Now, both the Caliph and the Crown Prince wish for the bulk of the Baghdadi forces to be thrust back towards the Persian border.'

Hasdai pointed at a map as he spoke. 'The main Khazar forces are waiting here, north of Mosul. When the main fleet and the advance flotilla rendezvous just off Latakia, the Caliph's army will ride towards Mosul to join the Khazars. Once they've taken the city they'll march on Baghdad and force their troops back towards the border. The Persians will see the Baghdadi retreat as an aggressive march on its own territory and will more than likely retaliate. Thus Baghdad will be forced to fight on both fronts as it gets squeezed.'

'We know all of this Vizier,' said Siraj. 'We worked with the Admiral of the Fleet and the generals to draft the plan in the first place.'

'Indeed you did. But what you haven't been party to, until now, is that the main fleet isn't following the same route as your advance party.' The Vizier paused to allow the significance of his revelation to sink in.

'It isn't? Why on earth not?' said Bandar. His cheeks flushed red as he looked at Siraj.

'Because that is exactly what popular wisdom, or rather popular navigation wisdom would dictate,' said Hasdai. 'And it is precisely what Baghdad will be expecting.'

'I don't understand,' stammered Siraj, 'Surely we have to know where the ships under our command are heading?'

'I completely agree,' said the Vizier looking from Vice Admiral to the other, 'and once you and your men have mastered the art of the astrolabe, and the Admiral of the Fleet and I are satisfied with your progress, all will be revealed. Now, shall we go and see the Crown Prince? Remember you two have been chosen because of your seniority and because you worked with the Admiral of the Fleet on the campaign plan. And Siraj bin Bahram, for the sake of your head, you be careful how you speak.'

Chapter 6

'Has the body been removed?'

'Yes sir,' said the corporal of the guard.

'Good,' said General Ghalib. 'Did you get a message to the Vizier?'

'I tried Sir. But I couldn't get to speak to him. He was in a meeting with the vice-Admirals and the Crown Prince. I was told he could not be disturbed.'

General Ghalib nodded. 'Very well,' he said as he sat down on a stone bench and massaged his knee. 'I'll go and see him myself later.'

He looked around the courtyard of the funduq which was empty now save for one soldier guarding the door to Omar Jaziri's office.

'Where are the mule-drivers?'

'Omar has put them in the stables and given them some hot tea.'

'It's not like him to be so generous. And no-one has left the premises?'

'No sir.'

'Have you found Lieutenant Haytham?'

'Not yet sir.'

'Right. I am going back to talk to Omar now and I want you to be there.'

'Yes sir.'

'Who's in there with him?'

'A cloth merchant from Sevilla.'

'Good. I'll also want to speak to whoever found the body.'

'Yes sir. I'll arrange for that to happen. According to Omar the man recognised the body.'

'Recognised as in he knew who he was, or he'd seen him before?'

'I don't know sir. I think…' a glare from Ghalib silenced the corporal.

'When we're in there you leave the talking to me. You listen but say nothing. Do you understand? Nothing! Let's go.'

'Yes sir.'

As they approached the office the guard at the door first snapped to attention then stooped to open the door for his commanding officer.

When the two men sitting at the desk jumped to their feet the cloth merchant knocked over his bowl cascading tea all over a pile of documents. As Omar opened his mouth to complain he caught the General's eye, thought better of it and sat down.

Both of them were scared. The cloth merchant was fighting to control the shaking in his pudgy hands.

'Well, who have we got here?' asked Ghalib. 'Sit down.'

The men obeyed.

'So,' said Ghalib, 'he was a sailor then, was he?'

'I think so sir,' said the cloth merchant quietly.

'Speak up. What is your name?'

'Antonio sir.'

'Very well Antonio. Now what did you say?'

'I said I think so sir.'

Ghalib sighed.

'Why do you *think* he was a sailor?'

'That's what he told me sir,' said Antonio. He was twisting his head cloth in his hands.

'When?'

'When we met sir.'

'And when was that? Last night?'

'No sir. I met him two nights ago. At the bathhouse.'

'Which one?' said Ghalib, his eyes firmly fixed on the merchant.

'The one run by the old Yemeni, near the…'

'I know it,' said Ghalib. 'What were you doing there?'

'Sir, I went with one of the traders from the suq to play a game of knucklebones,' said Antonio.

Ghalib rolled his eyes.

'Gambling. If I had a dinar for every time that I have heard that death follows gambling. Who was this suq trader you went to the bathhouse with?'

'He's called Nasim.'

'How do you know him?'

'I know him from the suq. He buys burlap cloth from me to wrap up his perfume bottles when they are being transported.'

'So what happened with you and this Nasim at the bathhouse?'

'Well sir, we played several games and then two other men joined us.'

'And who were they?' asked Ghalib.

'I don't know exactly sir. But one of them was…'

'The man we found lying in the courtyard with the side of his head missing?' said Ghalib.

Antonio stared at the floor and nodded.

'Tell me what happened in the bathhouse,' said Ghalib. 'You played knucklebones is that right?'

'Yes sir.'

'You said that was two nights ago. What happened last night?'

'Last night he came to see me here at the funduq.'

'Why?' said Ghalib.

'I owed him money from the game.' The merchant hung his head to escape Ghalib's glare.

'So why did he come here?'

'I have a secure storage area here where I keep my goods and valuables,' said Antonio.

'I don't understand. If you owed him money why didn't *you* go and see *him*?'

Antonio wiped his brow with his head cloth. 'He said he wanted to come here sir.'

'What on earth for?'

Antonio said nothing.

Ghalib leant in close to Antonio and said in a whisper that cut the cloth merchant to the bone, 'If you like I can ask the others to leave so we can talk in private.'

Antonio's fat cheeks wobbled as he shuddered.

'I had arranged some entertainment for after dinner,' he said quietly.

'Entertainment,' said Ghalib. 'Do you mean whores?'

'Well, sir... yes, sir, whores.'

'Was it just the two of you?'

'Yes.'

'Speak up!'

'Yes, it was just the two of us and of course the girls.'

'So,' said Ghalib, 'you have to be my chief suspect for the murder then, don't you? And you know what we do with murderers? We nail them up in the suq.'

Now it was all Antonio could do to speak coherently. 'I didn't murder him, sir. Why would I murder him? I didn't know him, sir.'

'But you were the last person to see him alive.'

'No sir. I wasn't, sir. I left him with the whores. He was alive when I left him with the girls. They saw him alive after I did. I didn't do it. I didn't kill him.'

'Well,' said Ghalib. 'Omar's entertainments, as you call them, may be the luckiest things you've ever paid for.'

He turned to Omar Jaziri. 'I need to speak to the girls. You,' he said pointing to Antonio, 'go to your quarters and stay there until my corporal sends for you. Corporal, put a guard on this man's door.'

'Yes sir,' said the corporal. 'Come with me.'

As the cloth merchant stumbled out of the office Ghalib turned to Omar.

'Bring me the girls.'

*

A few minutes later the office door opened and the funduq owner shepherded in the three girls. General Ghalib, now sitting behind the desk, motioned for them to sit down. He was dismayed at how young they were. They must have been about the same age as his younger daughter. But unlike his beloved Khalila these girls were tired and their sunken, kohl-lined eyes spoke of a lack of sleep and the abuse which had taken the shine from their features. Their flimsy sequined clothes gave no warmth in this the coldest month of winter and they each clutched a threadbare blanket about their shoulders. With them into the room came an odour of cheap attar of roses, wine and sadness. Ghalib noticed that one of the young women had livid red bruises about both her wrists and she had long scratches on her left forearm.

'Omar,' said the General, 'bring these young ladies some hot tea and some dates. Then see to it that we are left alone to talk.'

The owner of the funduq knew better than to show the slightest flicker of annoyance at being treated like a servant in front of his 'young ladies' and went immediately to do Ghalib's bidding.

'Now,' said Ghalib gently, 'don't be afraid. I am just here to find out exactly what happened. Tell me everything that went on and everything he said.'

'Who?' asked one of the girls. 'The dead man?'

Ghalib nodded.

'Well,' she said, 'to be honest they didn't seem interested in us at all. They spent most of the time looking out of the window down into the courtyard. But that's fine for us because we still get paid. We drank some wine with them then we sang and danced for them but they really didn't seem bothered.'

There was a knock at the office door and Omar Jaziri came in with a tray of tea and a large bowl of dates.

'Put it on the desk,' said Ghalib, 'then leave us.'

The girls took up their drinks and warmed their hands round the cups as Omar backed out of his own office.

'You say you danced for them. Was there a musician there that you haven't told me about?'

'No,' said one of the girls, 'it was him, the man who was killed. He played for us. There was a lute in our room. He just took it off the wall and started to play. He could play it really well.'

'Now,' said Ghalib, 'this is important. Did the man stay on after the merchant?'

The girl with the bruised wrists hung her head and nodded.

Ghalib pointed at the livid marks. 'Did he do that?'

She shook her head. 'No it was the merchant. He just grabbed me and wouldn't let me go. He had an incredible grip. He just shook me around. He kept shaking me.'

One of the other girls spoke. 'He started to shout. All she did was look out of the window to see what he was staring at. We had to get him to be quiet. It was almost the middle of the night by this time. Eventually we calmed him down by offering him more sherry and he finally let her go to have something else to drink. I thought he had broken her arms.'

The General sighed. 'So why did he leave you? How did he go eventually?'

'One moment he was playing the lute and getting up now and then to look out of the window. Then he just went.'

'What do you mean?'

'It often happens like that. The men simply stop what they are doing and leave. The last we saw of him he was walking across the main courtyard. Maybe the murderer was waiting by the stairs and lured him into the yard. There were people sleeping in the alcoves round the courtyard. It could have been one of them.'

Ghalib chose not to react to this proposition but said, 'Thank you ladies. What you have told me is very helpful. You can finish your tea and leave now. Take the dates with you.'

*

Alone in the office Ghalib thought over everything that he had just been told. The Admiral of the Caliph's Royal Fleet had been murdered on his watch and Lieutenant Haytham who had been assigned to protect him was nowhere to be found.

Chapter 7

Crown Prince Hakam, son of the Caliph of Cordoba Abd al-Rahman III, and heir to the kingdom of Al Andalus, rubbed his temples then stood up and walked briskly to the door of the balcony and stared out at the garden. Two white doves fluttering in the orange tree seemed to hold his attention. Hasdai could hear the dry scutter of their feathers as they tried to settle. As the prince stood with his hands on his hips the breadth and strength of his upper body was evident through his elegant silk brocade robe. Like his father the Caliph, he was not a tall man but his military training had given him a solid physique allied with speed and economy of movement.

He reached up and adjusted his red silk turban then turned and strode over to the divan where he sat back against the sumptuous cushions and clasped his hands in his lap. He stared at his Vice Admirals. First at Bandar bin Sadiq then at Siraj bin Bahram. Then he peered at the charts that lay on the small camphor wood table between them. The birds had flown and the only sound now was the soft crackle of the fire which warmed the room and gave off the sweet smell of pine resin.

Eventually the Crown Prince spoke without looking up. 'How long before our advance flotilla reaches Malta?'

'Your Highness we expect to receive word of their arrival any day now,' said Bandar.

'Once they've reloaded with provisions,' said Siraj, 'they will sail down to Benghazi along the coast to Alexandria then north east towards Cyprus to the rendezvous point off Latakia where they will wait for the main fleet.'

The Crown Prince looked at the Vizier who gave the slightest of nods.

'I take it you two know,' said Prince Hakam, 'that there will be a change to our plan?'

'Your Highness, we know the plan has changed,' said Bandar. He glanced at Hasdai. 'But we are not party to the details.'

'The details are not your concern,' said the Crown Prince. 'And do not come to any hasty conclusions about the fact that they have been kept them from you. The Caliph wishes it to be this way. Only the Caliph, the

Vizier, the Admiral of the Fleet and I are aware of the plans. You will be told all you need to know in due course.'

'Of course Your Highness,' said Siraj.

'Now,' said the Crown Prince. 'When I spoke with the Admiral yesterday he told me your contacts in Baghdad had some up to date reports about the Baghdadi forces. Tell me what you know.'

Bandar reached for one of the maps and turned it around so that it faced the Crown Prince. 'According to our sources outside of Baghdad the main bulk of their forces are arranged in a staging pattern to the west of the Tigris River which is the border with the Khazar lands. From what we can ascertain from our man in Baghdad the forces are located in blocks of approximately seven thousand five hundred men every five farsakhs until just before the border…here. That's every fifteen roman miles, sir.'

The Crown prince's look was glacial enough to make Bandar shudder.

'I don't need you to tell me what a farsakh is. Now how far is the Khazar border from Baghdad?' said the Crown Prince.

'It is about ten days march sir once we take Mosul,' said Siraj.

The Crown Prince nodded and thought for a moment. 'Have your sources said anything about Baghdad's relationship with the Berbers?'

'Yes Your Highness,' said Bandar. 'According to what we've been told it is clear Baghdad has been sending agents to the Barbary Coast, but at this time we don't believe that the Berbers pose a threat to Al Andalus.'

'Good, thank you,' said the Crown Prince. 'This has been very useful. Now, I am sure you two need to get back to your studies at the University. I understand there is still much for you to do before the Caliph returns.' The Crown Prince got to his feet as he gestured towards the door. 'The sooner you and the others are able to use the new astrolabe effectively the sooner you can be briefed on our plans for the main fleet. Leave us.'

'Very good Your Highness.' Both Vice Admirals bowed low then walked slowly towards the door.

As the door closed the Crown Prince turned towards Hasdai. 'There's something about that man from Qartajana that I don't like,' he said.

'I know what you mean Your Highness,' said Hasdai, 'but by all accounts he's the best navigator of the lot.'

'Well, perhaps that'll save his neck. How much longer will the training take?'

'Well, Your Highness, if there are no distractions then they should be ready to leave for Almeria and re-join the main fleet within a few days.'

'Then tell the Admiral of the Fleet to make sure there aren't any distractions. I don't want anything to get in the way of this campaign, and neither does the Caliph.' The Crown Prince stared at the pile of charts and maps on the table. He waved an arm over the papers. 'Are we absolutely sure this will work? Nothing like this has been done before.'

Hasdai paused then said, 'Your Highness, we are as sure as we'll ever be. We've been preparing for this for almost two years.'

Prince Hakam sat back down on the divan facing the Vizier.

'Good,' he said picking up one of the maps. 'Now take me through this again will you? When the Caliph asks me why we are going against almost a century of navigational wisdom I need to be able to explain exactly why it is a good idea.' He let the map fall back on to the table. 'More importantly I need to be able to tell him why Baghdad won't see it coming.'

Chapter 8

Bandar and the three other Vice-Admirals were in a narrow, closely guarded room at the university with their instructor Yunus ibn Firnas, the Astronomer Royal, a small, bright-eyed, man of about sixty years of age whose close trimmed beard was startlingly white against his mahogany complexion. They could hardly believe what he had just told them.

'You mean,' said Siraj bin Bahram, still incredulous, 'that we'll be able to plot our latitude while out of the sight of land?'

Yunus looked at the four seamen and nodded. 'Precisely,' he said, 'and that's exactly why the Admiral of the Fleet should be here. If anyone needs to know about this it's him.'

'But where did these new astrolabes come from?' asked one of the navigators.

'They are based on a design by Abdul Rahman Sufi who works in Shiraz,' said Yunus.

'How did the design get here?' Bandar bin Sadiq asked.

'There is no need for you to know that. However what you *do* need to understand is exactly how important these instruments are and what they are capable of. I must stress that these matters must remain absolutely secret. The instruments have been manufactured under the instructions of my assistant astronomer who is, as I have already explained, my daughter Miryam.'

As they contemplated this information the navigators heard the guards outside come to attention and the door opened to admit a strikingly beautiful woman of about thirty years of age. She was dressed in a knee-length, sky-blue tunic of heavy raw silk over matching trousers which were tucked into fur-lined leather boots. Over her head and shoulders and covering much, but by no means all, of her bright auburn hair was a heavily embroidered shawl of the finest Egyptian wool. She was followed into the room by two soldiers, one carrying a stack of seven books while the other carried seven identical red leather instrument cases. The soldiers placed the books and the instrument cases on the table before the Astronomer Royal and left.

'Good morning gentlemen,' said Miryam, then she turned to her father.

'Where is the Admiral of the Fleet?'

Nobody seems to know,' said Yunus. 'You had better carry on without him.'

Miryam took one of the almanacs then opened one of the instrument cases and lifted out a calibrated brass circle with two cross-pieces. A moveable sighting bar was fastened in the centre of the circle where the cross-pieces met.

'I take it that my father has already explained that the power of these astrolabes is in that, unlike the instruments we have had available until now, they are universal and can be used anywhere at sea to determine the latitude of the observer. To put it simply, these instruments can be used to navigate the oceans on ships which are out of the sight of land.

'Let me explain. There are two ways in which the latitude of a ship may be calculated using the device and the book. The first is by measuring the altitude of the sun when it is at its zenith.' She pointed to a small round window high in one wall then held up the astrolabe. 'Let that window be the sun at its highest point in the sky. First I sight the sun along this moveable bar. Then I read off the angle of altitude of the sun. Next I look in the almanac for the declination of the sun for today's date. Do you see? Here it is on page forty six. Now I subtract the measured altitude from ninety degrees and add the declination which I read from the almanac. The result is the latitude of my ship.'

The four navigators were astounded. At last one of them found his voice. 'Is that it? Is it really as simple as that?'

Miryam smiled and nodded. 'Yes,' she said, 'except you can do it at night as well. If you locate Al Jadi, the North Star, and use the astrolabe to measure how many degrees it is above the horizon then subtract that number from ninety you get an approximate value for your latitude. It is not quite as accurate as using the sun but it is good enough to see whether or not you are still on course. You'll have an enormous advantage over other naval fleets with these instruments and almanacs.'

Yunus watched as the amazement at these revelations slowly etched itself on the faces of the navigators. These men knew the huge significance of being able to determine latitude at sea and just what the ability to set a fleet's course while out of sight of the coast would mean for the success of a naval task force.

'Good,' said Yunus. 'Thank you Miryam. Now gentlemen, can you please take your instruments and copies of the almanac. I don't need to tell you how important these things are and that you must protect them with your lives and keep them absolutely secret. You may go now. Except for Bandar and Siraj, I want to speak to both of you. Miryam, thank you. I'll see you back at the observatory.'

When the others had gone Yunus spoke. 'Now, you two are the senior officers. Can you please explain to me why the Admiral of the Fleet is missing? I needed all five of you to be here so that there could be no doubt that you all knew how to use these instruments.'

'We really don't know why he isn't here or where he is,' said Siraj, 'but I am sure he would welcome some time alone with your daughter.'

Yunus took a step closer to Siraj, fixed him in the eye and spoke in a low, precise voice. 'Vice-Admiral you have not been long in Cordoba. Perhaps you don't know the kind of very important friends that my daughter and I have. Let's pretend you didn't say what you have just said. Now go.'

Chapter 9

Hasdai stopped speaking as two of the Crown Prince's personal servants entered. One tended the fire, making the pinewood crackle and spark as the flames were coaxed into life, while the other set down a laden tray on the table. The man cut three oranges in half and squeezed their contents into a stoneware jug to which he added sugar and a cup of water. He then unfolded a damp cloth and placed it on the edge of the tray. As the door closed behind the servants the Crown Prince nodded for the Vizier to continue.

Hasdai flattened the map. 'The advance party left from Almeria and sailed east here.' He traced a route along the north coast of Africa. 'Once our men have reached Malta they should be safely out of range of the Berber pirates that operate between the African coast and Sicily. When they arrive in Malta our captain will send pigeons with coded messages. Two to naval headquarters in Almeria and two here to Cordoba. There is of course no doubt that the pirates will see our ships but they are not likely to engage such heavily armed boats.'

'They might not engage with us but they'll certainly get word to Baghdad that our ships are under way,' said the Crown Prince.

'They will indeed, Your Highness. According to our man in Baghdad the Berbers are still in the pay of the Baghdadi court. They are probably waiting for the main fleet to pass by their watching posts before they make their next move.'

'Now as Bandar bin Sadiq pointed out,' said Hasdai, 'the advance flotilla will then sail to the rendezvous point off Latakia.' Hasdai paused as the Crown Prince poured and drank down a cup of the orange juice. 'The main fleet will also leave from Almeria but instead of following the advance flotilla they'll head straight for open water.' Hasdai traced the route across the map as he spoke. 'Using the new astrolabe the main fleet will be able to navigate out of the sight of land. They will sail in a straight line east of Almeria, take a south easterly tack between Pantelleria and Malta then sail directly east again to the rendezvous point. It will be a much quicker journey and they will always be out of the sight of land except for the passage between Pantelleria and Malta.

The biggest advantage is that if the Berbers are watching the coast they won't see the main fleet.'

The Crown Prince nodded approvingly as Hasdai continued his explanation.

'Once the fleets join up the army will make landfall just north of Latakia when they have a long but fairly easy march to Mosul. Tracks and caravan routes already exist there and the countryside is not at all densely populated. The ground is well watered and fertile so there will be lots of supplies available to keep the army going. Mosul will, by the time the army arrives, be under siege by the Khazars. Baghdad's forces will be marching to relieve Mosul but when they arrive they will find not only the Khazars but our forces as well. This combined army will force the Baghdadis back towards the Persian border where they will be squeezed like a bitter orange.' Hasdai paused before adding, 'Given our overwhelming strength I'd be surprised if they didn't just surrender as soon as they realise what they are up against.'

The Crown Prince cut open another orange and squeezed it into the jug. He smiled as he rubbed the sharp smelling orange peel into his hands which he then wiped with the cloth.

'Excellent. Tell the Admiral of the Fleet I want to talk to him. Have him sent here. One more thing. Have you worked on the Caliph's address to the people yet? He will need time to approve it before he delivers it.'

'It is in hand Your Highness,' said Hasdai. 'The first draft from the Chamberlain's office is on my desk.'

'Good,' said the Crown Prince. 'I hope you are wrong about one thing though.'

'What's that Your Highness?'

'The part about the humiliating surrender of our friend the Caliph of Baghdad.'

'Sir?'

The Crown Prince placed his cup back on the tray and settled back into the divan.

'I suspect that, having sailed all that way, our men may be most disappointed if all the Baghdadis do is surrender.'

Chapter 10

The crisp afternoon sunlight streamed in through the windows of the office in the heart of the funduq. As General Ghalib looked out at his men searching the courtyard and the stables he warmed his hands around the cup of hot tea that had been brought for him. There was a knock at the door which swung open to reveal the corporal of the guard.

The General gestured to one of the stools. 'Sit down.'

The two men sat facing each other and Ghalib rubbed his aching knee.

'Did you escort the girls back to their rooms?'

'Yes sir. They are still quite shaken up but they were very grateful to you for the tea and dates and the extra blankets that you got for them.'

The General nodded. 'Have you found Haytham yet?'

'Not yet sir, no. We've got men all over the city but nothing yet.'

Ghalib frowned. 'All right, so what *do* we have?' he asked.

'Well sir, it seems that the merchant's story is accurate enough. They played chess, had a lot to drink and then left the sailor with the whores. Antonio says that was the last he saw of him.'

'And Omar Jaziri?'

'Sir, he says he was here, in his office, for most of the evening. In fact he was here when one of the staff came to report the discovery of the body.'

'And you've spoken to the person who found the body?'

'Yes sir. He is waiting outside.'

'All right, we'll speak to him in a moment. Have you got the details of who was at the bathhouse two nights ago?'

'We are getting them sir. Two of our men have gone there to talk to the owner.'

'That's good,' said Ghalib, 'we can go and meet them once we've finished here.' He gestured towards the door. 'Now, let's get this man in.'

The corporal rose, opened the door and summoned the man inside.

'Sit,' said the General. 'Now, tell me what you do.'

'I am one of the night porters, sir.'

'One of them?' asked the General, narrowing his eyes.

'Yes sir, there are three of us. The night is a busy time for us during the winter.'

'How so? The gates to the city are closed shortly after evening prayers.'

'Of course sir. What I mean is that our merchants, or their men, often spend all night tending to their goods in the stores. They always need something from us, extra wicks or oil for the lamps, or fresh hay for the horses. Speaking of which we have to look after the stables, the courtyard has to be mopped and...' The porter stopped and hung his head as the General raised his hand to silence him.

'Tell me about the body.'

'Sir, I was doing my rounds and came across the murdered man in the yard next to the staircase. I told Omar straight away. A few people started to gather round the body, until the corporal here arrived. I think they just wanted to see who it was...'

'You think? You see corporal?' said Ghalib turning to the soldier. 'I told you this funduq is full of thinkers. We should alert the universities.'

Once again the porter hung his head.

'Sir, forgive me. I just assumed that's what they were doing.'

'I don't want to hear about your assumptions. Now, tell me about the body.'

'Well sir, it's like I told the corporal...'

The porter cowered as the General smashed his fist down on the table scattering cups and papers.

'It's me who's asking the questions,' he shouted, 'not the corporal of the guard.'

The night porter was terrified and fought to control his hands.

'Now,' said the General. 'Tell me about the body.'

*

'Corporal,' said Ghalib once the night porter had been sent away, 'instruct your men to keep this Antonio secured in his room until further notice. He will have food and drink brought to him but until I have had time to investigate further I want him kept to his quarters. He will speak to no-one. Also, instruct Omar Jaziri and the three girls that they are not to go beyond the city limits until I say so. I want to know where they are at all times. In fact it might be better for them to be confined to the funduq here.'

42

As Ghalib turned to stare out of the window there was a knock at the door. The corporal of the guard opened it, spoke briefly to the young soldier outside and then closed it again. He stood watching Ghalib's back with his hands flat against the door and a look of utter terror on his face.

'Sir,' he said quietly, 'we've found Lieutenant Haytham, sir. He's at the bathhouse.'

'At last,' said the General turning round and rubbing his knee. 'Let's go and talk to him shall we? When we've done that I shall have to go and meet the Vizier.'

Chapter 11

The young soldier couldn't hold it in any longer. He vomited through his fingers into the pool and the gobbets that didn't spatter onto the mutilated corpse formed long yellow strings in the steaming, blood-crimson water of the hot water pool.

General Ghalib drew himself up, wiped his moustache with the back of his hand, took a deep breath and turned away from the tiled bath in which the naked, purple-grey body was bobbing gently. Now he remembered what the smell was like; it was mutton soup.

The General tipped his head in the direction of the body and spoke to the old Yemeni. 'Have you any idea who this is?'

'Yes sir. I'm very sorry. I know you and the Lieutenant were close.'

'Never mind that,' said the General. 'Who found him?'

'My man came to tend the boiler fire and test the waters after prayers and found him where he is now. It looks like he's been here most of the night. He's half cooked.'

'Well, we'll hook him out and have a closer look at him. We shall have to be careful, though, that the head doesn't come off altogether. Whoever cut his throat made a pretty thorough job of it. Let's get the knife out too. What's this?' he asked, pointing to a bundle on a stool by the entrance. 'Are those his clothes? Who brought them here?'

'I did,' said Yousef. 'I brought them from the changing room.'

'Is that everything?'

'Everything that was there. I can't recall whether he was wearing a cloak or not,' said the old man.

'Well,' said the General, 'he certainly doesn't need a cloak now. Keep these things safe. The bathhouse is closed until I tell you otherwise.' Yousef nodded and Ghalib turned to address the soldiers. 'Nobody comes in or out of here without my permission. Is that clear? I'll be back shortly to examine the body. If anyone needs me I'll be at the palace.'

Ghalib stood alone at the doorway to the bathhouse and slowly breathed in the cool, clean winter air while looking up at the skyline of Cordoba dominated by the minaret of the Great Mosque. The air had the sharp tang of wet stone. The General allowed himself a few moments of

44

the most profound sadness at the brutal murder of his young friend before he flung his cloak around his shoulders, drew it close to his chest and stepped out into the narrow alleyway.

He set off for the Alcazar.

Chapter 12

'Ah General Ghalib,' said Hasdai. He held the door open and waved the guard away. 'Come in. I received your message. I understand you want to speak to me. Whatever it is it needs to wait. I am sure you remember Ali. I think that what he has to say may be very important.'

The General nodded to Hasdai, wondering what could possibly be more important than the brutal murders of the Admiral of the Fleet and Lieutenant Haytham.

As he stared at the stooped, slightly-built man standing by the Vizier's desk he could see by the light of the oil lamps that his clothing was heavily stained and he was clearly exhausted.

'I thought you were working for us in Baghdad. You look all in,' said the General.

'I was and I am very tired, but my master ordered me to come back to Cordoba and report immediately what we have discovered to the Vizier. It has taken me seven weeks to get here.'

'That's not bad,' said the General as he sat on the divan and massaged his knee. 'But why didn't you send a message by bird? What is it you have to say that's so important?'

Ali looked at the Vizier who had picked up his prayer beads. 'Just sit down and tell the General exactly what you told me.'

'My master said we couldn't take the risk with a bird in case it was intercepted. He said that this information is so important that he wanted me to bring it personally.'

'Just tell him what it is,' said Hasdai, the click of his beads showing his mounting impatience.

'Yes sir, sorry sir. Just over three months ago we started to get information that something strange was happening at one of their Caliph's farms one and a half day's march from Baghdad. There were reports that prisoners were being taken to the farm as well as different kinds of animals... sheep, horses, camels, goats.'

'What's unusual about that?' said Ghalib.

'Well, in the first place the men were all prisoners who had been condemned to death. Then it was the numbers,' said Ali. 'Just a few animals and men were going into the farm, not enough for a working farm and none were ever coming out again. Nothing was ever taken to market.'

'So what did you do?' said Ghalib.

'We kept a watch on the place. My master told me to go and see what was happening. The farm is hidden away in a deep valley. There is one vantage point upwind from the farm where you can see what is going on. It was horrible. All the different animals were diseased and so were the men. They were dying like flies.'

'Are *you* all right?' asked Ghalib.

'I must be,' said Ali. 'I have been travelling for weeks. If I was infected I would be dead by now.'

'Is that all?' asked Ghalib. 'You came all this way to tell us that there is a farm full of dead and dying people and animals and that you are all right? It sounds like an outbreak of anthrax.'

'That's precisely what I thought,' said Hasdai. 'But tell him the rest. Tell him what they were doing.'

'The prisoners were practically dead on their feet but they were shearing the animal carcasses and putting the wool into small earthenware pots. Then they sealed the pots with beeswax.'

'They were shearing the dead animals? So they didn't burn the bodies?'

'No, not until they had got the wool off, chopped it up and sealed it into the pots.'

'But the anthrax in these jars would kill anyone who opened them,' said Ghalib.

'That's exactly what my master thought. They were making the disease into weapons. If the jars were opened or broken there would be an immediate outbreak of anthrax.'

'Imagine what would happen to an army if one of these jars were broken open in a camp,' said Hasdai. 'It would be decimated within days.'

Ghalib sighed deeply and shook his head. 'I have never heard anything like this in my life,' he said. 'I've heard tales of the Romans poisoning their stores and letting their enemies loot them and wells being poisoned in India but to make a weapon out of a plague. This really does tell us what we are up against when it comes to fighting Baghdad.'

'Do you know if they have been able to make a lot of it?' said Hasdai.

Ali nodded. 'We think they have, sir, yes. From what I was able to uncover it seems they've had some help in making and testing it.'

'Help from whom?' said Ghalib.

'From the Berbers sir,' said Ali. 'We think that Baghdad sent a shipment of the anthrax to contacts on the Barbary Coast. It is likely that there is a considerable quantity of it available by now.'

'What do you mean "by now"?' asked General Ghalib. 'How long have they been making it for?'

'Sir,' said Ali, addressing Vizier Hasdai. 'My contacts in Baghdad told me that Malik Al-Qadar, the Baghdadi Emissary who was sent here to Cordoba the year before last brought it with him. His ships docked in Tripoli on the way. We think the anthrax was unloaded there and given to Baghdad's Berber contacts.'

General Ghalib sighed deeply. 'I never trusted him,' he said.

'What we don't know is where it is now. It is possible that it is still in the hands of Baghdad's contacts. But there is a possibility some of it will have been sold.'

'Sold to whom?' said Ghalib.

'We don't know sir. The Baghdadi alliance with the Berbers is a strong one. But I've never met a trustworthy Berber in my life.'

Ghalib snorted. 'I think that's a bit harsh,' he said.

Hasdai held up his hand to silence Ghalib then the Vizier smoothed his hair and thought for a moment. 'This must be kept absolutely secret,' he said. 'If it gets out that Baghdad has such weapons it will cut the morale of our troops to pieces before we even set sail. Ali, go now to the barracks and rest. Speak to no-one of this.'

'Sir, will I have to go back to Baghdad?'

'No,' said the Vizier. 'I think you have done enough. I am sure General Ghalib will find something here for you. We'll get a message to your master in Baghdad. In the meantime you need to rest. Go and have some tea and barad at the Al Bisharah teahouse. Now please leave us.'

Ali took the Vizier's right hand and clasped it between his own. He bowed deeply then slowly turned and left the room.

As the door closed Hasdai turned to Ghalib. 'Now General,' he said, 'whilst we need to keep a watch on what Baghdad is up to I must say that I am extremely optimistic about things. The Crown Prince is going to

Madinat al-Zahra at first light tomorrow so I will at last have a few days to attend to diplomatic matters and hopefully spend some time with Miryam.' He got to his feet and collected his headdress from its hook on the wall beside the door. He draped the cloth over his shoulder. 'I almost forgot,' he said holding the door open. 'You wanted to talk to me. What was it that you wanted to discuss?'

The General adjusted his belt then smoothed his moustache with his fingers and said, 'I think you'd better close the door again sir.'

Chapter 13

Day 3

'Oh God,' said Hasdai, breaking at last the silence which had hung between the two men. 'The Admiral *and* Haytham! Who could have done that? And why? Especially Haytham. Why would anyone want to kill Haytham?'

General Ghalib, sitting forward on the divan with his elbows on his knees, continued to stare into the fireplace. The fire had practically burned out. It would be dawn before long and a chill air was beginning to creep out of the thick stone walls of the Vizier's office. Only one untrimmed lamp burned on the table between the two men. They were both exhausted, their faces grey in the flickering light.

The General spoke. 'What are you going to do?'

Hasdai shivered, crossed his arms and rubbed his shoulders.

'Well,' he said, 'you know as well as I do that we are going to have to get the Crown Prince to promote one of the two senior officers to Admiral of the Fleet.'

'He's bound to ask you for advice on which one to promote. Which one do you think it should be?'

'That depends really.'

'What do you mean?'

'Well, Siraj is the better navigator. According to Yunus he is very, very able but he is also much less predictable than Bandar.'

'Being predictable is sometimes not an advantage in an officer,' said Ghalib. 'I know when I was in the field I would want a man in charge who could think on his feet and adapt to changes in battle situations.'

'It's not that so much,' said Hasdai. 'Siraj is probably as good a tactician as Bandar but occasionally he just doesn't seem to be as serious as Bandar is. He may not be ready for the top position yet.'

'Either way,' said Ghalib, 'the Prince will have to decide. But you sound like you favour Bandar.'

'I shall have to think about it,' said Hasdai.

'About the Prince,' said Ghalib. 'Wasn't he supposed to be going to Madinat al-Zahra immediately after prayers this morning? I got Colonel Zaffar to ride here so he could command the guard taking him back.'

'He was supposed to be going but he won't go now that this has happened,' said Hasdai. 'So what will you do with Zaffar now?'

'Well, he could go to the funduq and start questioning the people there.'

'Very well,' said Hasdai, 'get him to do that.'

'There's something else,' said Ghalib. 'Whoever the Crown Prince promotes to Admiral of the Fleet he is going to need a close personal bodyguard. We don't want any more dead admirals.'

'I am sure you can find the right man for the job. Just do what you have to. Another thing, once we know what the prince has to say about all this and we know what he wants to do, we'll have to get a messenger to the Caliph to tell *him* what's going on.'

'I wouldn't want to be the one carrying that particular message to the Caliph,' said Ghalib with a shudder.

'No,' said Hasdai. 'Anyway... what do you think? Could it have been the cloth merchant?'

'What, that killed the Admiral? I don't think so really. He doesn't look like he has the guts to kill an ant, never mind an admiral. He was terrified when I was questioning him.'

Hasdai looked up at the General. 'I wonder why,' he said with half a smile. 'What else have you got though? What about this man from the perfume suq?'

It was Ghalib's turn to smile now. 'The perfume suq's not exactly known for breeding warriors is it? They all waft about on clouds of frankincense and musk down there with dabs of attar of roses behind their ears! They are hardly killers.'

'I don't think you can dismiss him though just because you don't like the way he smells.'

'No, of course not,' said Ghalib. 'Perfume sellers are just as capable of cutting throats as proper men are. I know who he is. I'll send for him later this morning. What are we going to do now?'

'We shall have to go to the Crown Prince and tell him what's going on. The best we can hope for is that he is already awake.'

'I think the best we can hope for,' said Ghalib in a very low voice, 'is that he is alone.'

'Indeed,' said the Vizier, shivering as he stood up. 'Let's go.'

*

When the two boys were ushered out by one of the bed-chamber guards they smirked at Ghalib and the Vizier and it was all that the General could do to stop himself from booting their behinds. Ghalib knew the guard. The man tightened his lips and gave the slightest shake of his head as he caught Ghalib's eye. The General nodded in both recognition and understanding.

Hasdai knew better than react to any of this and waited, impassive, for the summons by the prince. When it came they were shown into the ante-chamber to the royal bedroom. The domed room was draped in red silk with pale gold panels which glistened in the lamplight. The panels were exquisitely embroidered with fabulous scenes from the hunt, the bullfight and other, rather more intimate, earthly pleasures. On the ivory and gold inlaid table between the two low divans an incense burner glowed, filling the room with the heady scent of frankincense and ambergris.

As the two men stood looking at the ornately grilled window they saw the black dark of night give way to pre-dawn grey and heard the melodic call of the muezzin summon the faithful to the Fajr prayer. As if on this signal, the door to the royal bedchamber opened and Crown Prince Hakam came in. Both Ghalib and Hasdai put their hands on their heart and bowed towards him. The prince, his jaw set, was obviously seething with rage but his years of training in both battle and diplomacy had taught him to control his temper. In any case, although he was the second most powerful man in the Caliphate, he did have some respect for both the General and the Vizier and knew that there was little point in venting his anger on them. They would only be here if something significant had happened. When he sat down the Crown Prince actually forced a smile and waved them towards the second divan. They sat with their backs to the window.

'Well Vizier Hasdai,' he said, 'what can be so important as to merit the interruption of my night's rest?'

'Your Highness, we have bad news. There were two murders in Cordoba last night.'

'I am surprised there have only been two,' said the prince. 'With the number of children that have been screaming around the city I should

52

have thought that many more would have been done away with!'

'Sir,' said Ghalib, 'with respect sir, these were not children. One was a lieutenant in the Palace Guard and the other...' The General hesitated.

'Well,' said the prince, 'who was it?'

'Sir, it was Suhail bin Ahmad, the Admiral of the Fleet.'

The prince sat perfectly still looking past them to the now brightening window. In the long moments that followed the only sounds they could hear were doves cooing and scuffling in the pomegranate trees beyond the grille.

At last Prince Hakam turned to the General and spoke. As he did so the only sign of his now absolute fury, was the tightly clenched fist of his right hand. 'You will find who did this. You will bring him to me and *I* shall be the one to tell him that he shall be crucified, flanked by dogs.'

'I understand Your Highness,' said Ghalib.

'Do you though General?' asked the Crown Prince. 'Do you understand what this means for our campaign in the east... our campaign with the Khazars against Baghdad?'

'I do sir. Vizier Hasdai and I have discussed this matter.'

'So Hasdai ben Shaprut,' said the prince, 'what have you to suggest?'

'Your Highness,' said the Vizier, 'at this stage in the campaign I don't think we have any alternative other than to promote either Bandar bin Sadiq or Siraj bin Bahram to the position of Admiral of the Fleet.'

Prince Hakam fell silent and again they listened to the dry scuffling and cooing of the doves. It was now bright day and the sunlight was broken into a thousand narrow shafts by the grille at the window. Crown Prince Hakam unclenched his fist and stood up. Hasdai and the General got to their feet.

'Promote Bandar bin Sadiq to Admiral of the Fleet,' said the Prince. 'Send a message to the Caliph in Madinat al-Zahra that this has been done on my authority and that I will remain here in Cordoba to await his return. Get this message taken by a trusted officer whom the Caliph will know and speak to in private. Go now and bring the new admiral of the fleet to me. Bring the man from Qartajana too as senior vice admiral.'

'Your Highness, they should be at the university about this time,' said Ghalib.

'Well, get them here as soon as possible and make sure this Bandar is given the protection he needs. When the Caliph addresses the people in a few days he will want to bask in the glory of the Royal Fleet. Let's make sure there is someone to command it.'

The Vizier and the General bowed to the prince as he walked to the door of his bedchamber. As he grasped the handle Prince Hakam turned to face the two men and said, 'Find whoever killed Admiral Suhail and remember, *I* tell him. Crucified with dogs.'

Chapter 14

'Right, I'll lend you this but don't forget to give it back to me. You lost the last knife I lent you. Oh, and when you do give it back you can also give me the five dirhams you owe me for the musk.'

It was just after morning prayers in Cordoba's perfume suq; three narrow, winding alleyways which ran between the cloth-sellers' row and the metalworkers. The merchants were preparing for the day's business. Here palm frond shades held both the sun and breeze at bay and kept the air close; heady with the multitude of fragrances which were concocted in the perfume merchants' shops.

Ever since Ziryab the Musician had fled to Al Andalus from Baghdad in 822 bringing with him his courtly style, fashion fads and what he had called his "scented refinements for daily living" there had been merchants selling perfumes, sweet unguents, soaps and incense in these ancient, cramped alleys. Here too were the barbers and beauticians who, when pampering the well-off citizens of the capital, skilfully added the grist to keep the city's gossip mills grinding effectively. There wasn't much that happened in Cordoba that wasn't talked about, primped and embellished in the perfume suq. The serving-boys from the Al Bisharah Tea House were often run off their feet providing enough mint tea and fruit juice to wash down the scandal which was peddled in this part of town.

'Don't worry, Harun,' said Nasim, 'I'll give you your knife back. As for the musk, I weighed that and I think you overcharged me for it but I'll give you your five dirhams if you get the tea this morning. Look here's the boy coming. I have got to open up this package. I hope that idiot in Murcia has sent me the right bottles this time.' He turned from his neighbour. 'Hey! Get your bloody mule away from the edge of my stall! Look at it! Look what it's doing! And clear that up. That's one perfume I don't want anywhere near my shop. Here!' Nasim flung the muleteer an old piece of burlap cloth and a palm leaf broom to clear up the steaming dung and then sat cross-legged on the carpet, took the knife from his neighbour and started to cut through the straw ropes on the parcel of Murcian glass bottles which the mule-driver had just delivered from the funduq.

The old muleteer shook his head as he bent to his task. He hated making deliveries to the perfume suq. The merchants and barbers here were a strange lot and none more so than Nasim bin Faraj... a loud mouthed oaf of a man with everybody except his customers. With them he could be as oily as the scented ointments he sold.

'Look at these,' said Nasim to Harun. 'These are going to be a huge success. The glass makers in Murcia certainly know their trade. Look how the glass rod is a stopper as well.' He held up a green glass vial which glinted like jade in a shaft of sunlight that had found its way through the palm leaf shades. 'I can practically double the price I charge for stuff in glasses like this.'

'I don't know how you can afford to get bottles like these shipped in from Murcia and you can't afford to pay me my five dirhams.'

'Stop moaning about money will you?' said Nasim. 'Who said I can't afford five dirhams? If you must know I have been quite lucky recently playing at knucklebones. You'll get your money. Then you can give me some of it back if you want to buy some of these fine bottles!'

'You are always the same, aren't you?' said Harun. 'All you ever think about is money and gambling.'

Nasim smirked. 'I think about my lovely customers too. After all they are the ones who supply me with the stakes. Especially the ones who need that extra special something to give their love-life a lift. My tinctures have done a lot of good in this city!'

'Some day you are going to kill someone with those potions of yours. If the doctors ever find out what you are up to you'll be in real trouble.'

As Harun spoke the mule-driver tapped his animal's rump with his goad and it moved off to reveal two of General Ghalib's palace guards striding towards Nasim's stall. The men were so big they could hardly walk side by side in the narrow street.

'It looks like you're in trouble already,' said Harun.

The guards stopped in front of Nasim's stall.

'Which one of you is Nasim bin Faraj?'

'Him!' said Harun immediately, pointing with a trembling finger.

The other soldier gave a snorting laugh. 'It's good to have a friend Nasim! We've been sent here by General Ghalib. You may have heard of him, although I don't think he is much of a perfume man. You're coming with us to the Alcazar. I am sure your good friend here will shut up your shop for you.'

Nasim's knees were suddenly so weak that Harun had to help him to his feet.

Chapter 15

This was really quite intolerable now. For the life of her Miryam couldn't understand why the Admiral of the Fleet, Suhail bin Ahmad, would miss yet another class. Who did he think he was? He was a good navigator but he wasn't by any means the best in the group. If anything that accolade was Siraj bin Bahram's. He seemed to have a natural gift for astronomy and understood everything he was told the first time it was explained to him. The other three were good enough but didn't have Siraj's natural talent. It was just a pity that Siraj was such an arrogant man. Tall, fair complexioned and good looking too, thought Miryam, but his arrogance would be his downfall. Of the remaining three Bandar was probably the best. He seemed to be very competent in everything he did. They would all be fine though. They'd all be competent to navigate their ships with the new astrolabe.

It was some time after morning prayers and the four vice-admirals were sitting with Miryam and her father in their room in the university. As they were waiting for Suhail, Yunus was filling in the time regaling the younger men with tales of his student days in Shiraz.

The Astronomer Royal had done a few daft things during his studies in Persia and none more so than the antics he had got up to with his very good Christian friend, Aidun banu Qasi. Aidun had been a brilliant mathematician and chess player who had spent much of his time taking money from rich Persian merchants who were foolish enough to bet that they could beat him on the board. Aidun had always won and had kept Yunus and himself in the best of food and wine until one day he had fleeced someone who was just that little bit too powerful and he had had to flee from Shiraz in the middle of the night.

Although Aidun had returned to Cordoba to become the first Christian professor of mathematics in the university, it always saddened Miryam to hear her father talk of him as two years previously he had been brutally murdered following a rigged chess match in a bathhouse. The killer had never been found and Miryam could see how the lack of a resolution to his friend's terrible death had been eating away at her father.

'I think we have heard enough reminiscing about the past now gentlemen,' said Miryam briskly as she stood up. 'We are going to have to start without the Admiral of the Fleet.' She turned to her father. 'The Astronomer Royal is going to have to find out exactly what is going on with our colleague Suhail. Now, can you all please take your instruments and almanacs and we shall do the exercises for a final time to make sure you have understood the process completely. When we have finished with the astrolabe we want to make you familiar with these charts.' She held up a roll of heavy papers bound by leather thongs.

'What are they?' asked Siraj.

Yunus looked at his daughter who nodded. 'I shall explain briefly what they are,' he said, 'and we can go back to them once we have done the astrolabe exercise. These are the very latest charts of the Roman Sea showing the coastline from Jebel al-Tariq in Al Andalus to the coast of Syria in the east.' He unrolled the charts and held one up and pointed to it. 'Here is Jebel al-Tariq, then Cordoba and here to the south east of the capital is our naval base in Almeria. This is the north coast of Ifriqiya and Egypt. And here we have Malta. Sicily. Italy. Cyprus. This is Constantinople. And to the east of Cyprus this is the coast of Syria. Baghdad and the Persian border.'

Siraj bin Bahram spoke up. 'This is not the chart we usually use... al-Khwarizmi's.'

'Well,' said Yunus. 'It is and it isn't. This is based on al-Khwarizmi's original chart but it has been improved by the addition of information discovered by the geographer Ibn Hawqal.'

'Is that the same Ibn Hawqal who is the ambergris expert, the alchemist?' asked Bandar.

'That's him,' said Yusuf. 'But he has also been working for us through General Ghalib the Commander of the Alcazar Guard, as a cartographer. His interest in alchemy gives him the ruse he needs to travel and travelling has given him the chance to learn the configuration of the coasts and islands of the Roman Sea. It was Ibn Hawqal who updated al-Khwarizmi's chart. When we have finished the astrolabe training we shall spend this afternoon working on the chart.'

'How different is it?' asked the youngest of the navigators.

'We should be able to work that out for ourselves,' said Siraj.

'Yes indeed,' said Yunus, 'but to answer your colleague's question, the most important changes are the distances. On al-Khwarizmi's map they were not nearly as accurate as they are on this new edition. Anyway, we'll come to that when I take you all through Ibn Hawqal's changes after Miryam has completed the astrolabe exercises. Suhail should have been here to see these charts too. Now we are going to have to have an extra training session just for him.'

Yunus was rolling up the charts when a knock came to the door. 'Aha, this is probably Suhail now. I wonder what he's got to say for himself. Come in!'

One of the soldiers on guard duty put his head round the door. He took a long look at Miryam before speaking to Yunus.

'I'm sorry to interrupt you sir but there is an officer and two men here from Hasdai ben Shaprut, the Vizier.'

'I know who Hasdai ben Shaprut is thank you!' said Yunus. 'I had dinner with him two weeks ago. Send the officer in.'

'Yes sir, sorry sir,' said the guard and pushed open the door to admit the officer who spoke directly to Yunus.

'*A salaam u aleikum*, Your Excellency.'

'*Wa aleikum a salaam*,' the Astronomer Royal replied.

'There are two men here, Bandar bin Sadiq and Siraj bin Bahram?'

'They are here.'

'They are to come with me now to the Vizier's quarters,' said the officer, who then took from his pouch a folded piece of paper, 'and this is for you.' The paper was sealed with a silk thread below which in the Vizier's own hand was his personal 'alama or motto "Ask counsel of all that are wise and despise not any counsel that is profitable".

Yunus broke the seal, unfolded the message and read "*Miryam, Yunus. You must both come to my office immediately following the Asr prayer. Hasdai ben Shaprut.*"

He looked from the paper to his daughter. She was not at all happy with this latest interruption to her tuition. Now she would need yet another session with Bandar and Siraj to explain the charts to them. And she would have to spend extra time with the Admiral of the Fleet.

The old astronomer turned to the group of navigators. 'Bandar, Siraj, both of you, go with this man. You others must work quickly now. We have to finish the work with the astrolabe and the charts before the afternoon prayer. Miryam can you carry on please?'

Chapter 16

Bandar bin Sadiq and Siraj bin Bahram were admitted into the Vizier's office to find Hasdai ben Shaprut staring out of his window at the pearl-grey morning light. Despite the fire of pine-cones which crackled and spat in the grate the Vizier was wearing a woollen cloak about his thin, hunched shoulders. Anyone who didn't know any better would think he was just absentmindedly fingering his prayer beads.

As the door closed the Vizier continued to look out of the window. 'I think it is going to rain,' he said.

'Yes Your Excellency,' said Bandar, 'I can smell it on the wind.'

'Ah indeed,' said Hasdai as he turned to face them. 'You sailors have a way of telling which way the wind is going to blow and what it is going to bring. Sit down.'

Bandar's look suggested that he had no idea why the vizier had said such a thing. Siraj just looked smug as he sat down on the divan.

'I have sent for you both as I have matters of the utmost importance to tell you. The first of these,' said Hasdai, 'is that the Admiral of the Fleet, Suhail bin Ahmed, is dead.'

The Vizier saw the colour go out of Bandar's knuckles as his hands clamped tightly together.

Siraj seemed curiously unmoved by the news.

'When did this happen?' asked Bandar.

'Was it sickness?' asked Siraj.

'I had no idea he was ill,' said Bandar. 'Is that why he wasn't at the university again this morning?'

'That's certainly why he wasn't with you this morning, but he wasn't ill. He was murdered.'

'Murdered!' said Bandar. 'How?'

The Vizier tipped his head to one side and looked again at Bandar's white knuckles. 'Does it make any difference "how"?'

'Well, no... but who did it? Who do you think killed him?'

'I have no idea. That is for General Ghalib to find out. But you both knew Suhail far better than I did. I thought perhaps one of you could tell *me* who might have done it. Did he have any enemies here in Cordoba?'

61

'No,' said Bandar. 'At least I don't think so.'

'He was an important man,' said Siraj. 'He had been allocated a personal bodyguard. He must be dead too.'

Again Hasdai's head tipped to the side as he looked quizzically at the man from Qartajana.

'That's an interesting observation,' he said, 'but for the moment it's not important. What is important is your assessment of how the Admiral's death affects our naval expedition against Baghdad.'

'May I ask you a direct question, Your Excellency?' said Bandar.

The Vizier waved his hand.

'Why are you asking us about this?'

'It is very simple. We need to know if the death of Suhail bin Ahmed will in any way delay the sailing of our fleet. We think this is a question you may be able to answer.'

'That depends on whether or not he is replaced quickly by a competent officer,' said Siraj.

'The Crown Prince himself has spoken to me about this matter,' said Hasdai, 'and his wishes are very clear. He is promoting you, Bandar, with immediate effect to the position of Admiral of the Fleet.'

As he said this Hasdai could see the blood begin to flow back into Bandar's fingers as he relaxed and leant back on the divan.

'Well,' said Bandar. 'This is a surprise.'

'It certainly is,' said Siraj.

'Good,' said Hasdai and he paused for a moment. 'That's settled then. It is now your mission to ensure that the Andalusi fleet is ready to set sail from Almeria as soon as possible. Official notification of your appointment has already been sent to naval headquarters there. Siraj, you are to be the first vice-admiral. The Crown Prince has specifically said that the chain of command will be from Bandar to Siraj then from you Siraj to your two navigating vice-admirals and then directly to ships' captains. Do you understand?'

'Yes, Your Excellency,' said Bandar as Siraj nodded in agreement.

'Very well. This afternoon you are to discuss the departure of the fleet with the others. Report back to me immediately after evening prayers to give your assessment on when the fleet will sail. And be aware that I shall pass your assessment word for word to Prince Hakam so it is in both of your interests to get this right. And Bandar, the officer who brought you here will now act as your personal bodyguard.' Hasdai turned and looked out of the window again. 'Go now or you will be caught in the rain.'

Chapter 17

Harun tugged nervously at his straggly beard as he looked through the arched doorway of the teahouse and out to the brightness of the street. The man, who wore a sleek brown fur cap, lingered for a moment in the entrance, saw him, waved, then, leaning his considerable bulk on his silver handled walking cane, made his way slowly between the crowded tables through the bustle and chatter to where Harun sat at the back of the cramped room. The air, already full of the aromas of mint tea, lemons and warm honey, was made heavier still when Simon, the huge, barrel-chested Christian proprietor, came from the kitchen carrying above his head a tray of steaming-hot sweet buns; his barad for which the Al Bisharah teahouse was famous throughout Cordoba.

Harun looked again at the table next to his where a group of smiths from the metalwork suq were engrossed in a game of knucklebones. He watched as one of the men, who had hands like legs of mutton, threw one bone in the air and then attempted to scoop up the other four from the table in time to catch the first one again in the same hand. A great roar of laughter came from his mates as the falling bone landed in a pot of hot water in the centre of the table. To still more laughter one of the men cried that even he could do better than that and held up his right hand which was missing the thumb.

As the laughter settled Harun rose to greet Hamid al-Mursi the Suq Inspector who, supported on his stick, was squeezing his large frame between Simon and a serving-boy who was clearing tables. As usual, the Al Bisharah in the heart of the suq was full of tradesmen, merchants and market workers, a fact that the Suq Inspector never failed to notice. As he edged his way closer the men from the metalwork suq pocketed their knucklebones, drank down their tea and got up to head back to work.

'You know how I disapprove of gambling in tea-houses,' said al-Mursi rather louder than he needed to as the men tried to avoid his glare. Simon shook his head and looked at the ceiling.

As they left, one of the smiths muttered, 'It's all right if it's chess in one of the bathhouses you own though, isn't it?'

As they made their way to the door, the smith tried to move aside as a scrawny beggar child brushed past him. He then bade the market inspector goodbye with a wave of his hand. With his other hand he grasped the note that had been slipped into the pocket of his robe.

'Get back to work,' said al-Mursi with half a smile on his sleek, fat face. 'You know the regulations as well as I do.'

As he sat down he turned to Harun. 'Now, I hope this is important. But before we start let's see if we can get any service in here... Simon!' he cried. He banged his cane on the floor and clicked his fat fingers at the teashop owner, signalling for his customary tea and a plate of barad. As the nervous serving-boy rattled towards them carrying a tray with two cups of hyssop tea and a plate of the small, soft buns al-Mursi opened up his green woollen cloak, smoothed his immaculate silk robes then leant his cane against the wall. He straightened his fur cap. 'Well,' he said, 'what is it that requires my immediate attention?'

'Nasim bin Faraj has been taken to the Alcazar for questioning. Two soldiers came for him just after morning prayers.'

Al-Mursi ate a barad then helped himself to honey and stirred it into his tea. 'What did the soldiers say?'

'Nothing, other than that they'd been sent by General Ghalib and Nasim was to go with them immediately. They told me to shut up his shop. That's when I asked one of the market officers to get word to you. I was just worried that this has something to do with ambergris.'

Al-Mursi grabbed the sleeve of Harun's robe and leant forward close enough for him to smell the honey on his breath. The tea house fell silent at al-Mursi's sudden move. 'How long have you worked in the suq?' he said under his breath.

Harun's brow furrowed with confusion. 'What do you mean?' he said eventually. 'Why is that important?'

'It's not,' said al-Mursi helping himself to another bun. 'I just wanted to make you shut up for a moment. Look around you,' he whispered. 'Most of the people in this tea house are pretending not to listen to our conversation. And those who aren't pretending have probably heard enough already.'

Harun hung his head.

'Now, tell me, quietly this time, what were you saying about ambergris?'

As the hubbub from the rest of the tables bubbled up again Harun spoke, hardly above a whisper. 'I think Nasim has ambergris at his perfume shop.'

Al-Mursi glanced around the room. 'But that trade has been expressly forbidden… by the Caliph himself.' He sipped his tea. 'If this is true then General Ghalib will be doing more than just talking to him at the Alcazar.' He took another of the barad and this time nibbled at it delicately. 'How long have you known about the ambergris?' he asked, looking intently at the bun.

Harun hung his head and tugged once more at his beard. 'Not long. I broke a jar in his shop two days ago. I thought it was bitter orange jam but there was another jar inside it which was full of ambergris.'

Al-Mursi's eyes hardened in his plump cheeks as he chewed. 'I see. And is there anything else I need to know?'

Harun shook his head. 'I don't think so.'

'Very well. If you find out any more about this be sure to contact me. Any of the market officers will know how to reach me.' With that the Suq Inspector drank off his tea, reached for his cane and, with two hands on its silver handle, heaved his large frame from the stool. He helped himself to the last barad and made his way out of the tea house nodding to Simon on the way.

Chapter 18

The rhythmic clicking of the prayer beads stopped abruptly as Hasdai shivered and pulled his cloak closer about his shoulders.

Ghalib winced and rubbed his knee as he got up off the stool. He scooped a couple of handfuls of pine cones from the basket and threw them on the fire. 'Enter,' the General shouted as a servant knocked at the door. Hasdai gave a half smile and shook his head. This was his office after all. He was the Vizier but Ghalib just couldn't be kept down!

The servant came in, bowed and placed a tray with cups, a plate of lemons cut in half, a bowl of honey and a steaming jug of hot water onto the desk.

Ghalib poured hot water into two cups, added some honey and then squeezed half a lemon into each one. He handed a cup to the Vizier who warmed his hands on it and breathed in the scent of the lemon. Hasdai had stopped smiling.

'I never said how sorry I am,' he said as he sat down behind his desk.

'Sir?'

'About the young Lieutenant. I know you were very close to him.'

'Thank you sir,' said Ghalib as he stared into his cup. 'Yes, I have known him since he was a boy.'

'Has his mother been told?'

'Yes sir. Although I haven't been to see her myself yet. I was going to talk to her this evening once we've spoken with Bandar. You know it wasn't just a son she lost.'

'What do you mean?' said Hasdai.

'Suhail, the admiral, was her step-brother,' said Ghalib. 'That's one of the reasons I wanted Haytham to be his bodyguard.'

'Poor woman,' said Hasdai reaching again for his prayer beads. 'Make sure you make time to go and see her. How well did you know Suhail bin Ahmed?'

'Not that well. I knew him by reputation of course, but before he came to Cordoba I had only met him a couple of times in Almeria and never for long enough to really get to know him.'

'Tell me about his reputation then.'

Ghalib refilled his cup. 'Well sir he was only in the post for just over a year. From what I heard he wasn't that skilled as a navigator but they say he was a first class naval commander. He could get his men to do anything for him and he had the total trust of the Caliph and the Crown Prince. He had other people to do the navigation for him, although I'd heard that when Suhail was promoted everyone had expected Bandar to be given the job.'

'So the man from Qartajana, Siraj, was never considered then?' said Hasdai.

Ghalib nodded. 'That's right. Bandar was the most senior of the Vice-Admirals. When the old Admiral of the Fleet died, I think even Bandar himself expected to get the job.'

'What happened then?'

Ghalib shrugged as he sipped his drink.

'I honestly don't know. The old Admiral of the Fleet had been sick for a few weeks before he died. I can understand that the Crown Prince wanted the best man for the job, but Bandar had been next in line for many years and you know how important that is in the military. I have no idea why the prince insisted on Suhail getting the promotion.'

'Well no matter,' said Hasdai. 'Bandar's the Admiral of the Fleet now.' As he spoke he let two of his prayer beads click down their chain and looked up at the window. Raindrops were gusting against it and he could hear the trees thrashing in the wind. He looked back at his desk and sighed. He picked up a document. 'I've still got this to finish.'

'Is that the Caliph's address to the people?'

'Yes. I'll have to remove the references to Admiral Suhail. Now, tell me again, where exactly are we with these murders? What do we know?'

Ghalib put down his cup and wiped his moustache with the back of his hand.

'Well, I think we can assume that the Lieutenant was killed first, which means…'

'Why can we assume that?' asked Hasdai, puzzled. He put his beads down on the desk and stared at the General.

'Well, it's obvious sir.'

Hasdai tucked in his chin as his wiry frame stiffened in his chair. 'Then enlighten me with your wisdom General. I seem to have missed this obvious fact.'

The General didn't rise to the Vizier's sarcasm but bowed his head and smiled.

'I agreed that Lieutenant Haytham should be the one to look after Suhail bin Ahmed during his stay in Cordoba. As Admiral of the Fleet he had to have a bodyguard.'

'But why is it obvious the bodyguard died first?'

'Well sir, the Haytham would never have left Suhail's side. He would have put his own life in danger to save his uncle.'

The Vizier ran a hand through his sparse brown hair and thought about this for a moment.

'General, please understand I am not doubting the bravery of the young Lieutenant, nor his commitment to you and his post. But you must stay neutral in this matter until we have all the facts. We may yet prove that Haytham was killed first, but until I have absolute proof of this it would seem imprudent to leap to conclusions.'

Ghalib nodded.

'Based on what you know to be true, and only that, is it possible that the Admiral was killed after Haytham?'

'Yes sir. It is possible.'

'Let me ask you another question. Do you think it is likely?'

Ghalib paused for a moment. 'That depends sir.'

'On what?'

'On what the killer's motive was.'

Hasdai nodded as he felt the water jug. It was still fairly warm so he poured himself more water and added some honey.

'Exactly General. So let's talk about that. Tell me again what you told me last night. Tell me about the game of knucklebones.'

'According to Antonio, Haytham was with the Admiral the night before last when he was playing knucklebones with Antonio and the suq trader at the bathhouse. Yousef, the owner of the bathhouse confirmed this, but he also said there were other people there. He said it was a busy night as people were relaxing prior to the festival of Night Journey the next day.

'You said it was a good-natured game.'

The General nodded. 'Antonio said it was all very friendly. He said the Admiral was in a good mood, presumably because he'd won a good deal of money.'

Hasdai held up his hand, 'We'll come to the money in due course. Tell me about the bodies.'

'Sir, the Lieutenant was killed by a single slash to his throat. It was a terrible wound which nearly took his head off. I can't be absolutely certain but I would guess he was already in the water when he died as there was no blood around the pool, only in the water itself. The knife we found in the water is consistent in terms of size with the wound to Haytham's neck.' Ghalib nodded at the cotton-wrapped bundle on the Vizier's desk. As the Vizier unwrapped the cloth the pattering of the rain on the window grew louder with the rising wind.

'What can you tell me about this?' he asked, handing the knife to the General who hefted it in his hand. 'Do you think it belonged to the Lieutenant?'

Ghalib turned the knife over in his hand then peered at the blade. 'If it is a knife that belonged to Haytham then we didn't supply it. This isn't an army issue weapon.'

'Could it have been a personal weapon?'

'No, I don't think so. When he was on duty he would have had his sword and possibly a falcata.'

'A falcata?' said Hasdai. 'Why would he have one of those?'

'Quite a few of our young officers have taken to carrying them. They have them made by our armourers. They are a fearsome weapon for close combat.'

'So where are these weapons now?'

The General shook his head. 'I don't know sir. They weren't with his belongings at the bathhouse.'

'What *was* with his belongings?'

Ghalib stayed silent. He tried to remember what the old Yemeni had said to him at the bathhouse.

'General,' said Vizier Hasdai gently, 'I know Lieutenant Haytham meant a lot to you but we need to be certain about the facts. We can come back to that. Tell me again about the Admiral.'

'His body was dumped in a small yard behind some stairs off the main courtyard of the funduq.'

'Was there anything else there?'

'Just the usual rubbish... empty wine casks and rotting vegetables.'

'You seem sure he was dumped there,' said Hasdai.

'Yes sir. When I spoke to Antonio and the girls at the funduq they seemed to think that when he parted from them Suhail was intending to leave the funduq. As you know, the main gate is right in the centre of the south wall but the body was found off to one side.'

'Behind the stairs.'

'Exactly.'

'Where do the stairs go?'

'Up to the lodgings... the sleeping quarters. If he was leaving he wouldn't have gone that way.'

Hasdai nodded. 'Right. Then if his body was dumped there someone may have seen it being dragged, or carried. Have your men spoken to all the mule-drivers?'

'They should be finished today sir. As yet nobody remembers seeing anything.'

Hasdai stared intently at Ghalib. 'No General,' he said slowly, 'as yet nobody has told us they remember seeing anything. Whether they actually remember is a different point entirely. Tell me about the wound.'

'His head had been opened by some kind of heavy sword or axe. He'd been there for some time when I arrived as his body had attracted the attention of a cat and lots of cockroaches.'

Hasdai stood at the window and watched the rivulets of rain distort in the wind. It was a miserable day. He rubbed his temples and closed his eyes for a moment.

'Well, until we know more we can't make any assumptions. As far as we are concerned the game of knucklebones, the money that Antonio owed and the visit to the funduq may be completely unconnected to the murders.'

The General sat still, his brow furrowed in concentration.

'Sir,' he said after some time, 'I think we need to start with the premise that the murders are connected to the gambling.'

The Viziers' prayer beads started to click again. 'No General. We need to start by determining whether or not the two murders have anything to do with to each other.'

As Hasdai stared at the rain, which was now lashing against the window, he could just make out the muezzin's call to prayer which was being tugged at by the wind.

'General, after you have prayed we can go and have a look at the Admiral's room. Once we've done that we can speak to this perfume trader. Tell your men at the funduq that I want to speak to them all this evening. We'll go and see them just after the evening prayer.'

Chapter 19

'How much longer will this take?' asked Colonel Zaffar al-Din as he stood in one of the arched doorways to the stables and watched the rain bounce off the cobbled courtyard. The downpour which had begun just before prayers showed no sign of abating and a dank smell of dung, horse sweat and damp straw filled the air. The raw January cold sank through to the bones of the two soldiers behind him, who were huddled round a small, smoky brazier. The sputtering fire had little impact in this freezing weather.

'I hope we can get through the ones we have left before afternoon prayers,' said one of the soldiers rubbing his hands in the smoke. 'There are only about ten more men to question.'

'Let's be a bit more than *hopeful* Lieutenant. Let's have some certainty. I've had word that the Vizier and General Ghalib are on their way here to inspect our progress.' The Colonel waved his hand at the muttering queue of muleteers in their sack-cloth capes who were waiting, stamping in a line along the wall outside the stables. 'I don't want this lot still hanging around when the General arrives.'

'Yes sir.'

Zaffar was the Colonel in charge of the Madinat al-Zahra Royal Guard, whose primary responsibility was to protect the Caliph, Abd Al-Rahman III. As a solider he had distinguished himself in the campaigns on the Northern Frontier and General Ghalib had personally sponsored his promotion. Zaffar had also been Lieutenant Haytham's senior officer and it was he who had suggested to Ghalib that Haytham be the Admiral of the Fleet's bodyguard. He had received news of the young lieutenant's death at first light that morning. He had been told to report to General Ghalib who had told him that the Admiral had also been brutally murdered. Ghalib had assigned him to interview all of the funduq's residents and workers and also to make sure that Antonio the cloth merchant and the whores did not leave.

'Ah, good,' said Zaffar to a porter who came into the stable carrying a board with three steaming cups of strong, hot hyssop tea. 'It has taken you long enough to get these here.' The colonel and his men wrapped their hands around the cups.

There were porters everywhere in the ground floor galleries of the funduq. They carried goods to and from the strong rooms and warehouses, darting between the horses and mules which clattered over the cobbled courtyard as they were led to drink at the troughs. It was the porters who shovelled away the dung, oblivious of the steam which rose from the torrents of horse urine that ran in channels in the cobbles.

Zaffar shivered and pulled his cloak closer around his shoulders.

'Have you got anything from any of the interviews?' said Zaffar to his lieutenant.

The lieutenant put his fingers to his lips and pointed behind the colonel to a porter who had slipped in to tend the brazier and the pitch pine torches which lit the gallery. He spoke when the porter had gone: 'The stories, as far as they go, are consistent sir. A few of the men remember seeing the Admiral arrive and some of them even said they saw Lieutenant Haytham too. The Admiral and the cloth merchant spent some time in the merchant's stores. Some say it was to do with collecting money, and then they went upstairs. But no-one seems to recall seeing the Admiral leave. Most of them can't remember anything though and I don't have much hope for these either,' he said gesturing to the line of men waiting in the rain.

'Don't bother with your *hope* Lieutenant. General Ghalib will want facts, not fancy or anything you hope for.' He drank down the rest of his tea and shivered again. 'The night before last,' he said. 'That was the celebration of the Night Journey wasn't it?'

'Yes sir. I was on duty at the Alcazar. The guards who came back from the city gates said there were hundreds of people on the streets with their lanterns. There were children running everywhere. The celebrations lasted until just before dawn.'

'Was the funduq busy?' said Zaffar.

'Extremely busy sir. According to the clerk's books all the rooms were occupied and Jaziri had got in extra staff to work in the stables and the warehouses.'

'Has anyone left the funduq since yesterday morning?'

'It's difficult to be precise sir,' said the lieutenant.

Zaffar looked hard at the man.

'What I mean, sir, is that there is a chance that some of the guests left in the time between the murder and General Ghalib arriving. The Corporal of the Night Guard is talking to the clerk to get list of people who had reserved rooms for that night, and comparing it with the list of men we've been able to speak to.'

'All right,' said Zaffar. 'Make sure I see a list of anyone we can't account for.' The lieutenant nodded. 'Do you not think it's strange Lieutenant?'

'What sir?'

'A city filled with people, a funduq full of guests and workers, and we can't find a single person who saw anything. The Admiral had his skull split open, probably with an axe, and his throat cut from ear to ear and nobody heard a thing. Surely someone heard the commotion, even if they didn't see it.'

'Sir that's possible but with the noise from the Night Journey celebrations and all the activity here at the funduq we might have to concede...'

'Listen,' said Zaffar, 'the Admiral of the Royal Fleet and his bodyguard, Lieutenant Haytham, have been murdered. We concede nothing until we have caught whoever is responsible. Do you understand?'

The lieutenant hung his head. 'Yes sir.'

'Good. Now get the rest of these interviews finished and then meet me in Jaziri's office as soon as the afternoon prayer is finished. We need to prepare what we are going to say to the General and the Vizier.'

Chapter 20

Hasdai ben Shaprut's breath hung in the air like smoke as he faced the door and looked around the Admiral's room once more. As he did so he manipulated his amber prayer beads in a futile attempt to keep his fingers warm. There was no fire now so the room was damp and dank and Hasdai could hear the rain and wind outside sweeping through the Alcazar gardens. He shivered in the harsh, bitter cold.

According to the officer in charge of the palace guard no-one had been into the Admiral's room since he'd left it two days ago. He had been collected by Lieutenant Haytham and now they were both dead.

On the desk in front of the Vizier lay a pen beside a pot of ink and a small pile of papers on top of which was a dish of knucklebones. Next to the papers were two, small, round green jars with tight fitting glass stoppers. Pocketing his prayer beads Hasdai reached out and picked up a couple of bones from the dish. They felt cold and smooth as he rolled them around his palm as if they were his beads. He heard the guard outside the door snap to attention as the sound of heavy footsteps in the corridor grew louder. There was a sharp knock at the door just before it was opened.

'Come in General,' said Hasdai without looking up.

'Thank you sir,' said Ghalib, drawing his cloak closer about him as he felt the chill in the cold, damp room. 'Let me see to this lamp,' he said and went to attend to an oil lamp which was almost burnt out. 'My men tell me Colonel Zaffar will be ready to receive us at the funduq after evening prayers.'

'*Ready* to receive us?' said Hasdai quietly as he placed the knucklebones back in the bowl.

Ghalib said nothing.

'We can go there later before we speak with Bandar,' said Hasdai. 'He should have worked out how much more training his men need by the time we return.'

'Have you found anything in here sir?' asked Ghalib as he gazed around the room.

Hasdai nodded. 'Do you know what these are General?' he said, pointing to the glass jars on the desk.

The General lifted one of the jars and held it up to the lamp while he peered at the contents. 'I found them in the Admiral's trunk,' said Hasdai.

'Well, they're jars,' said Ghalib. 'But I've no idea what that is inside them.'

'Open it,' said Hasdai. 'Here, let me...'

He took the jar from Ghalib and removed the glass stopper. 'Smell it,' he said, offering the open top to Ghalib who took a deep sniff and then recoiled in disgust, spluttering and coughing.

'What on earth is that?' he said wiping his mouth and gulping in a deep breath.

'That General,' said Hasdai putting the stopper back in the jar, 'is ambergris.' He placed the glass back on the desk then opened the second one. Offering it to Ghalib he said 'And so is this. Go on, I promise this one won't hurt you.' The General took the jar and sniffed at it tentatively.

'You see,' said Hasdai. 'This one's actually very pleasant.'

'I don't understand sir,' said Ghalib. 'I thought ambergris was a perfume. That first one smells like something that's died.'

'It *is* a perfume General, but only after a long period of ageing. When it's young it's black, soft and smells as you said, rancid, like something that's died. However, once it has become exposed to seawater, the weather and the open air it turns grey, or in some cases a deep yellow like this stuff here. That's when it develops the pleasant odour, and that is when it becomes extremely valuable.' Hasdai held the two glass jars up to the lamp and watched as the light shone through. 'Very valuable indeed.'

The General wiped the moisture from his eyes and smoothed his beard. 'Are they important sir? I mean, are they relevant?'

'I don't know General,' said Hasdai as he clicked his prayer beads.

'Is there anything else?'

The Vizier sat down on a stool next to the desk. 'I'm not entirely sure,' he said. 'There are some personal papers here which are about naval matters.' He held up one of the sheets of paper. 'This one's a list of names. We can check with Bandar later on if any of these men mean anything to him.'

'It might be a list of the officers serving under him,' said Ghalib.

'It might be I suppose,' said Hasdai. 'But none of the navigators' names are there.'

'Ah,' said Ghalib. 'Where did you find the jars of ambergris?'

'In the trunk over there. They were wrapped in a naval cloak.' Hasdai rubbed his eyes. 'There were some robes and other personal clothes in the closet, but other than that, nothing.'

The General looked at the jars for a moment. 'Do you think the Admiral…' he said before the Vizier raised his hand to silence him.

'I don't know General. And I'm not sure I want to know either,' said Hasdai. 'But I do know as well as you do that trade in ambergris, of any kind and in any form, has been expressly forbidden.'

'Not just trade sir. It is one of the goods that the Caliph has decreed can't even be moved between cities.'

'Exactly. Whatever the Admiral was doing, even if he didn't get this ambergris here in Cordoba, just having it was against the direct orders of the Caliph. And that is a big risk to take, even for a man in his position.'

The General peered again at the two small jars. After a silence during which the only sound was the rain and wind lashing outside, he spoke. 'I am certain the Admiral would not have deliberately gone against the Caliph's decree sir.'

Hasdai looked quizzically at the General. 'We spoke earlier about the fact that neither of us knew the Admiral that well. How certain can we really be?' He took his prayer beads from his robes and the rhythmic sound of the beads competed with that of the rain and the wind.

'We need to talk to the suq trader your men brought in earlier,' said Hasdai eventually. 'The one you said played knucklebones with the Admiral. He works in the perfume suq so he might be able to tell us where this ambergris came from. In the meantime we'd best not speak of this to anyone. I don't want it to be known that this stuff was found in the Admiral's room. At least not until I know how and why it got here. Have your men bring this suq trader to my office. Meet me there when you have told them.' With that he got to his feet, picked up the two jars and the papers from the desk. Folding the papers he wrapped them carefully, together with the jars, in an oiled cotton cloth which he produced from his pocket. He held the package inside his robe and ushered General

Ghalib towards the door.

Chapter 21

'What are you doing here? Come in! Quickly! I thought I asked you not to come here.'

Yazid al-Haddad looked up and down the cloth suq, slipped into the barber's shop and closed the door behind him.

'Who are you to tell me what to do? You Baghdadis are all the same. Who do you think you are? I may be just a blacksmith but I've got as much right to come to the cloth suq as anyone else.'

'Yes, yes,' said Bilal bin Safwan, the barber, as he turned the key in the lock. He was beginning to regret ever having agreed to work with Yazid. He was obviously unstable. 'Of course you have, but we mustn't be seen together. It's dangerous. This has already gone badly wrong. Sit down and tell me what you know. Why didn't you meet me at the teahouse?'

Yazid glanced round the small shop. Along the right-hand wall there was a low divan seat above which hung a five string lute and on the back wall, a stone hearth with a copper basin of water bubbling on the charcoal fire. Next to the fire three smaller bowls gleamed. These were Bilal's blood-letting bowls. Yazid could see the handle of the lancet he had made for the barber poking over the rim of one of them. In front of the hearth were two stools and a low table with more of the barber's accoutrements. The three folding razors and two pairs of shears were also Yazid's handiwork. There were two boxwood combs lying on a pile of towels next to a bowl of sweet smelling soap. On the wall to the left under a framed piece of calligraphy extolling the genius of the Baghdadi musician Ziryab there were two shelves cut into the stone. They were filled with jars of perfume and hair creams and bottles of pure alcohol which the barber used to stem the bleeding from the cuts he inflicted on his patients.

Yazid sat down on a stool and screwed up his nose. He hated all this perfume stuff. He thought the place smelt like a whore's pillow... cloying, heavy perfume with a taint of blood. Picking up one of the razors he flicked it open with his good hand and while looking Bilal in the eye, he drew the edge across the back of his own wrist. He licked the trickle of blood then said, 'This needs grinding again. If anyone asks you just tell them I am bringing you some new razors.'

'Yes, yes! All right, but what do you want?' said Bilal.

'Well first of all I could do with a drink. It's thirsty work in a forge all day. Have you got any wine?'

'No, but I have some water.' Bilal reached behind a curtain next to the hearth and pulled out an earthenware bottle and a squat, heavy mug. 'Here!'

Yazid took the bottle in his left hand and held the mug on the table with his right. Bilal watched as the blacksmith used his right hand. The fact that the thumb was missing seemed to make very little difference to what he could do. Yazid looked up and saw Bilal staring at his hand. 'I've got used to it now,' he said. 'Obviously you still haven't.'

'It must affect your work,' said Bilal.

'Not really. You know the things I make. Small, delicate things... very sharp things!' He pushed the cut on his wrist towards Bilal's face and gave a loud laugh. 'You know, razors, knives, shears. My apprentice does the rough cutting and I do the finishing and grinding. I sharpen them up. I can manage. Just as I can manage without you.'

'I'm sure you didn't come here to talk about your missing thumb,' said Bilal quietly. 'Tell me what happened last night? You didn't turn up at the teahouse as arranged. We were supposed to take those crates away. They needed to be out of the storage unit during the Night Journey celebrations. Now there are soldiers all over the funduq asking questions about a dead body.'

'How do you know that?' asked Yazid.

'When you didn't turn up at the teahouse I went to the funduq. There were soldiers everywhere and one of the farriers told me what was going on.'

'What did he say?'.

'Just that. There's an officer of the guard interviewing everyone who works in the funduq.'

'What else do you think they know?' asked Yazid. Again he licked the cut on the back of his wrist.

'I don't know. My main concern is how we get to those crates.'

'Do we know what was in the crates?'

'Does it matter?' asked Bilal. 'Two men were nailed to the city gates in Balansiyya four days ago. They were caught trying to smuggle a shipment of cloves to Toledo.'

Yazid laughed. '*Y'Allah*, crucified for a basket of cloves! I hope the nails were sharp.'

Bilal looked quizzically at Yazid. Sometimes he had no idea what he was talking about.

'We don't need to think about that now,' said Bilal desperate to change the subject. He took a risk. 'If you ask me I think you didn't turn up last night because you were scared.'

'Me?' said Yazid. He laughed once more then flicked the razor open and shut, open and shut.

'Yes,' said Bilal. 'But we've got to hold our nerve. Whatever is in those crates must be worth a fortune given how much we got paid to put them there in the first place. Who are we doing this for anyway?'

'I told you,' said Yazid, 'It is best you don't know. It is safer that way.'

Bilal sighed. 'This could be our last job,' he said.

'We can't do anything about that now,' said Yazid. 'Here! Look at this.' He handed a folded piece of paper to Bilal. 'I got this message at the teahouse earlier.'

Bilal looked at the paper quickly and his head sank into his hands. 'So that's it? The job is off?'

Yazid shrugged.

Bilal knuckled his eyes and drank from the earthenware bottle. 'We have to find another buyer,' he said.

'We'll never get near the stuff.'

'We have to try,' said Bilal. 'We could have enough money to stop, if this comes off.'

'You say that every time,' said Yazid. 'And every time when we have paid off all the people we need to pay there is never enough left for the risks we are taking.'

'You mean there is never enough left for you to gamble away,' said Bilal. 'Why do you *do* that?'

Yazid stared into the mug of water as if he would find an answer at the bottom. It made him angry when anyone talked about his gambling addiction. And when he was angry he could do strange, very violent things. 'I know why I do it,' he said quietly. He opened the razor again and held it up at eye level. 'I do it to forget what I am. That's why I keep going back to it.' As he looked at Bilal the barber could see a profound emptiness in the blacksmith's eyes when he said, 'I've nothing left. It's all gone.'

'All of it?' said Bilal. 'We've been smuggling for months. We've split about six thousand dirhams. How could you lose that much?'

Yazid laughed again. 'Believe me,' he said, 'once you start it is not difficult. Knucklebones in the bathhouse is just the beginning. I lost most of it at the cockfights.'

Bilal was angry enough now to risk speaking out. 'How can you risk being nailed to a plank in the suq for the few minutes of excitement you get in the cockfight? We all like a bet on the birds but you seem to lose control whenever you do it. And don't forget you're risking *my* life now too. Do you think you will be able to keep my name to yourself once they've started on you? You think you know all about hot metal. Have you seen the state of some of these bodies by the time they are nailed up? The city guards could tell you a thing or two about what to do with red hot iron. I'll have to think about what to do with these crates. Then you'll have to help me. Do you understand?'

Yazid looked long at Bilal. He could see that the barber was frightened of him. He'd seen that look in victims' eyes many times before. 'So what do we do now?' he said.

'Please go,' said Bilal. 'Go and do nothing. Wait until I've worked out what we need to do. Once I've done that I'll tell you.'

Chapter 22

'Because,' shouted Hasdai, 'very early yesterday morning the Admiral's body was discovered in a heap of rubbish at the funduq! Someone murdered him, probably with an axe or some weapon like that. Someone, maybe the same person, also murdered the Admiral's bodyguard. We know that the bodyguard was murdered in the bathhouse where you all played knucklebones together and we also know that whoever killed the bodyguard did so with this knife. *Your* knife as it turns out. So I think that now you should try and remember where you were two nights ago and when you last remember having this knife.'

This outburst from the Vizier drained the colour from Nasim bin Faraj's features. The perfume trader looked down from the Vizier's face to the knife on the desk next to the two glass vials of ambergris. He swallowed and nodded gripping the sides of his stool so tightly that his arms quivered.

'I... I was in my shop in the suq until the evening prayer,' he stammered. 'After prayers I went to the bathhouse run by al-Mursi, the suq inspector; the one near the Bab al-Jadid.'

'Can anyone confirm that you were there?' asked General Ghalib.

Nasim thought for a moment. 'I think al-Mursi was there, and that his clerk was in the office. Yes, the clerk saw me. There were some other people there playing chess. Once I had bathed I went home and returned to my shop again in the morning.'

'We'll talk to al-Mursi's clerk,' said Hasdai. 'Now, tell me again about the knucklebones.'

Nasim wiped his mouth with the back of his hand.

'I go to Yousef's bathhouse most weeks to bathe and play chess or knucklebones. Three nights ago I met Antonio the cloth merchant there.'

'Had you agreed to meet him there?'

'No. I met him by chance. He was having tea and we got talking. Yousef, the bathhouse owner, introduced us. After a while I invited him to join the knucklebones game. Then we...' Nasim broke off as the Vizier raised his hand to silence him.

'Say that again,' said Hasdai.

Nasim looked blank. 'Which bit? We got talking and I invited him to join the game of knucklebones.'

'Are you saying that the game with the Admiral was already arranged?' asked Hasdai.

Nasim nodded. 'Yes.'

Hasdai glanced at General Ghalib who had raised his heavy eyebrows.

'So who arranged it?' said Hasdai.

'The Admiral did. He came to my shop in the suq several times in the days before the game. The last time he came he invited me to join him at the bathhouse.'

'When he visited your shop,' said Hasdai, 'did he buy anything?'

'He bought some scent which he said was for his wife.'

General Ghalib opened his mouth to speak but the Vizier held up his hand.

'Did he say anything else?' said Hasdai.

'Not really,' said Nasim.

'I find that hard to believe,' said Hasdai.

Nasim wiped his mouth again. 'What do you mean?'

'A man you'd only ever met a couple of times when he came to your shop invites you to play knucklebones. Are you absolutely sure you didn't discuss anything else?'

Nasim shook his head. 'We didn't really talk about anything.'

'So you expect me to believe he simply asked you to play knucklebones with him? Just like that.'

Nasim glanced first at General Ghalib and then at the Vizier.

'Yes,' he said gripping the stool once more. 'Because that's exactly what happened.'

The Vizier stared at the perfume trader. 'Very well,' he said eventually. 'We are finished...for now.'

As Nasim made to stand up the Vizier spoke again. 'Until further notice you are to remain here in the Alcazar.'

Ghalib could see the panic Nasim's eyes. 'I don't understand,' he said.

The Vizier leant forward and clasped his hands together. 'Then let me enlighten you. The Admiral of the Caliph's Royal Fleet and his bodyguard have been murdered. A knife belonging to you was found at the scene of one of those murders. If I share this information with the Crown Prince I would be surprised if anyone, other than your executioner, ever saw you again.'

Nasim leant back on the stool and stared at the floor sucking the cold air into his lungs in an attempt to calm himself.

'Look,' he said, hoarse with fear, 'I didn't kill that man.'

'Which man?' said Hasdai.

'The bodyguard.'

'And what about the Admiral?'

Nasim shook his head. 'I didn't kill him either.'

Hasdai looked at the glass vials on the desk in front of him. 'But you *did* sell him this ambergris.'

Nasim breathed deeply several times. 'No,' he said, his voice cracking. 'I didn't sell him anything apart from some scent for his wife.'

*

'He's clearly hiding something sir,' said General Ghalib once the guard had taken Nasim away.

'I worked that out for myself, General,' said Hasdai. He rubbed his temples as he saw on his desk the draft of the Caliph's address to the people. He sighed deeply. He would have to find time to get back to this document. He smoothed his beard and took up his prayer beads. The beads clicked on their chain as Hasdai pointed at the jars next to the papers on his desk. 'From what your men told you about his shop, these vials could have come from Nasim, right?'

The General nodded.

'As for the ambergris inside I'm not sure,' said Hasdai. 'But as a perfume trader Nasim will have had direct access to it from his suppliers. The only problem he has is the fact the Caliph has forbidden its sale or movement. Which means getting rid of it is very difficult.'

'Why do you think the Admiral wanted it?' asked Ghalib.

'I don't know that he did want it General. I just know that I found these jars in the trunk in his room.'

'What do you want to do with him sir?' asked Ghalib.

Hasdai thought for a moment. 'As I said earlier, we'll check with al-Mursi's clerk. If he was there the clerk will remember him and he'll be able to tell us who else was there. But even if Nasim was at al-Mursi's that still doesn't rule him out. If he stayed in his shop until evening prayers and then went to bathe, he would still have had enough time to kill Lieutenant Haytham. Don't forget Haytham was probably killed late in the night. We've got Nasim's knife, which we have good reason to believe was used to kill the Lieutenant. We have these two glass vials which we found in the Admiral's trunk and which we think came from Nasim's shop, and we both suspect he is lying. The only thing I don't know is which bit he is lying about. We'll keep him here in the cells to give him time to think about telling the truth.'

General Ghalib bent down to rub his knee and grimaced as he did so. 'Would you like me to get my jailer to talk to him?' he said.

Hasdai stared once more at the knife and then the two glass jars. 'No,' he said eventually. 'You know what I think about your jailer's ways of talking to prisoners. But I'd like you to make Nasim think I want your man to talk to him. Is that clear?'

'Yes sir,' said General Ghalib. 'Very clear.'

Chapter 23

Hamid al-Mursi was hardly a timid man but he never felt entirely safe in the metalwork suq. The crowded, claustrophobic alleyways of shops hung with sickles and plough blades, iron chains, copper basins and weapons of all kinds seemed to press in on him. There were too many blind corners here, too many people, too many strong men with ready access to knives, hot metal and fire. The constant clatter and ring of the blacksmiths' trade played on his nerves and the acrid smoke from the forge fires made him hack and cough. In every charcoal-carpeted alley was the strident hiss and sulphurous stench of red hot iron being quenched in bubbling tubs of greasy water. In a place like this a man could disappear quite easily... even a suq inspector in disguise.

He stopped and scratched violently at his waist as he leant against a wall, careful to maintain the crooked posture he adopted whenever he put on the rough, dun-coloured Tuareg clothes which were his favourite disguise. The voluminous robes and the enormous head-cloth reeked of the stable but they also obliterated his shape and covered everything except his eyes. Even so he had taken the precaution of smearing his face with dirt and his hands and feet were filthy. His silver handled cane had been replaced by a long, gnarled staff of hawthorn which he leant on with both hands as he stumbled along. This formidable weapon, the stench from his clothes and a constant mumbling and spitting made sure he was left alone in the suq.

He was in the heart of the metalwork suq now and had to squeeze against the wall as a donkey whose panniers were laden with charcoal came towards him. It was driven by a child of no more than eight years old who was almost as dirty as the donkey. The boy had the temerity to shout at al-Mursi to get out of the way. Confirmation indeed that the suq inspector's disguise was complete. But he had reached his destination. A sackcloth curtain hung over the entrance to Yazid al-Haddad's workshop and he could hear the smith yelling and cursing at his apprentice over the din of the anvil. Al-Mursi swept back the cloth and lurched inside. As he did so Yazid strode in from the forge yard, saw him and shouted, 'Clear off! No alms today. Go to the mosque. See if you can get something there.'

Al-Mursi drew himself up to his full height and tugged down the head cloth to show his face. 'It's me,' he rasped before pulling up the cloth again. 'Now get rid of your apprentice. I want to talk to you.'

Yazid wiped his hands on a filthy cloth at his waist then went back into the yard. When he came back with his apprentice to push him out of the doorway al-Mursi had turned his face to the wall.

'Come into the forge,' said Yazid. 'No-one can overhear us there.'

There could be no preamble to what al-Mursi wanted to say. He was aware of Yazid's reputation for violence but he would have to face him down. The market inspector knew that he would have to come out on top after this conversation.

'I know what you and that blood sucker Bilal bin Safwan have been up to. And I also know how much you have gambled away at the cockfighting. More money than you can earn making razors and lancets. I know that you two are up to your necks in smuggling and that it was your contacts who were crucified in Balansiyya for smuggling cloves.'

Yazid looked up; his face completely devoid of expression. He slowly shook his head and opened his mouth to speak.

'No,' said al-Mursi and he brandished his staff. 'Don't even try to deny it! If you do I'll split your skull right now and save the executioner the trouble. Let me tell you what I want... let me tell you what you are going to do. You are going to stop betting on fighting cocks. You always pick the wrong one anyway... and you are going to start betting on chess games. You're going to bet on the matches I run in my bathhouse. You are going to deal with my clerk. And you are going to lose. Do you understand? You are going to lose regularly. Which means I am going to win... regularly. My clerk will tell you the stakes. And if I don't win enough of your money I may come back and visit you again. But this time it'll be dark.' He pointed to the stick. 'Do you understand?'

The smith said nothing. He was violent but not stupid. It was clear that he understood.

'Or perhaps I won't come back. Perhaps I'll just tell the right people in the Alcazar what I know about you and that perfumed vein-cutter. I'll tell them what you are up to. That way I won't have to do anything except turn up on the day they nail you up in the suq.'

Yazid knew now that he would have to wait for his revenge on this fat cripple.

'Oh,' said al-Mursi, 'There's one more thing.'

Yazid's eyes narrowed as he wondered what the suq inspector could possibly add to what he had already said.

'I have heard that the Vizier, Hasdai ben Shaprut, has been asking a lot of questions about smuggling. He is particularly interested in finding out about a ring who may be trying to smuggle ambergris out of Cordoba. You know that the Caliph has specifically forbidden the movement of ambergris in a decree. I hope for your sake you are not involved in that. That could be very serious. Now you be sure and tell your barber friend everything I have told you,' said al-Mursi. 'I'll find my own way out.'

Back on the crowded street al-Mursi breathed a sigh of relief and allowed himself a smile behind his stinking veil as he heard Yazid vent his fury on the anvil.

Chapter 24

It started to rain again just as Miryam and her father got to the Alcazar. The soldiers huddled at the gate knew the Astronomer Royal and his daughter as regular visitors to the palace, so there was a minimum of formality on their arrival and the corridor guards outside the Vizier's office greeted them almost like acquaintances. Despite his position at court, Yunus was a modest man who didn't stand on ceremony and for this he was much admired by soldiers and courtiers alike. As for Miryam, there wasn't a soldier in Cordoba who didn't admire her.

Usually Miryam enjoyed coming to Hasdai's office, in fact she enjoyed his company altogether. Theirs was a warm relationship and one which had given rise to all manner of speculation in both the court and the suq. The Crown Prince himself had once asked Hasdai why he didn't just marry the woman and be done with it. It wasn't at all unusual for Jews to convert and take Moslem wives. The Vizier, as head of the diplomatic corps in the Caliphate, had needed all of his skill as a diplomat to change the subject.

'Ah, Yunus, Miryam, shalom, come in, thank you for coming... come in.'

Miryam waited for the door to close before she took Hasdai's note out of her pocket and held it up. 'I don't think we had much choice, did we? What's going on? The Admiral of the Fleet has not turned up at the university for two days and Bandar was spirited away this morning. Are you behind all of this?'

Yunus tutted at his daughter. Hasdai was a very good friend of theirs but he was still the Vizier.

'No, Yunus, she's right. I need to explain. But first have you eaten? I have asked for some chicken soup and bread and olives. I hope that's all right. Let's have a cup of sherry. I have some salted almonds somewhere.' Hasdai rang a bell to summon a servant who he instructed to bring the soup.

'Let me get the drinks,' said Miryam who knew exactly where the sherry flask was *and* the almonds. Miryam loved this room. She loved in particular the way in which it reflected the best in Hasdai ben Shaprut.

The way it smelt of leather, pine resin, herbs and Hasdai's scent. In the early evening light, the fire flickering in the grate on the north wall bathed the room in a gently undulating glow which picked out the gold embroidery on the red leather of the divans and the bindings of the books with which one wall was lined; books in Arabic, Hebrew, Latin and Greek. On one end of the oak desk was a pile of exquisitely detailed drawings of medicinal herbs each one annotated in Hasdai's graceful Arabic script. On one side of the fireplace there were exquisite pieces of Arabic and Hebrew calligraphy while on the south facing wall on either side of the window to the courtyard there were two pieces of art, one a framed Persian tile mosaic of deep red roses surrounding a pair of golden orioles and the other a richly embroidered mizrach, the Jewish icon which showed the direction of Jerusalem.

As they sat down to eat Miryam asked the inevitable question. 'So why have you got us here? This is not just a social call for chicken soup and sherry is it?'

'It's nice soup though,' said Yunus.

Hasdai smiled as Miryam glared at her father.

'No,' said Hasdai, 'it's not a social call. The Admiral is dead.'

'Dead?' said Yunus, his olive-wood spoon half-way to his mouth. 'How can he be dead?'

'Quite easily,' said Hasdai. 'Somebody cut the side of his head off and for good measure cut his throat as well.'

'Well,' said Miryam. 'This is not good news. I didn't particularly like the man but he didn't deserve that. Didn't he have a bodyguard though?'

'Yes, he did, but he was killed too. You might well know him. He was out at Madinat al-Zahra. It was young Lieutenant Haytham bin Tariq. General Ghalib knew him as a boy. In fact the General is quite close to the family.'

'Actually I know who his family is too,' said Yunus.

'Do you?' said Miryam.

'Yes. We're not friends, but they live over by the synagogue on the other side of the suq. I know who they are.'

'Were they together?' Miryam asked Hasdai.

'Who?'

'The Admiral and Haytham.'

'Why do you ask that?'

'Well, it seems like the kind of thing you would ask, or Ghalib. Where is the General by the way? He usually gets involved when something like this happens or when there is chicken soup.'

'He is very much involved. He is examining the case. The Admiral was found dead at the funduq and Haytham at the old Yemeni Yusuf's bathhouse.'

'What was the Admiral doing at the funduq?' said Yunus.

'We are not altogether sure, but it seems the Admiral was gambling at Yousef's place. He may have gone to the funduq with someone to collect a gambling debt, but we don't really know. Haytham was with the Admiral of course. At least they left the bathhouse together but we are not sure what happened after that. One thing we *do* know is that the bathhouse seemed to be empty when it was locked up for the night. The people in the bathhouse have no idea how or why Haytham got back in. He had had his throat cut too and was found half-cooked in the hot tub.'

Miryam shuddered, 'Oh dear, that's not a nice image,' she said.

'So where is Ghalib now?' asked Yunus.

'He has gone to the funduq. His men are questioning the people there. Ghalib has gone to hear what they have found out,' said Hasdai. 'One thing I wanted to ask you two... did anyone say anything out of the ordinary to the Admiral when you were teaching them? How were the relationships in the group?'

'Everything seemed perfectly normal,' said Yunus. 'They all seemed to get on well with each other. They weren't all as good as each other but that's to be expected in any class.'

'What's going to happen as a result of these deaths?' asked Miryam.

'You are going to have to speed up the training of Bandar,' said Hasdai. 'The Crown Prince has promoted him to Admiral of the Fleet and he has to get back to Almeria to get the navy underway as soon as possible.'

'There's not much more for him to do,' said Miryam. 'We have to go over some of the details of the almanac and then look at Ibn Hawqal's map and that's it. We finish tomorrow.'

'All that has to happen after that,' said Hasdai, 'is that he will need a briefing from Prince Hakam and then he can get off to Almeria to sort out the departure of the fleet.'

Yunus asked, 'Are we finished now?' He pushed his empty bowl to the

93

centre of the table.

'I think so,' said Hasdai. 'Why?'

'I thought I might go down to the Al Bisharah teahouse for a while. I said I would meet someone there tonight.'

'You never told me you were going to the Al Bisharah this evening,' said Miryam.

Yunus smiled. 'I don't need to tell you everything. But I'll tell you anyway. He's an instrument maker who works in the metal suq. He is making a new sundial for one of the gardens in Madinat al-Zahra.'

Hasdai got up and looked out of the window. 'I'll lend you a rain cape,' he said, then he laughed, 'Can he not make a rain dial? That would be more use in weather like this!'

'Very droll,' said Yunus. 'I am sure he could make a rain gauge if I asked him to but I will leave it up to you to tell the Caliph the next time you see him that you changed his orders.'

Hasdai laughed. 'Well you go off to the suq. I'll get a guard to take Miryam home when she's ready.'

As the door closed on Yunus, Miryam turned to Hasdai. She smiled and said, 'Let's get the fire built up. Is there any more sherry?'

'There's a flask in the cupboard under my desk. But I can't have any more.'

'Why not?' said Miryam.

'I still have to go to the funduq and then come back here to speak with Bandar tonight. I've also got to work on the Caliph's speech.'

'*Tonight*?' said Miryam. Hasdai could sense the exasperation in her voice. 'I thought you were finished for the day.'

'I'm sorry,' said Hasdai, 'I have to see him tonight. But we still have some time. He is not coming until just after the Isha prayer.'

'Well,' said Miryam, 'you really are working late! I'll be gone long before then.'

Chapter 25

Yunus shook the rain from Hasdai's oiled silk cape as he stood under the awning at the entrance to the Al Bisharah teahouse. Simon, the proprietor, had already spotted him and was making his way between the tables to the door wiping his huge hands on a cloth which he then draped over his massive shoulder.

'Yunus, my friend! *A salaam u aleikum*! Come in. It's good to see you.' Simon towered over Yunus as he clasped both of the astronomer's hands in his and shook them vigorously. 'In fact it's good to see anyone in weather like this. How are you? Come in and I'll get you some ginger tea to heat you up. Sit here by the kitchen door; it's warmer.' As he pulled out a stool for Yunus he shouted at the serving boy. 'Salah! Get some ginger tea with honey and some barad for my guest here and be quick about it!'

'*Wa aleikum a salaam*!' said Yunus as he sat down. 'I'm fine thanks, Simon, but I'll be better once I have warmed myself up and had a few of your barad. I see the rain is keeping away most of your customers.' He looked around the teahouse which was empty save for a couple of men at one of the tables at the back who were playing knucklebones to see who would buy the next cups of tea.

'Yes there is not much business really. People are staying at home after the Night Journey celebrations. The only regular customers we have lately are the navigators and their guards, and our friend in the corner.' Simon nodded towards the man wearing the black burnus.

'He's here again?' asked Yunus.

Simon nodded. 'I've never seen someone take so long over one cup of tea. But never mind him, how are you? What's happening with Miryam?'

Yunus waited until the boy who had come with the tea and barad had gone back into the kitchen.

'Miryam is fine. She is with the Vizier at the moment.'

'Ah, so that's why you have come,' said Simon.

'Well, yes,' said Yunus, 'but I was also supposed to meet Mohammed Al-Garnati here.'

'The instrument maker? He hasn't been in. He has not been in good health recently. Maybe this weather has kept him at home.'

'That must be it,' said Yunus, then he gave his friend a broad smile. 'In that case I shall just have to talk to you. Can I have some cinnamon for this tea?'

'Cinnamon?' said Simon. 'You'll be lucky! I don't have any. Ever since the Caliph banned the movement of foodstuffs, spices have become very hard to get. You're lucky I have any ginger left. I'll be glad when things get back to normal. Either this war is going to happen or it isn't. Not knowing is the difficult bit.'

'So the Caliph's ban is beginning to take effect is it?' said Yunus. 'I was wondering when that was going to happen.'

'Well,' said Simon, 'you can't just ban the city to city movement of all foodstuffs and expect *nothing* to happen. We can still get local supplies of course but some of the stuff we need is running very short. I suppose it makes sense though. If there is going to be a long drawn out campaign it is probably not a good idea to have hundreds of thousands of dinars' worth of food being traded all over Al Andalus. But it's not just food. Other commodities are being affected too. I get all sorts in here from the suqs and I hear that metal is being bought up by the armourers as fast as they can find it. It is the same with timber, the army agents are buying as much as they can lay their hands on... even the perfume trade has been affected.'

'The *perfume* trade?' said Yunus. 'How?'

'They say that it has now become a capital offence to move any kind of luxury goods from one city to another. Anything that ties up large sums of money. Ambergris for example. That can't be traded at all because it is so valuable.'

'Yes,' said Yunus, 'we are living in strange times.'

'*You* must know what's going on with your connections to the Vizier.'

Yunus smiled as he replied, 'Simon you know very well that even if I did know I wouldn't tell you. I knew Hasdai ben Shaprut long before he became Vizier. He is almost as old a friend of mine as you are. You wouldn't expect me to report our conversations to anyone would you?'

'No, indeed not,' said Simon. 'Let's have some more barad. I think I'll join you this time. Now, apart from spending time with the Vizier, what's Miryam been doing with herself?'

'She's got a new pupil. A girl who is absolutely brilliant. Miryam is spending a lot of time tutoring her.'

'What's her name?'

'Lubna bint Marwan.'

'Is that the daughter of Marwan the fur trader? She must be about eighteen years old now?'

'That's right, that's her. She is a very clever young woman. Miryam is teaching her mathematics and astronomy. She is already a very proficient grammarian in Arabic and an excellent scribe. She writes poetry too.'

'Well,' said Simon, 'I'm sure we'll hear a lot about her in the future. Are you sure she's Marwan's daughter though? Every time he comes in here he seems to forget how many cups of tea he has to pay for. He's always one short.'

Yunus laughed and said, 'Her father's not daft then. Maybe that's where she gets it from. And you *will* hear a lot about her in the future. Crown Prince Hakam wants her to start working as a scribe in his private office as soon as she is finished her studies with Miryam.'

'Hmm,' said Simon quietly, 'I am not sure that's such a good idea.'

'It's not really a matter of choice, is it?' said Yunus. 'But she'll be all right. Miryam is already working on the Vizier to make sure Lubna is looked after when she goes to work for Prince Hakam.'

'Well, if only half the rumours are true at least he won't try to bed her.'

'I think the less that's said about that the better,' said Yunus.

'Yes, perhaps you're right,' said Simon. 'Anyway I hear there are other things going on. The suq is full of talk of the murders. I suppose General Ghalib and the Vizier are concerned with them as well, aren't they?'

'And the prince,' said Yunus. 'He is taking a very personal interest in the investigation. But don't ask me any more about it. I'm sure you get all the information you need from your sources in the markets.'

'Most of what I hear is just speculation and idle talk. I hear all kinds of wild nonsense in here. I've learned to ignore most of it.'

'That's the best way,' said Yunus. 'Right, I think I'll be off back home now. The rain seems to have eased off a bit. How much do I owe you?'

'Ach, never mind,' said Simon. 'Invite me for a meal some time when Miryam is cooking.'

Yunus laughed. 'Oh well, in that case I'll take a couple of these barad home with me and you can come round for dinner next Sunday when you are closed. And this time bring your wife with you to keep you under control with the sherry!'

'Well, you certainly know how to spoil a good evening, don't you?' said Simon laughing with his friend. He shouted for the serving boy. 'Salah! Wrap up six barad for this customer and send him on his way.' Simon got up, 'Right, I must go and see to my oven. *Ma as-salaamah* Yunus, I'll see you on Sunday.'

'Yes, goodbye Simon. And thanks for the barad.'

Chapter 26

'Where did you find it?' asked General Ghalib as he hefted the falcata in his hand. The weapon glinted in the light of the oil lamp on the table.

Colonel Zaffar pointed to the dark at the back of the stables. 'There's a trough over there. One of the muleteers found it in the water, wrapped in the cloak. He was taking one of his animals to drink.'

Hasdai peered at the cloak, which had been wrung out and draped over the side of one of the stalls, then looked back at Ghalib. 'What do you think General? From what you saw of the body, could this be the murder weapon.' He looked at the falcata, a large heavy knife with an angled blade broader at the tip than at the hilt… a fearsome chopping weapon.

Ghalib nodded. 'Yes sir. Very much so. He would have needed something as heavy as this to make a wound like that.' As if to emphasise his point the General swung the falcata round his head and downwards, stopping just short of the table around which the three men were gathered. "Yes,' he said with a grunt of satisfaction. 'I think it is very likely that this is the weapon.'

'And what about the cloak?' asked Hasdai. 'Could that be Lieutenant Haytham's?'

'Possibly sir. As I recall, when we found him at the bathhouse there was no cloak amongst his belongings. Whoever killed him could have taken the falcata and his cloak. What I don't understand is why, having gone to the trouble of doing that, he would hide it in such an obvious place,' said the General. 'The murderer must have known we'd look in the water troughs.'

'Maybe he didn't have time to do any better than that,' said Hasdai. 'If he exploited a sudden opportunity to kill the Admiral, rather than having planned to do it, then he might not have had time to hide the things anywhere else.'

'Sir, one or two of the men we've spoken to said they thought the Admiral was with Lieutenant Haytham here at the funduq,' said Zaffar. 'That could be another reason why the cloak was found here. If Haytham was here, it seems logical his cloak was too.'

'But it isn't logical as to why his cloak was found here and his body was found at the bathhouse,' said Hasdai. 'No I think it more likely Haytham was already dead by the time his cloak turned up here at the funduq. We know the funduq was full and with all the people on the streets celebrating the Night Journey maybe whoever the murderer is just needed to get rid of the weapon and the cloak quickly, so he dumped them here.'

'Well, we don't know that do we?' said Ghalib

'No, General,' said Hasdai, 'we don't.' He showed his exasperation by bringing out his prayer beads and clicking them furiously.

The Vizier took a deep breath. 'Colonel, tell me about the interviews you have had with the people here.'

'Yes sir,' said Zaffar. 'We have spoken with all of the muleteers and funduq workers. None of them gave us much to go on. We have gone through the funduq's register and spoken to all but three of the guests. As you ordered, we've got men guarding the three girls and the cloth merchant. He is still being held in his room.'

'Good,' said Hasdai. 'I want to speak to him later. What can you tell me about these guests you haven't spoken to? Anything?'

As Zaffar took two sheets of paper from inside his tunic a young soldier approached the three men.

'Excuse me sir,' he said to the Colonel, 'the funduq owner is here as you requested.'

Zaffar nodded and gestured for Jaziri to join them.

'You asked to see me,' said Jaziri.

'I did,' said Zaffar. 'Tell the Vizier what you know about these three people.' He handed one of the papers to Hasdai and other to Jaziri. They both bent to the lamp to read them.

As he read the names Hasdai's eyes widened. He reached inside his robe and pulled out the pages he had found in the Admiral's room. 'Look General, this name here on Admiral Suhail's list…Shahid Jalal. It's the same as one of the funduq guests.'

Ghalib nodded. 'What do you know about this Shahid?' he said to Jaziri.

'Not much. He arrived about six weeks ago. I haven't seen a lot of him really. He didn't speak much to any of the other guests or staff. He has a small secure storage area that he occasionally goes into, but other than that, there isn't anything much to tell.'

'Where is his room?' asked the Vizier. 'I want to see it.'

'Of course,' said Jaziri. 'It's over on the other side of the courtyard.'

'So it's away from the main gate?' said Ghalib.

'Yes,' said Jaziri.

'Take us there now,' said Hasdai.

'We'll need this light,' said Jaziri and lifted the oil lamp from the table.

The other three men pulled their cloaks tightly about them and set off across the courtyard behind the funduq owner. As they did so Hasdai couldn't help noticing that General Ghalib was limping badly again. He'd been standing too long in the cold on that leg.

When they reached the bottom of a flight of stairs Jaziri said, 'Shahid's room is up there.'

General Ghalib stopped abruptly. 'This man's room is up there?'.

'What's the matter General?' said Hasdai.

Ghalib pointed to a tiny rubbish filled courtyard behind the staircase that they could just make out by the flickering light of the lamp. 'This is where we found the Admiral's body, sir.'

'Is it indeed?' said Hasdai as he turned to Jaziri. 'Let's see what is inside this Shahid's room then.'

The four men went up the stairs and a few steps along a walkway, with Jaziri holding up the lamp to light their way. He stopped outside a room and unlocked the door then stood back to allow the others to pass.

General Ghalib pushed him by the shoulder. 'You get in first and light the lamps,' he said. 'You can't expect the Vizier to stumble about in the dark, can you? *Ya Allah* it stinks in here. Don't you ever clean the rooms?'

With a mumbled apology Jaziri entered the room and lit the lamps. He looked from Hasdai to General Ghalib. 'Of course, we *do* clean the rooms, every morning after prayers but this man specifically asked for his room not to be cleaned.'

'Bah!' said Ghalib looking about him with his moustache bristling. 'What kind of a man was this?'

'Thank you, General,' said Hasdai as he looked around the room. 'That's exactly why we're here... to find that out.'

Whatever kind of man Shahid Jalal was, he had clearly left the funduq in a hurry. There was a head cloth on a nail at the back of the door and a belt with a broken buckle on the floor of the closet beside a discarded pair of worn-out sheepskin slippers. On a shelf by the window there was a large earthenware bowl still a quarter full of scummy water on which stubble still floated. The man had washed and shaved. On the side table by the mattress were the rotting remains of a meal of bread, olives and rice with fish, all of which had obviously had the recent attention of mice. A wine flask stood next to a toppled beaker, the spilled wine now nothing more than a dry red stain.

Hasdai turned to Jaziri. 'Remind me, when did this man arrive?'

'About six weeks ago sir,' said the funduq owner.

'And how long did he intend to stay?'

'He didn't say. But he paid in full for two months.'

'In full?' asked Hasdai.

Jaziri nodded.

'Is that normal?'

Jaziri shrugged. 'It happens sometimes.'

'When was the last time you saw him?' asked General Ghalib.

Jaziri thought for a moment. 'I can't exactly recall, but I don't think I have seen him for two or three days.'

'By the look of this room I think it's unlikely you will see him again,' said the General. 'Assuming he hasn't been here for a day or so is it possible that anyone else could have been in here since he left?'

Jaziri shrugged.

The General frowned and fixed his eyes firmly on Jaziri.

'Let's be very clear here,' he said facing up to him. 'A man has been murdered on your property. It might help speed up the investigation if you gave us as many details as possible about who this Shahid was and what you discussed. It would help even more if I didn't have to beat every little detail out of you. Am I making myself clear?' He was now close enough for Jaziri to see the individual hairs in his thick black moustache.

'Yes sir,' he croaked.

'Good,' said Hasdai. 'Now leave us. We'll talk to you again later.'

'Sir, what do you make of all this?' said Zaffar once Jaziri was well out of earshot.

'I'm not sure,' said Ghalib as he looked around the room and walked slowly over to the window which looked out over the walkway to the courtyard.

'So, tell us what your immediate thoughts are General,' said Hasdai.

'Let's explore the possibility that the Admiral had arranged to meet Shahid on the night he died. The door that leads into the courtyard from the room where the Admiral met the girls is over there,' he said, pointing to the far corner of the building. 'So if the murderer was waiting for him in here then he'd have been able to see him coming.'

'Wouldn't it have been too dark?' asked Zaffar.

'Yes. You may be right,' said Ghalib. 'And actually, if he was waiting in here why did he kill him down by the stairs in full view of the courtyard?'

'Unless Shahid is the murderer and he killed him in here,' said Zaffar. 'He could have dragged the body downstairs. Or maybe the Admiral wasn't actually dead and staggered down the stairs to try and get help?'

'With his throat cut from ear to ear and half his head missing?' said Hasdai. 'I really don't think so colonel. But if he was killed in here then someone has done an excellent job of cleaning up the blood but not the food and wine. And why go to the trouble of doing that if you are then going to dump the body a short distance away?'

'Well sir, the murderer could be trying to distract attention away from this room, or he may have been disturbed whilst moving the body. Rather than be discovered he simply left the body and ran.'

'I'm not sure, colonel,' said Hasdai. He came to the window and peered out into the courtyard.

'Sir, we may be reading more into this than is actually there,' said Ghalib. 'Shahid Jalal could be the name of one of the Admiral's men. It may simply be a coincidence that it is also the name of someone who was staying close to where his body was found.'

Hasdai turned from the window and looked around the room again. 'I think that's too much of a coincidence to be true General. Now, Jaziri mentioned that this man had a secure storage area. Zaffar, go and get Jaziri. I think it's time for us to see what this Shahid has in store.'

Chapter 27

Yunus knuckled his eyes and sat up as he heard the key turn in the heavy oak door to the courtyard of his house. He was sitting by the fireplace in his majlis from where he could see the door through a window. He listened to his daughter thank the palace guardsman who had escorted her home then saw her step over the threshold.

Miryam shivered and pulled her cloak closer about her as she hurried past the date palm in the centre of the courtyard then came into the sitting room.

'Shrrr! It's cold,' she said making straight for the fire.

'I didn't expect you back so soon,' said Yunus stifling a yawn. He watched as Miryam sat down on a pile of cushions and warmed herself by the fire. The oil lamps on the walls cast a soft glow bringing out the deep reds of the carpets and cushions in the room.

'The Vizier had some state business to attend to,' said Miryam, taking off her shawl and shaking out her long auburn hair. 'It's lovely and warm in here.'

'What was Hasdai doing this late?' asked Yunus. 'It must be important.'

'I think it is to do with the poor Admiral,' said Miryam. 'It is so sad. Who could want to do such a thing?'

Yunus shook his head. 'I don't know. Bandar was with the navigators all afternoon. It must be a heavy blow to them to lose their commander like that. I hope we can get them through the rest of their training before the Caliph returns.' He took a plate from a low table and offered it to his daughter. 'Here, would you like one of Simon's barad?'

'Thanks,' said Miryam. 'Have you already had some? How *was* Simon?' She slipped off her fur-lined boots and put her feet up to the fire.

'He was very well. I invited him and his wife for dinner on Sunday. He asked after you.'

'That was kind of him.' She took a bite out of the cake and sank back into a cushion. 'It's strange but this will probably mean that the men will finish their training sooner,' she said. 'I know it all has to be done by the time the Caliph returns to Cordoba but the Admiral really wasn't that skilled with the astrolabe. I think without him they'll finish things without any more problems.'

'He didn't meet your high standards did he?' said Yunus with a grin. 'You are just like your mother.'

Miryam blushed.

'I'm only teasing you,' he said laughing. 'But those high standards will serve you well when you take over as Astronomer Royal.'

'Come now,' said Miryam, 'you know that'll never happen.'

'Oh, I don't see why not,' said Yunus. 'I have no intention of carrying on forever. I think you are the perfect choice.' Miryam was about to speak before her father carried on. 'Let's look at the situation,' he said. 'You are teaching that lovely girl Lubna who is about to start working as a scribe in the Crown Prince's private office. You wouldn't have been asked to do that if they didn't value you highly now would you?'

Miryam shrugged. 'There's a difference between a woman being valued and one getting a court position.'

'You are also close friends with the Vizier and you have been trusted with the training of the naval officers.'

'That may be the case,' said Miryam, 'but I'll never get the position. In any case all I want to do is get on with my observations. I'd rather stay in the position of assistant to the Astronomer Royal. I don't want to spend my time casting horoscopes. I want to do proper science.'

Yunus squeezed her arm. 'Your mother would be so proud see what you have become. Now, shall we have a drink?' Yunus got up and fetched the wineskin which hung on a hook in the corner of the room. 'It is a shame your time with the Vizier was cut short,' he said yawning again. 'Did you make any plans to see each other again?'

Miryam shook her head. 'No, he is very busy. Things might be easier once the training is finished and the officers have left for Almeria.'

Yunus poured two cups of wine. They sat next to each other and stared into the fire.

'Just out of interest,' said Yunus putting his cup down on the table, 'how much of a problem was it with the Admiral and the training?'

'What do you mean?'

'What you said earlier,' said Yunus. 'I didn't really spend that much time with the officers as individuals. Was he really not as skilled as the others?'

Miryam took a sip of wine and leant her head against her father's knee. He stroked her hair gently.

'I don't know,' she said. 'He seemed to grasp the mathematics, and how to set up and use the astrolabe itself. But he just seemed, well, distracted. He always seemed at odds with the others. Once I heard him shouting at one of them when I wasn't in the room. I think it might have been Siraj.'

'I don't like that Siraj,' said Yunus.

'No, neither do I but he *is* an excellent navigator. Maybe Admiral Suhail was just confused. Perhaps he didn't understand.' Miryam sighed. 'I don't know really. I asked them all, several times a session if they had any questions. He never asked me a thing. I don't think...' Miryam broke off at the sound of her father's gentle snoring. She smiled then got up to pull a rug over his legs. She gently kissed the soft white hair on the crown of his head and stared into the glowing embers as she drank her wine

Chapter 28

'This is the one,' said Jaziri. He pointed to a stout wooden door deep in the shadow of an arch.

'Bring that light here,' said Hasdai to Colonel Zaffar who was standing behind General Ghalib holding a torch.

They could see that the door was secured with a heavy iron padlock.

'Where is the key to this?' asked Hasdai.

Jaziri shrugged his shoulders. 'I don't know. Shahid had it.'

'Do you have a copy of the key?' asked Ghalib.

'No. Why should...'

'Listen Jaziri,' said Ghalib, 'don't ask us any questions. Just give us the answers we need. Nothing else. Do you understand?'

'Yes,' said Jaziri. 'I'm sorry.'

'Good,' said Ghalib. 'Now, do you have a heavy hammer? We'll need a hammer and some kind of iron spike to break this lock.'

'I'll get one of my servants to...'

'No you won't,' said Ghalib. 'You'll get it. We don't want every stable-hand in this place to know what's going on. Bring us a hammer and the poker from your fireplace in your office. Colonel Zaffar should be able to get us in here without too much trouble.'

Moments later Zaffar had smashed the padlock and they stood in the small, musty storeroom with Jaziri holding the torch. In the flickering light they could see that the room contained four wooden crates which, piled one on the other, reached the height of a man.

'Zaffar,' said Ghalib. 'Get that top crate down.'

'This is heavy!' said the young officer as he heaved the box to the floor.

'Open it up,' said Hasdai and they watched as Zaffar levered off the top of the crate with the poker then rummaged in the straw packing inside the box.

'It's full of earthenware pots,' said Zaffar, 'and they are all sealed with beeswax.'

'Here,' said Ghalib. 'Put one on the box so I can open it up.' He took his dagger and scraped at the wax which sealed the pot.

'Be careful!' said Jaziri. 'You don't know what's in there. It could be anything.'

'Will you shut up until you are spoken to,' said Ghalib, much to the amusement of Zaffar and the Vizier. 'Bring the torch down to give us some light. Here Zaffar, let's have a look.'

The two soldiers hunched over the pot as Ghalib, a bit more carefully now, opened the seal. As the wax broke the smell of bitter oranges filled the storeroom.

Ghalib couldn't help but laugh. 'There you are Jaziri! There's nothing to be frightened of. Four crates of bitter orange jam.'

Zaffar looked up at Hasdai who did not appear to be sharing Ghalib's mirth.

'What do you think of this Your Excellency?' the colonel asked.

'It makes no sense,' said Hasdai. 'Why would anyone go to such trouble to keep four boxes of bitter orange paste in a secure storeroom like this? The cheapest fruit in Al Andalus. Hand me the pot.' He leant forward.

As Zaffar picked up the pot in both hands he snagged his forearm on one of the nails in the lid of the box and opened up a gash from wrist to elbow.

'Aaach!' he shouted and dropped the pot at Hasdai's feet where it smashed in a mess of orange jam, beeswax and pottery.

'I am really sorry Your Excellency, did you get splashed?' said the young soldier as he bound his arm with his head cloth.

'No, don't worry,' said Hasdai. 'I'll see to your cut as soon as we get back to the Alcazar. But I think your injury may have been worth it. Look!' He pointed at the mess on the floor.

'Bring the light down,' said Ghalib to Jaziri as he poked in the jam with his dagger. 'There's a smaller jar here inside the jam.'

Hasdai spoke. 'I think you'll find that there is something in that jar which is a lot more valuable than bitter oranges. Zaffar help the General up then get two guards on this door. No-one but General Ghalib is to enter here without my permission. Jaziri bring this jar to your office. We can wash it there and open it up. But I'd be prepared to wager anything you like that what we have found here is one of the biggest shipments of ambergris which has ever been put together in Al Andalus. If I am right the contents of these crates are worth an enormous amount of money.'

Chapter 29

'Look,' said Bandar bin Sadiq, 'it's happened and nothing we can do can bring the old admiral back to life. We just have to get on with things and do our duty as best we can.'

The four navigators were in Bandar's room in the Alcazar, huddled up on stools close to the fire, each with a cup of arak of sugar cane.

'Well,' said the man from Qadiz to Bandar as he raised his cup, 'I think we should drink to the memory of our Admiral. I have nothing but good memories of him. He was a fair and just commander and a real prince of the sea, a true *amir al-bahr*. I served with him, you know, on a voyage on the *Bahr al-Zulumat*. We sailed north for weeks on that Sea of Darkness from Qadiz. He could read the ocean like an almanac. It was him who taught me how to use a compass.'

Here the navigator from Abdera chimed in. 'All four of us have served under him man! Why do you sailors from Qadiz always think your sea is more important than ours in Abdera and Almeria. Our *Bahr al-Rūm* is no less of a sea because we know the extent of its shores.'

'Pah!' said Siraj. 'The Romans knew the extent of the *Bahr al-Rūm* centuries ago. Why do you think it's called that?'

'Listen to me Siraj,' said Bandar, 'this is no time to squabble over which sea is more or less important than another. From now on, what is important is the voyage we have to complete for the sake of our Caliph and Admiral Suhail. You've all done well. I think we're almost there. The Admiral would be proud of you. You should be proud of what we have achieved in a few short days.'

The men nodded, each silent in their private grief, taking comfort from Bandar's words.

'I sense we will be here in Cordoba for two more days and then depart for Almeria to re-join the fleet,' said Bandar. 'You know that I cannot say much more about our plans until we leave port, but you should know that Admiral Suhail's plan is a brilliant one. What's more, you should take courage from the fact he wanted you to be the ones to lead the fleet as we set sail.' He watched as all the men except Siraj met his gaze. 'I need to leave you now. I have to go to my briefing with the Vizier. Let's meet here again at first light. Make sure the door is closed when you leave and tell the corridor guard my room is empty.'

Bandar put his cup on the table and bade his three colleagues goodnight. The door closed behind him and the men sat in silence until Bandar and his bodyguard were gone.

Siraj put his empty cup down on the table. 'That's enough for me for tonight,' he said. 'I am going to bed. I wish you all goodnight.'

Siraj had no sooner left the room when the man from Qadiz spoke. 'We should say something,' he said.

'No. We should say nothing.'

'Look, I really think we should say something about what happened. You heard what…'

'I heard nothing. Neither of us heard anything. Is that clear? Bandar is in command now and Siraj is second in command. We follow their orders.'

'I'm not disputing that. I'm just saying that someone needs to know what we heard.' He got up and moved towards the door. As he did his companion blocked his way and the two men grasped each other's arms.

'Listen to me,' said the man from Abdera, his eyes filling with tears. 'Admiral Suhail is dead. There is no need for you to do this. Let him die with his reputation intact.'

There was a short pause. 'Very well.'

'Come on. Let's get another drink. I have a wineskin in my room.'

The man from Qadiz nodded and they stepped out into the corridor.

As they walked away a figure slipped out of the shadows and watched.

What do they know about Admiral Suhail? thought Siraj.

Chapter 30

'Sir, I think the Admiral was either killed for the money which he got from Antonio after the knucklebones game, or because of the ambergris... probably by Shahid Jalal.'

General Ghalib's face twisted as he spoke and he bent down to rub his knee. It felt like someone was pushing red-hot needles into his bones. Hasdai sighed. He knew the General was reluctant to let him treat his knee.

The rhythmic clicking of Hasdai's amber prayer beads filled the silence. The two men were alone in Hasdai's office in the Alcazar Palace.

Ghalib grunted as he got up to scoop two handfuls of pine cones from the basket and throw them on the fire. He settled on a stool opposite the Vizier and stretched his leg so that his knee could get the warmth of the fire.

'I could believe it was a robbery,' said Hasdai, 'but I'm not sure about Shahid Jalal. I'm not sure about the ambergris.'

'Why not?' said Ghalib flexing his leg.

Hasdai thought for a moment before he placed the beads on his desk next to the draft of the Caliph's speech. He opened a drawer. He took out two small squat cups and reached for a wineskin which hung on its hook next to his bookcase. Hasdai held up a cup and Ghalib nodded.

'I am prepared to concede that ambergris plays a part in this somehow,' said Hasdai as he poured two cups of wine. 'But I am not sure how it is connected to the Admiral.'

'What if the Admiral were planning to buy the ambergris we found at the funduq,' said General Ghalib taking the cup of wine. 'You found those vials in his room and Jalal was on a list of names amongst his notes. It isn't too much to assume he was looking to get a quantity of ambergris.'

Hasdai sipped his wine as he thought. 'General, if we assume that the Admiral was planning to buy ambergris and smuggle it out of Cordoba, then we must conclude he had a significant amount of money available to him.'

Ghalib nodded. 'That's my point sir. The money could have been taken by whoever killed him.'

'Are you suggesting that Jalal arranged to sell the ambergris to the Admiral only to kill him, or have him murdered, and take the money?'

Ghalib nodded. 'It's a possibility,' he said.

'Then why would he take the money, but leave the ambergris in the funduq? You saw that storage area. It's worth a fortune.'

The General frowned and emptied his cup.

'Before we get too far ahead,' said Hasdai, 'we need to think this through carefully. It is clear that the murder is related, in some way, to the ambergris. It is just too much of a coincidence not to be connected. Now, if you were planning to smuggle ambergris out of a heavily guarded city, how would you do it? What would you need to make it happen?' He offered the wineskin to Ghalib.

The General refilled his cup. 'You would need help for one thing. If you were planning to move all the ambergris you couldn't do it on your own.'

Hasdai nodded. 'Agreed. What else?'

'You would need a way of diverting attention away from what you were doing. You would also need to break it down into smaller quantities. What we found is too large to transport at the same time.'

Hasdai sipped his wine as he thought. 'When was the body found? It was the night before last?'

'Yes sir,' said Ghalib.

'That was when the Night Journey of Mohammed was celebrated. Think about it General, that would have been an excellent opportunity to move the ambergris. The city gates were all open, there were crowds of people out on the streets and the noise alone would have allowed someone, or possibly more than one person, to move it. The chances of getting stopped and searched would have been very slight.'

'It's still taking a big risk though sir,' said Ghalib.

'I'm not denying that General. But it is considerably less of a risk than moving it at any other time. Let's assume for the moment that that was the plan, and that is how they intended to get it out of the city. Presuming they were intending to sell it on, what would they do next?'

'That depends on who they were selling it to. If it were to someone here in Al Andalus they could arrange for whoever it was to collect it.'

Hasdai looked into his wine cup and thought for a moment. 'What if you were looking to move it abroad?'

Ghalib's eyes widened. 'You mean the main fleet?'

Hasdai shook his head. 'I didn't mean anything General. I simply asked what you would do if you were looking to move it abroad.'

'Well sir, if the Admiral was involved in this then he would have had an excellent method of transporting the ambergris straight to the fleet. The amount of supplies that we are sending to Almeria to support the war effort is huge. You can't get hold of anything here in Cordoba at the moment. It is all going straight to Almeria and on to the main fleet. The Admiral could have hidden it easily in the daily transports from the stores.'

Hasdai nodded. 'Very good General. That's right. But there's something that really doesn't make sense.'

'What's that sir?'

Hasdai held out his cup and Ghalib refilled it from the wineskin. 'The Admiral had the Caliph's fleet under his command and he could have used this to transport the ambergris abroad, he had the perfect cover to move it out of Cordoba and he could have used the war supply network to transport it all the way to Almeria without arousing suspicion. It is a brilliant plan.'

'What is it that doesn't make sense then?' asked Ghalib.

Hasdai sipped at the wine. 'What doesn't make sense, General, is that on the night that provided the best opportunity to move the ambergris out of Cordoba the Admiral, and the bodyguard we assigned to look after him, were murdered. Someone didn't think the plan was quite so brilliant.'

The sound of a soldier snapping to attention came from the corridor outside the Vizier's office.

'This will be Bandar,' said Hasdai. 'Not a word of all this until we know more.'

'Shouldn't we tell him though sir? Surely he has right to know what the Admiral was planning to do?'

Hasdai placed the cups back in the drawer and hung up the wineskin. 'We don't know for certain what the Admiral was planning to do though, do we? And until I have some proof I don't think it would be wise for me to accuse a well-respected Admiral of the Royal Fleet of smuggling ambergris. Particularly not one who has just been brutally murdered.'

'Yes, you're right.'

There was a knock at the door.

'Enter,' called the Vizier.

'Sir, the Admiral of the Fleet is here as arranged,' said the Chamberlain's clerk who showed Bandar in to the office.

'Good evening Admiral,' said Hasdai. 'Leave us,' he said to the clerk. 'Please, take a seat,' he said gesturing to a stool. 'How are the men?'

'Shocked,' said Bandar smoothing his thick beard. 'We all are. It is difficult to take in.'

'I quite understand,' said Hasdai. 'Will you be ready in time?'

Bandar nodded. 'Yes, we'll be ready. The Caliph is not due back until the day after tomorrow. That gives us time to complete the work with the astrolabe and finish the charts with Yunus and his daughter. Have we had any news from the advance flotilla?' As he spoke he scratched at the bandage on his arm.

'No, not yet,' said Hasdai. 'Do you want some more chamomile and thyme for your wound?'

Bandar noticed that the General was smiling as he shook his head. 'Thanks, it's fine. What about the Admiral's killer?'

'We have two main suspects, a cloth merchant who is being held at the funduq, and a suq trader who is here in the cells in the Alcazar.'

'Have they confessed to the murders?'

Hasdai shook his head. 'Now,' he said, 'something else. You need to know the arrangements for when the Caliph returns to Cordoba. There is to be a reception here at the Alcazar in the evening at which you and the vice-Admirals will be the guests of honour. The following afternoon, after the Asr prayer, the Caliph will address the people and send you on your way.'

Bandar nodded. 'Very good, sir,' he said. 'It will be a great honour for me and my men to meet the Caliph. Will there be anything else?'

Hasdai shook his head. 'Not tonight, no. If you should need me for anything then one of the clerks in the Chamberlain's office will know how to contact me. If not then we shall meet at the reception the evening after tomorrow.'

Bandar bowed to the Vizier then the General and took his leave.

Ghalib drew in his knee. 'What do you want to do now?' he asked.

'After the dawn prayer tomorrow morning I want you go to the camp and talk to the quartermaster. Find out how difficult it would be to access the supply chain in order to smuggle something into it. And get a list of all the people who work there. Once you've done that go and check the suq trader's alibi with the clerk at al-Mursi's bathhouse.'

Ghalib nodded 'Very good sir. I can do that.'

'Good. I'll go myself and talk to Yousef at his bathhouse to see if I can find out anything about this game of knucklebones. I'll also talk to our man from Baghdad, Ali, to see if he knows of anyone there who might be looking to secure a large quantity of ambergris. He should have recovered from his journey by now. If there is something going on with the supply chain then we can get Ali to keep a watch on it. Tell the quartermaster Ali will be coming to work for him. Oh, something else... I presume you are going to get Colonel Zaffar to ride to Madinat al-Zahra so he can command the Caliph's escort back to Cordoba?'

'Yes, I am going to do that,' said Ghalib. 'Do you think we have enough time, sir?'

'Do you mean to find the Admiral's killer before the Crown Prince and the Caliph expect to see a crucifixion with dogs in front of the people? I don't know General. But I'd wager that the crucifixion will go ahead regardless, and either our friend at the funduq or the one in the Alcazar prison will be invited. Quite possibly both.'

Chapter 31

Day 4

'Welcome Your Excellency,' said Yousef, 'welcome!' He shut the grille then pulled open the heavy door to the bathhouse. 'I am glad to see you! I was beginning to think you would never come here again!'

Hasdai smiled at his old friend. 'Thank you Yousef. It's good to see you too, and yes you are right, I am long overdue for a visit.'

'Please come in out of the cold,' said Yousef as he led the Vizier inside and then into his office where Hasdai sat down by the fire. 'I trust the Caliph is keeping you busy?'

Hasdai laughed. 'Yes you could say that.'

The two men had been friends for many, many years, ever since Yousef had taken over what had become Hasdai's favourite bathhouse in the city. At that time Hasdai had been a rabbi and an academic. But since he had become Vizier to Caliph Abd al-Rahman III the bathhouse pools had often provided a sanctuary for him as he pondered the affairs of state.

'I assume,' said Yousef, 'that given recent events, you didn't come here to use my hot water pool. Let me organize some tea for you and then you can tell me how I can help you?'

As he overheard Yousef instruct his servant, Hasdai noticed a wooden bowl of lamb's knucklebones on the shelf above the fireplace. He leant forward and took a couple of the bones from the bowl. They were smooth from constant handling over many years and had a deep brown patina. The Vizier took one of them between finger and thumb and examined it in the firelight. He thought of how many fortunes had been won and lost on the four sides of bones like this one; the convex, concave, flat and snake-like sides. This is what men bet on, with four bones, how many of which side would turn up when they were cast on the table.

When Yousef came back in he saw the Vizier with the bones. He was clicking them together in his hand as if they were his prayer beads.

Yousef raised his eyebrows and said with a half-smile, 'You don't want to play knucklebones too do you?'

'No indeed,' said Hasdai. 'I don't get my money easily enough to lose it using these things. I always think of knucklebones as a game in which you throw a bone in the air and then try to collect the rest of them from the table with the same hand before you catch the first one as it falls.'

Yousef smiled and nodded. 'It is,' he said, 'for children and old men on doorsteps in the suq but you know as well as I do that they weren't playing that game here.'

It was Hasdai's turn to smile. 'So they play a different game when the Market Inspector's not looking,' he said.

'You'll have to ask Hamid al-Mursi about that,' said Yousef with a shrug and a smile.

Yousef's servant knocked on the door then came in with a copper pot of tea and two cups. Hasdai could smell the honey and mint. He looked up and thanked the servant and waited until he had closed the door. Yousef poured the tea.

'Do you know Nasim bin Faraj?'

'The perfume trader?' said Yousef. 'Yes I know him. He comes here regularly. Once a week at least.'

'That's what he told the General and me,' said Hasdai. 'He said he comes here to bathe.'

Yousef shook his head and laughed. 'Not quite Excellency. He does bathe when he's here, but he really comes to play knucklebones.'

Hasdai nodded. 'Nasim said that the night before we found the Lieutenant you introduced him to a cloth merchant from Sevilla?'

Yousef sighed deeply. 'That was a dreadful business. That poor soldier. But yes, Nasim's right. The cloth merchant said that someone at the funduq where he was staying recommended my bathhouse to him. He came that night after evening prayers, bathed for a while and then we got talking. He seemed interested in watching Nasim and the Admiral playing knucklebones so I introduced him to them when they stopped for refreshments.'

'So the game between the Admiral and Nasim was already taking place?'

'Yes. They arrived earlier that evening and played for a long while. They seemed to know each other fairly well. I saw Nasim give the Admiral a note and a small package. They talked for a long time.'

'What was it? The package.'

'I'm sorry Excellency, I couldn't say what it was, and I certainly didn't ask. I know there was a lot of money exchanged.'

Hasdai sniffed deeply at the steam from his tea then took a sip. He thought for a moment.

'So how were they betting?' asked Hasdai. 'The usual way?'

'Yes, but the stakes were pretty high.'

'From what we've learnt,' said Hasdai, 'the Admiral won a great deal of money that evening.'

'Yes I believe so,' said Yousef. 'I heard later that he agreed to meet the cloth merchant... Antonio I believe his name was, the following night to settle the debt.'

Hasdai frowned.

'Is there something wrong Excellency?'

'No Yousef. That's fine. Tell me... was the Lieutenant here the whole time?'

'Yes. He didn't play but he was in the room during the game. As far as I recall he was there all the time.'

'Can you remember who else was here that night?'

Yousef sipped his tea. 'There were a few other regulars, mostly workers from the metalwork suq. They come here quite often.' He paused for a moment before adding, 'Gambling is a terrible thing. I've seen it rob a man of his character.'

'Then why do you let it go on in your bathhouse?' said Hasdai.

'Excellency please understand, I am not here to judge, but nor am I responsible for the moral standards of the city. In any case, you should really talk to al-Mursi the chief market inspector. He is the one in charge of the suq traders and their workers.'

'I'll talk to him in due course,' said Hasdai. 'Out of interest though, how big a problem do you think it is, the gambling?'

Yousef shrugged. 'It happens,' he said. 'Some men can have their fill once in a while. Others struggle. It is those individuals I feel for. You can see in their eyes that they want to stop, but don't know how to.'

The Vizier nodded.

Yousef poured more tea for the two of them. 'Do you know Excellency, there used to be a group of men who met here at the bathhouse, a year or so before I owned it. By all accounts they would gamble vast quantities of money, or food, or whatever. But the risks were enormous.'

'What do you mean?' asked Hasdai.

'As I understand it, they would gamble for a year's pay at a time.'

'That's a lot of money to lose.'

'They didn't lose money Excellency. If you won, you could *win* a year's pay. If you lost, you would lose a finger, or a thumb.'

Hasdai stared intently at Yousef. He spoke eventually. 'Did you see the Admiral leave?'

'I did. He and the Lieutenant came to talk to me on their way out.'

'What did you discuss?'

'The Lieutenant asked me if he could come back the following evening once I had closed for the night.'

'Did you ask why he wanted to come?'

'He just said he wanted time on his own to relax.'

'That's unusual though. Did you agree?'

Yousef nodded. 'Yes. The Admiral gave me a rather generous amount of money. I saw no reason to object to the Lieutenant coming back. Did I do something wrong?'

Hasdai thought for a moment. 'I honestly don't know Yousef. But I do know that both the Lieutenant and the Admiral are now dead. Whatever happened to them is not clear, but we know that the Lieutenant's body was found here in the bathhouse. Would he have let himself in?'

'Yes. I gave him a key. We found it amongst his belongings after his body was discovered.'

'Did you? General Ghalib said there was no sign of the Lieutenant's cloak.'

'That's right. Just his robes.'

At that moment there was a knock on the street door to the bathhouse.

'Would you excuse me Excellency? That will be the cleaner.'

'Yes, of course. You've been very helpful,' said Hasdai. He held up the two bones. 'Can I keep these for a while?'

Yousef bowed slightly and made to leave. 'Of course,' he said.

'One final thing,' said Hasdai. 'What happened to the men who gambled here before you bought the bathhouse? The ones you just mentioned. Where did they go?'

Yousef shook his head. 'I can't be certain. They were a rough lot. After

I put a stop to their nonsense most of them didn't come back. I see a couple of them from time to time. As far as I know they still work in the metalwork suq. The rumour is they currently gamble on cockfighting down by the wharf.'

Chapter 32

General Ghalib knew exactly why he was here this morning. It had been playing on his mind. If there was movement of contraband going on it would need to start somewhere and to him this seemed as good a place as any.

He had walked from the Alcazar in the chill mist of the morning past the Funduq and through the Bab al-Jadid to the vast temporary military camp, Camp Maaqul, which had been set up just outside the city walls at the head of the road to Almeria. It was here that a significant part of the huge quantities of arms, equipment and foodstuffs necessary to supply the Caliph's army and navy was being assembled to be transported by camel and mule trains to the naval port of Almeria. Once there the supplies would be loaded on the second wave of ships to the east. He knew that there were other such camps closer to the coast but Camp Maaqul was important. It was from here that the armoury of the elite royal regiments was being shipped as well as preserved fruits and other important provisions requisitioned from the rich farmlands surrounding the capital. This was going to be a long campaign.

As the General walked past the guards into the teeming camp he fixed his jaw against his limp. He well remembered scenes like this. Trains of camels complaining and belching, the screaming bray of mules mingling with the sound of their jingling harnesses and the whooping cries of the drivers of the ox-carts echoing their screeching wheels. Grooms scampering about with bales of feed while sweepers cleared up the muck. And everywhere, tent after tent of equipment and materials for war to be organised and checked against the manifest lists. He would give anything to be back on active service again but as he stooped to rub his knee he knew it could never happen.

An officer of the guard approached and saluted him.

'Good morning sir. It's General Ghalib isn't it, sir? I was a cadet under you on the Northern Frontier. It was an honour to serve with you. How can I help you sir?'

For the life of him Ghalib couldn't remember the man's face. There had been dozens of cadet officers on that campaign and after all it was a few years ago now.

'Thank you,' said Ghalib. 'I need to find the sergeant quartermaster.'

'Certainly sir, I'll take you to him myself. Be careful here sir, there's a drainage ditch.'

They walked between lines of tents and half loaded caravans of pack animals towards a wooden stage which had been built up in the centre of the camp. This was where the quartermaster was based. From his operations tent erected on this stage he could look out over the whole camp and see exactly how the movement of supplies was proceeding. The tent itself was large enough to accommodate twenty or so military clerks who were busy ordering runners to every part of the camp and taking messages from others. Ghalib knew exactly how important this part of the war machine was. Once, on the Northern Frontier, his troops had almost run out of arrows...a potential disaster for a defending force. This would never happen now. The arms manufacturers in Cordoba were much better organised than ever before and could produce over fifteen thousand arrows and eight hundred bows every month of the year. The smiths in the royal armouries were producing spear heads and swords and shield bosses and daggers at an incredible rate and if necessary all the smiths in the metalwork suqs could be pressed into the service of the Caliph.

'I'll just tell the quartermaster you are here,' said the young officer and he leapt up on to the stage and ducked under the awning of the tent.

A few moments later he reappeared with an older man dressed in the livery of the royal armoury. The man spread his arms wide. '*Marhaba*, General Ghalib! Welcome, welcome. *A salaam u aleikum*. I haven't seen you since we prepared for your campaign to the north.'

'*Wa aleikum a salaam*,' said Ghalib, then he thanked the young officer who had brought him to the quartermaster. He turned again to the quartermaster. 'I never got a chance to say how grateful I was for your efforts.'

'Come General. Who needs thanks for doing their duty? How can I help you today? We can have tea first. Sit... please.' The quartermaster took Ghalib into the tent and they sat down on stools beside a clay brazier on which was bubbling a copper pot of water. A servant quickly made mint tea and brought some barad.

'I hope you like these,' said the quartermaster offering Ghalib one of the sweet buns. 'I have them delivered every morning from the Al Bisharah tea-house. Now, what can I do for you?'

Ghalib chuckled and said, 'Even quartermasters march on their stomachs! Now, is there somewhere private where we can talk?'

'Why of course,' said the quartermaster. 'Here! This is my office.' He stood up and clapped his hands twice. 'Out!' he shouted. 'Check on your lines! Now!'

As the tent emptied of personnel Ghalib thought that one of the clerks took rather longer to leave than the others. He was wearing a thick hooded burnus of black wool and had the hood pulled down over his eyes. Then the General shook his head. Surely he was imagining things now. He smiled again and looked around the empty tent. This was exactly the sort of thing he would have done himself. Show your guests that you have absolute command over your men.

'So, how can I help you?' asked the quartermaster.

'I'll come straight to the point. The Vizier and I have been investigating a killing.'

'Is that the Admiral of the Fleet?'

'Indeed. Nothing stays secret in the military!'

'No, it was a nasty business. And some of my men served with Lieutenant Haytham as well. It's one thing for a soldier to be killed in battle but to be slaughtered like a goat in a bathhouse is something else. Have you got anyone for it?'

'You wouldn't expect me to tell you that would you sergeant?'

'No, not really. I'm sorry sir.'

'Don't worry. But there is something I think you can help us with. And I must ask you to keep this absolutely confidential. We have reason to believe that there may be a smuggling ring in operation. As you well know His Majesty the Caliph has forbidden trade in a number of commodities. Particularly things which are needed for the war effort but also high value merchandise. He doesn't want any financial speculation at this time. And as usual circumstances like this bring out the rats who try to carry tasty morsels from one place to another if the price is high enough.'

'I know exactly what you mean,' said the quartermaster. 'But how does this concern me?'

'Well, you are responsible for a constant flow of goods from here to

Almeria.'

'Yes, but everything is registered by my clerks on the caravan manifests which are sent ahead by messengers to Almeria and the lists are checked again on arrival.'

'Do you think it is possible for contraband to be put on one of your caravans and then sent under guard to Almeria?'

'In theory it is possible, but it would need a good deal of organisation, and a traitor within Camp Maaqul. What kind of contraband are we talking about here?'

'Again, sergeant, I can't tell you that exactly, but say I wanted to ship four extra cases of foodstuff on one of your mule trains. How would I do that?'

'Well,' said the quartermaster, 'I suppose if whoever was doing it was able to forge the manifest all they would need to do then is add an extra mule to the train. Four standard cases is just one animal or at most two depending on what they are loaded with. You can see for yourself that some of these mule trains have over a hundred animals. One extra would probably not be noticed as once the trains are made up we never count the animals. We depend on the lists being accurate.'

'And all your staff know that?'

'Of course.'

'So it's not really *that* difficult, is it?' asked Ghalib.

'Well,' said the quartermaster, 'if you put it like that I suppose not. But I must say it's not something I have ever given any thought to. Should I be worried about something like this happening?'

'I am not here to find fault with your organisation,' said the General, 'but I *would* like you to be aware of what might be going on. And if you *do* find anything out about your manifests being tampered with I don't want you to confront anyone who is doing it. Just keep an eye on him and contact me immediately. There are two more things I need to ask of you.'

'Carry on. I'll do anything I can to help.'

'Do you have a list of the names of everyone who works here?'

'Yes. They are all on the military payroll. I can get a list to you in the Alcazar before afternoon prayers.'

'Can you use a messenger you can trust absolutely and send it to the office of Vizier Hasdai?'

124

'Of course. What is the other thing?'

'We have a man we would like to place in your camp. He is used to working undercover so he will blend in easily. He will call himself Ali and will be here later today. Can you set him to work checking the foodstuffs manifests?'

'Of course. Is there anything else?'

'No,' said Ghalib, 'I think that's all for the moment so I'll take my leave of you now. Thank you for the tea and barad.'

As the General was about to leave he turned and said, 'By the way, what's the name of the officer who brought me to you earlier?'

The quartermaster thought for a moment then looked up. 'Muhammad,' he said. 'Why?'

'Oh, no reason,' said General Ghalib. '*Ma as-salaamah*! Goodbye!'

Chapter 33

Colonel Zaffar al-Din bit his bottom lip as he immersed his forearm in the bowl of warm water. The nail in Shahid Jalal's store room had ripped his arm from elbow to wrist. He closed his eyes and winced as the lavender and chamomile water penetrated the wound. Vizier Hasdai had told him to soak his arm several times a day and to change the bandage each time he did so. He let his arm lie in the water for several minutes as he listened to the clatter of hooves on the cobbled courtyard and the footfall of his men as they went about their duties.

Zaffar had taken over Jaziri's office and his notes from the investigation at the funduq were on the desk in front of him. General Ghalib had instructed him to keep the funduq closed to both new guests and deliveries until his work was completed. Current guests and staff were permitted to leave the funduq building but they had to report twice daily to the lieutenant of the guard at the main gate. Until General Ghalib and the Vizier gave their approval, everyone in the funduq had been forbidden from leaving the city overnight. The General had also instructed Zaffar to keep Antonio, the cloth merchant, confined to his room at all times.

Zaffar's men had now interviewed all of the funduq staff, searched every storage area and guest room and spoken with all of the guests except Shahid Jalal. Zaffar couldn't help thinking that whatever Jalal and the Admiral were involved in, it was undoubtedly connected to the ambergris. He lifted his arm from the bowl and dabbed it dry with a clean cloth. As he wound a fresh bandage round his arm there was a sharp rap at the door.

'Enter! Ah good. Come in. You're just in time to tie this for me.' He held up his bandaged arm to the young officer who had put his head round the door.

'Sir, you asked for an update on our work,' said the young man concentrating on the bandage. 'Is that too tight?'

'No it's fine. Thanks. So, tell me.'

'We've finished everything you asked us to do here in the funduq itself. There are several men now searching the area around the outside of the building especially between here and the city wall. As you know there's a lot of dense shrubbery and bushes there so it'll take some time to search it completely.'

'Very good,' said Zaffar. 'I take it there is still no word on Shahid Jalal?'

'No sir, not yet. We've sent birds with Jaziri's description of him to all the usual locations. Jalal's only had about a day and a half, although probably in the saddle, so we have also sent messages to the river ports too.'

'That's good thinking,' said Zaffar. 'Let me know as soon as your men have checked the outer perimeter and then get someone to take these notes to General Ghalib at the Alcazar. Once he has read them I think he and the Vizier want to speak directly to the cloth merchant and then have a final briefing with me.'

'Very good sir,' the officer said. Then he hesitated a moment before he spoke again. 'There's one more thing sir.'

'What is it?'

'Omar Jaziri sir.'

'What about him?' said Zaffar.

'Sir, he says he is expecting a delivery of fresh hay for the stables.'

'And I suppose he wants me to reopen the funduq so he can receive it?'

'I think so sir.'

'Very well, bring him here.'

'Right away sir, in fact he's waiting outside.'

'Of course he is,' said Zaffar. 'I expected nothing else of a man like him. Give me a moment then bring him in.'

When he was alone Zaffar clutched at the bandage on his arm, grimacing as he did so. It felt as if he had been branded with a red hot iron. And now it was beginning to itch under the bandage just like Vizier Hasdai had said it would. He recovered his composure and wiped his forehead before shouting, 'Jaziri! Come in!'

'Colonel, how good of you to see me,' said Omar as he closed the door. 'I hope my staff are doing everything they can to…'

'What do you want?' said Zaffar. He couldn't bear Omar's fawning manner.

'Sir, forgive me, I simply wished to…' A look from Colonel Zaffar cut him off. 'Well Colonel,' said Omar 'I am keen to get things, ah…

moving again. I have supplies that need replacing, animals need to be fed, rooms that need cleaning and I also have several very unhappy guests?'

'Unhappy?'

'Yes sir. You see they need to go about their business and being made to report back here to the funduq twice a day is, well, inconvenient.'

Colonel Zaffar stared intently at the funduq owner and slowly rose to his feet. 'Inconvenient?'

'Yes sir.'

'I don't think you understand the seriousness of this situation,' said Zaffar. 'The Caliph is on the brink of war with his sworn enemy, Baghdad. Our ships are only days away from setting sail on a mission that could decide the future of our whole Caliphate, and the Admiral of the Royal Fleet, the man the Caliph has entrusted with this mission, has been found dead. Murdered. In *your* funduq. I am not sure that what *you* think is "convenient" is very high on our list of priorities at the moment!'

Omar hung his head. 'Yes sir,' he said.

'I will let you know when you can reopen the funduq. Until then the General's orders are to be obeyed.' As he looked out of the office window he saw two horses being led across the courtyard. 'In the meantime,' said Zaffar. 'You may receive your delivery of feed for the stables, but I want my men to check it as it arrives.'

'Thank you Colonel,' said Omar just as there was a sharp rap at the door before it opened.

'Yes?' said Colonel Zaffar to the same young officer. 'Have you finished your search?'

'Yes sir…' he looked at Jaziri. 'Sir, can we speak?'

'Yes. Speak man, what is it?'

The young man looked his colonel and then at the funduq owner. 'Don't worry about him,' said Zaffar. 'What is it?'

'Sir I think you need to come with me. We've found something.'

Chapter 34

General Ghalib stood at the gate to al-Mursi's bathhouse and breathed in the comforting smell of new bread from the bakery next door. He could hear the clatter of the bakers tending their ovens over the bustle of the people thronging the narrow street. Everywhere there were porters scurrying through the crowds, some with yokes for their burdens, while others were bowed down by the heavy baskets of goods on their heads. These tough, sinewy men were the backbone and muscle of the suq moving goods and fetching supplies for the merchants. At this time of day many of those merchants were turning into the Spicesellers' Row, some almost certainly heading for the Al Bisharah tea house for refreshment and gossip before prayers.

The market inspector's bathhouse was not far from the eastern gate to the city, the Bab al-Jadid, which led to Camp Maaqul and the main road to Jayen and Almeria. It was a popular meeting place for bathers and gamblers alike and got a lot of its clientele from residents of Omar Jaziri's funduq which lay between it and the city gate.

As he waited for his knock to be answered Ghalib bent down to rub his aching knee. His visit to Camp Maaqul had stirred his spirits temporarily but the searing pain in his leg served only to remind him that his days of active service were over. The battle field injury suffered during a skirmish on the Northern Border had consigned him to more sedate duties in recent years and done little to curb his temper. He banged once more with the massive iron ring of the door knocker.

A servant swung open the gate the General stepped into the entrance.

'Where is the clerk?' he said.

'Sir,' said the servant, cowed by the sight of the General. 'He is in the office. Please follow me, sir.'

The bathhouse was built round a garden the central feature of which was a large outdoor chess set with pieces a cubit and a half tall. On each side of this giant board there were benches and tables with chessboards and pieces.

Just inside the gate, water poured from the mouth of an alabaster horse's head into a shallow basin which fed irrigation channels for flowerbeds, oleanders and lemon trees. Here and there the water bubbled out of a channel where it had been blocked by fallen lemons. An old gardener was busy gathering up the fallen fruit, clearing the waterways. He bowed to General Ghalib as he crossed the courtyard. There were sparrows in the flowerbeds.

The baths themselves were on the other side of the courtyard. Shaded by elegant red and white brick arches were the tiled antechambers to a warm room, a steam room and a bitterly cold plunge bath. There was also a massage room where Ghalib could see piles of rough cotton towels on top of raised massage tables. In a private alcove next to the steam room there was a small office with a desk and two stools.

As they approached the office al-Mursi's clerk, Hamza, came out to meet them.

'General, *marhaba*! Welcome! Please come in.'

General Ghalib did no more than nod to acknowledge the clerk, walked into the office and sat down behind the desk. Stretching his leg out he gestured for the clerk to sit down. He turned to the servant who had lingered a little too long in the doorway. 'Bring me some tea,' Ghalib said. The man nodded and left as Hamza stood in the centre of his own office.

'How may I help you?' said the clerk.

'You can start by sitting down,' said the General as he tugged at his leather jerkin and settled himself on the stool.

Hamza sat down on the other side of the desk and plucked at his head cloth.

'Where is al-Mursi?'

'Sir, my master is doing his rounds in the metalworkers' suq. He will be back here after prayers if you would like to speak with him?'

'That depends on how helpful *you* are,' said General Ghalib as he looked round the office at the piles of papers and journals. 'How long has he had this bathhouse now?'

'Just over two years sir,' said the clerk. 'We are very pleased with how things have gone.'

General Ghalib thought briefly of Aiden, the Christian chess master whose body had been found in the steam room here nearly two years earlier. He too had been slaughtered like a goat.

'I wouldn't be too pleased,' he said. 'We all know what goes on here.'

The clerk sat in silence trying to fathom what he meant.

'Do you know Nasim bin Faraj?' asked Ghalib.

'He works in the perfume suq sir,' said Hamza.

General Ghalib stared at the clerk. He lowered his voice and said, 'I know where he works. I asked if you knew him.'

Hamza hung his head. 'Yes sir. I know him. He comes here regularly.'

'When was he here last?'

The clerk thought for a moment. 'I'd need to check the journal sir,' he said.

Ghalib glared at him.

'Sir, I'm sorry it is just that the journal is…well you are leaning on it sir.'

Ghalib grunted and lifted his arms. The clerk leant over and took the heavy book which was bound in pale brown leather. He opened it up and started to flick through the pages.

'Here,' he said, pointing to an entry. 'According to this he last placed a bet on the evening of the Night Journey of Mohammed.'

'I didn't ask you when he last placed a bet, I asked you when…look never mind that,' said Ghalib. 'Tell about that evening. When did he arrive?'

'Well sir, I couldn't be sure but I would guess it was just after the evening prayer finished. That is usually our busiest time.'

'Was it busy that night?'

'Yes sir. Very busy. The streets were full and there were a lot of people out to enjoy themselves.' The clerk turned the book round for Ghalib and pointed at the page. 'As you can see, there a number of names in the journal for that particular evening.'

'This man,' said Ghalib jabbing at the page. 'This Shahid Jalal. What can you tell me about him?'

The clerk peered at the journal. 'Well sir, it looks like he placed a few bets on, let me see, a chess game. I'd need to check with my master as this particular entry was written by him. I do recall though that my master spend some time talking with Jalal. He seemed to spend a good deal of money.'

'Is *this* your entry?' said the General pointing to Nasim's name.

'Yes sir.'

'So you remember seeing Nasim?'

'Sir?'

'It's not a difficult question,' said Ghalib. 'Do you remember seeing him?'

'Well sir, I must have done, look his name is in the journal. Here you…'

The clerk's eyes widened as General Ghalib gasped loudly, clenched his teeth and crashed both his hands down on the table. One of the shards of metal in his knee had moved and a white-hot spasm of pain seared through his leg. He struggled to stand up and as he did so the hilt of his dagger caught on the desk and lifted it up overturning a pot of ink. The clerk leapt to his feet as the ink poured onto the surface of the desk and seeped into a pile of papers.

'Ach,' said Ghalib, grabbing the now empty pot and getting his fingers covered in ink. 'Look, I know what it says in the book, but I want to know if you actually saw Nasim here, in this bathhouse, on the evening of the Night Journey of Mohammed.'

The clerk tried to mop up the ink with his head cloth as it dripped off the desk and collected in a pool by one of Ghalib's leather riding boots.

'Yes I remember,' he said looking up at the General.

'Leave that!' Ghalib shouted as he picked up the book in both hands and brandished it at the clerk. 'Tell me what you saw!'

'I remember he and the other gentleman, Shahid Jalal, spent some time talking. They seemed to know each other. At least that is how it appeared. I also recall they left together.'

'Are you certain?' said Ghalib. The pain had passed now and he sat down again.

'Yes sir. Absolutely; I watched them go.'

'What did they say to each other?'

'I'm sorry sir. I wasn't close enough to hear. Though, I did see Nasim and my master together at some point. My master might be able to help you.'

'Before that evening, had you ever seen Shahid Jalal, or heard his name in conversation?'

The clerk shook his head. 'No sir, never.'

The General thought for a moment then put the book down on a clean part of the desk.

'Give me that cloth to wipe my hands.'

132

When he had wiped off the worst of the ink he picked up the journal. 'I am going to take this.' The clerk winced as he saw how the General's ink stained fingers had left their mark on the pale leather covers of the book.

'Sir I ...'

'One more thing,' said Ghalib cutting off the clerk as he tried to speak. 'Tell al-Mursi I want to see him at the Alcazar Palace this afternoon. Let him know I want to discuss the contents of this journal.'

The clerk wiped his mouth with the back of his hand and nodded slowly.

'Good,' said Ghalib. He held up the book. 'I noticed you went straight for this betting journal when I asked about Nasim being here. Do you have any clients who come here simply to bathe?'

The clerk said nothing.

'I thought so,' said General Ghalib. He turned and stepped out into the garden where he was met by the servant who had returned with a tray of cups and some hot tea. 'You took your time,' said Ghalib. 'Fetch some towels. The clerk has made a mess.'

Chapter 35

It was always called the Chamberlain's office, but in fact it was a suite of seven separate departments under his direction situated at the far end of the same corridor as Hasdai's quarters. But, whereas Hasdai, because of his higher status as principal advisor to the Caliph, had peace and quiet and close proximity to the royal apartments the Chamberlain and his staff were at the front of the Alcazar overlooking the bustle of the main courtyard and the gate to the palace.

Apart from the headquarters of the royal guard, which was ultimately General Ghalib's responsibility but with the daily routines delegated to the Chamberlain, there was an office, reporting to Hasdai, which dealt exclusively with the relationship between Crown Prince Hakam's retinue in Cordoba and that of his father the Caliph Abd al-Rahman in the palatinate city of Madinat al-Zahra to the west. There was a Communications Centre staffed by hand-picked members of Ghalib's guard who read and analysed the dozens of daily reports from all over the Caliphate and beyond. They were the ones responsible for preparing the daily brief sent through the Chamberlain to both Hasdai and Ghalib. It was Hasdai who, in his position of Vizier, had to choose what the Crown Prince and the Caliph needed to be told of the occurrences in the Caliphate and other kingdoms where the Caliph's spies were at work. The Office of State and Legal Affairs was responsible for the administration of the Caliphate of Al Andalus through the twenty one *kuwar* or provinces and the collection of taxes and the supervision of trade and industry while the Office of Religious and Cultural Affairs ran the mosques with their associated schools, the hospitals, libraries and the universities. Another department had to do with the relatively mundane matters of running of the royal household; feeding and attending to the everyday requirements of the hundreds of people living in the palace. The last office was relatively new and had been established on the orders of the Crown Prince. This was the Army and Navy Liaison Bureau. It had been set up specifically to coordinate the activities of the Caliphate's armed forces for the forthcoming campaign against Baghdad. This was where close-mouthed military men worked on the Caliphate's strategy, and, while supported by the Chamberlain's secretariat, reported only to the Crown Prince through the Vizier. It was to this office that Hasdai was taking Ali the spy from Baghdad.

As they walked together down the corridor Hasdai glanced at Ali and couldn't help smiling to himself. How was it that spies, or at least the good ones, could manage to make themselves practically invisible like this? They seemed to have the knack of turning off their personalities and looking so ordinary. Ali with his slight, stooped figure walked down the corridor with his hands in the pockets of his robe, his eyes fixed on the floor and his face devoid of expression. This was a man who put his life in danger every day that he was on active service but he looked for all the world like some clerk in a tax office instead of the fearless frontline operative he was.

The Vizier had already instructed Ali that he was to report that afternoon before the Asr prayer to the sergeant quartermaster at Camp Maaqul. Once there he was to act as the eyes and ears of General Ghalib while working in the camp checking the manifests of the mule trains leaving the camp for Almeria. His task was to find and infiltrate the smuggling ring that Ghalib was convinced was operating in the camp. Ali had understood immediately what was required of him and accepted the mission as if it were a perfectly simple thing to ask him to do.

Hasdai clicked his prayer beads in time with their steps until they had passed the corridor sentries and reached the door of the Bureau. With his hand on the door latch Hasdai turned to Ali. 'I suppose I don't need to tell you not to elaborate on anything in here.'

Ali lifted his face to look at the Vizier. It was a complete blank.

'No,' said Hasdai after a second. 'I don't suppose I need to tell you anything.' He clicked his beads again and opened the door.

There were five officers, all navy captains, in the small room which was piled high with documents. Three of them were leaning over a desk near a window discussing a large scale map on which were dozens of small paper arrows of different colours all pointing in the same direction while the other two were reading what looked like long lists and seemed to be checking them off against ledgers. At the sight of the Vizier at the door they all stood up.

'*A salaam u aleikum*, Your Excellency,' said the man nearest the door

Both Hasdai and Ali replied, '*Wa aleikum a salaam.*'

'How can we help you sir? Our report is not due until tomorrow.'

'Thank you captain, I am not here because of your report. I'll get that from the Chamberlain in good time. I need access to your sea charts and maps. I…' Here the Vizier turned to Ali who had remained by the door and was standing with his hands clasped at his waist, staring, completely expressionless, at a spot on the wall above the window. '… or rather *we*, need to consult a map of the shores between Almeria and Latakia.'

The captain looked at his colleagues and then at Ali. 'But Your Excellency all our maps are…'

The Vizier held up a hand to silence him. 'I know captain. Your maps are all annotated and highly confidential. But I am sure you will allow me to judge who may or may not look at them. Now if you will show us the maps you and your colleagues can leave us. I suggest that they wait in the corridor sentries' alcove while you go and inform the Chamberlain that I am here. I shall send for you when we have finished. Tell the Chamberlain that there is no need for him to leave his duties to come and meet me. Is that clear?'

'Yes Your Excellency. The most accurate chart we have is the one we were working on when you came in. It is this one here by the window. Can I ask you not to move any of the arrows?'

Ali looked at the captain as if he were a child. 'I have worked with campaign maps in the past,' he said. 'I won't move any of your little arrows. And I'll try not to remember where they are all pointing.'

'Thank you Ali!' said Hasdai who again couldn't help smiling at Ali's demeanour. 'Now captain if you and your colleagues could leave us I'll let you know when you can return.'

Alone now Hasdai and Ali bent over the chart on the table by the window. After just a few seconds Ali frowned and straightened up. 'This is an Ibn Hawqal map,' he said.

'You are very well informed,' said Hasdai.

'Information is my profession Your Excellency.'

'Hmm,' said Hasdai, 'that's as may be but looking at this map can you make any kind of informed guess as to where someone from Al Andalus might want to land a shipment of contraband ambergris between Almeria and Latakia? Bear in mind that they would have the most sophisticated new navigation instruments to work with.'

'Well,' said Ali. 'The highest price a smuggler is likely to get for raw

Andalusi ambergris would be in Damascus. The perfume industry there is very highly developed and I know that in Baghdad damascene rose oil perfume is one of the most expensive but effective scents that money can buy because it is fixed with ambergris.'

'So how would a smuggler get the ambergris to Damascus?' said Hasdai.

'How much of the stuff is there?'

'I dare say it could all be loaded on to three camels.'

'That's the answer then,' said Ali. He traced his finger eastwards from Malta to Cyprus on the map then diagonally to the coast of Syria.

'If the ambergris were in one of the ships of the fleet, they could sail to this point just to the south of Cyprus then make for the shore of Syria here to a cove just south of Saida. The city you call Sidon in Hebrew, Your Excellency. A competent navigator with good instruments and a chart as good as this one would have no problem steering to this point. It would then be just a matter of unloading the ambergris and sailing north to rejoin the fleet.'

'There's only one problem with that as a plan,' said Hasdai. 'How could a single ship break out of the fleet and head south east when all the others are turning to the north towards Latakia?'

'That might not be as big a problem as you think, Your Excellency. In a fleet of that size there are always going to be ships which run into trouble… take in water… break their backs in storms or simply disappear in the night. Our smuggler's ship could easily be one of those. The captain could simply make up some tale of trouble and fall behind the fleet before setting a new course. However there is a much bigger problem for the smuggler.'

'What's that?' said Hasdai. 'It all seems pretty straightforward to me.'

'Oh it is!' said Ali. 'Perfectly straightforward. Except for the fact that if you take a ship of the line to a small cove in Syria to unload a cargo of contraband onto a camel train there are going to be about three hundred witnesses to what you have done.'

Hasdai straightened up, lifted his prayer beads from the table and fingered them as he looked out of the window for a few seconds. 'Ah,' he said. 'Perhaps you have found the flaw in the plan.'

As he spoke there was a knock at the door over which they could hear the voice of one of the captains.

'Your Excellency! Your Excellency! Please excuse me. I have a message for you from the Chamberlain.'

Hasdai turned to Ali. 'Open the door.'

The Vizier spoke to the officer. 'I thought I told you that I didn't want the Chamberlain to come here.'

The captain swallowed hard before he spoke. 'Sir, it's not that sir. The Chamberlain has asked for you... for you... to come to him, sir. I'm sorry, Your Excellency, but that's what he told me to say. He said he has a message for you which he can only give to you in his strong room.'

As Vizier, Hasdai was not used to being summoned by anyone other than the Caliph or the Crown Prince. However he realised immediately that the Chamberlain must have a very good reason for this departure from protocol.

'Very well, take me to the Chamberlain.'

As Hasdai, Ali and the captain walked towards the secretariat the corridor guards drew themselves up to attention. Through the open door Hasdai could see the Chamberlain, clearly agitated, standing by the entrance to an inner office. Hasdai knew that this was a sound-proof room where the Chamberlain could issue the most secret of orders or pass on the most confidential of messages.

'You two stay here,' said Hasdai. As he entered the secretariat the staff rose and bowed then, obviously following some order from the Chamberlain, they filed out of the office to congregate in the corridor.

The Chamberlain bowed. 'Your Excellency. I ask your pardon but I am sure that once you hear what I have to say you will understand my actions.'

Hasdai tried to put the official at ease. 'I am sure you know what you are doing,' he said as he entered the small windowless room and sat down on one of the two chairs which were the only furniture in the place. The yellow flickering oil lamps seemed to suck the air out of the room.

The Chamberlain closed the heavy wooden door and put the bolt in place. The room stank of lamp oil and smoke and Hasdai started to cough. 'I shall be as brief as I can Your Excellency. We have received a top secret coded message concerning the advance flotilla of our fleet. It was sent by bird from the island of Malta. As the flotilla approached the island one of our ships started to fall behind the others. There was an outbreak of pestilence on board and the rowers were unable to keep the vessel underway. She was taken in tow and a sailor from another ship put on board. The poor soul was condemned to death as soon as he set foot on the boat. He recognised the signs of anthrax and shouted that no other man should come aboard. The entire crew, the regiment and all the animals were dead. Three hundred men, sailors, soldiers and their mounts… gone! The captain of the adjacent ship ordered that the stricken vessel be set ablaze with fire arrows and it was burned to the waterline.'

Hasdai sat for a moment staring at one of the sputtering lamps while clicking his beads then he stood up. 'I see,' he said. 'You were right to call me here. Thank you. Now please open the door. Oh, and thank you for sending me the first draft of the Caliph's speech. I'll work on it as soon as I can. Did you include the information about Bandar bin Sadiq's service record?'

'I did Your Excellency,' said the Chamberlain as he opened the door. Then he turned to Hasdai. 'Your Excellency,' he said, 'I have a second message for you. It is on my desk in my office.'

Hasdai, glad to be out of the fug of the strong room was taking deep breaths of fresh air. 'Well, I might as well come and get it then,' he said.

'Thank you Your Excellency.'

Hasdai followed the Chamberlain through the empty secretariat to his private office which overlooked the main gate to the Alcazar courtyard. Here the pale light of the late morning flooded in at the window onto the desk with its heaps of papers. The Vizier sighed. It seemed that every desk in the Caliphate was full. He knew that his own paperwork would be piling up in his absence.

The Chamberlain spoke, 'Here is the message Your Excellency.' He handed him the document which was sealed with a silk thread.

Hasdai knew as soon as he saw the 'alama on the outside of the letter, "Serve Him and persevere in His service", that the message was from General Ghalib.

Chapter 36

The four navigators were sitting round a table in the back corner of the Al Bisharah teahouse while their guards had taken a table near the door, glad to be just that bit away from their charges for a while. Simon the proprietor was almost run off his feet supplying steaming tea and sweet cakes while a couple of young serving boys were collecting empty cups.

'Will you shut your mouth?' Bandar hissed. 'This is not the place to say such things. In fact there is no place at all that such things should be said about Admiral Suhail.' As he spoke he looked around the teahouse terrified that someone might have overheard their conversation.

The navigator from Abdera was furious that Bandar had spoken to him like this but he had enough sense not to say anything more. Siraj bin Bahram already had his arm in a firm grip in case he would lose control and lash out at Bandar.

'I'm sorry sir. But I though you would want to know.'

Siraj relaxed his grip.

'When was this?' said Bandar

'The day before his murder,' said the navigator. 'I was at the University and went back to the room where we study to collect something.'

'Who was he talking to?' asked Siraj.

The navigator shook his head. 'I don't know sir. I couldn't see.'

'Then how do you know it was the Admiral?' asked Bandar.

'He was shouting sir,' said the navigator. 'He seemed very agitated. He kept going on about ambergris. I didn't go in.'

Bandar shot a look at Siraj and they both glanced around the teahouse. Bandar gestured with his head towards the door and Siraj nodded.

'Stay here you two,' said Bandar. 'And keep quiet.'

Bandar and Siraj moved a short distance from their table. The guards at the door stood up. As they did so Bandar shook his head to reassure them and they sat back down again.

'If this gets out,' Siraj whispered, 'the Admiral's reputation will be ruined.'

Bandar nodded. 'I know.' He scanned the room and was relieved to see that Simon, the proprietor was now busy arranging barad and the boys were washing the cups.

'Do you think it is true?' said Siraj.

Bandar breathed deeply. 'I can't think about that now,' he said. 'But I hope for all our sakes that it isn't. The last thing we need at this stage in our preparations is something like this. The men worshipped the Admiral. If they found out he was a smuggler they might begin to have doubts about the rest of us.' Glancing over his shoulder he said, 'We need to keep this quiet, for the sake of discipline in the men.'

Siraj nodded. 'I agree. Look, we should get back to the University.'

Bandar gestured to the navigators. 'We need to go,' he said.

'Thank you Simon!' Bandar called. 'The barad were delicious, as usual.' He put a few coins on the counter and bade the proprietor farewell.

As the men filed out of the teahouse a serving boy went to clear away their plates and cups. In the corner of the room a man wearing a black burnus drank off his tea, pulled his hood over his eyes and stepped out of the teahouse into the street. He placed a copper coin into the palm of beggar child who approached him. Folded around the coin was a small piece of paper. He watched as the boy ran up the street towards the metalwork suq.

Chapter 37

'How may I be of service sir?' asked Hamid al-Mursi, the market inspector. 'My clerk told me you wished to speak about the journal.' As if to emphasise the point he gestured with his walking cane towards the ink stained notebook that lay in front of General Ghalib.

The two men were in an anteroom in the administration wing of the Alcazar Palace. As al-Mursi fiddled with the large ruby ring that adorned one of his fat fingers he could hear the bustle of the chamberlain's clerks as they passed up and down the corridor.

'I do,' said Ghalib. 'Specifically, I want to talk about Shahid Jalal. What can you tell me about him?'

'I only actually met him the once,' said al-Mursi.

'At your bathhouse?'

'Yes. He came to see us on the evening of the Night Journey. The journal will confirm that but as I recall all he did was spend some money and play a few games of chess. He didn't say much really. I thought he was a rather quiet man.'

'Did he talk to many people?'

'One or two. He seemed to know one man in particular. A trader from the perfume suq.'

'Nasim bin Faraj.'

Al-Mursi swallowed and nodded slowly.

'I assume you are aware we are holding Nasim here at the Palace?'

Al-Mursi nodded again.

'How did they know each other… Nasim and Jalal?'

'I don't exactly know but I expect that their work brought them into contact from time to time. From what I understand Shahid Jalal is a merchant specialising in scents and fragrances. He will probably have sold his goods to Nasim who may then have sold them here in his shop.'

'How often does he visit Cordoba?'

'I'm sorry sir, I don't know.'

'I find that hard to believe. I thought it was your job to know what goes on in the suq.'

'It is sir. What I mean is that I had I never met him until that night at the bathhouse. It is possible he has been doing business through a series of agents. That happens often. When I met Jalal I knew only that he was staying at Omar Jaziri's funduq and that he was a professional acquaintance of Nasim the perfume trader.'

General Ghalib frowned.

'However,' said al-Mursi sensing the General's impatience, 'if he does use agents then they tend to visit the city four or five times a year. Agents tend to be around just before a major festival or celebration, like the Night Journey of Mohammed.'

General Ghalib nodded then thought for a moment.

'Do travelling merchants and agents usually visit your bathhouse during their stay in Cordoba?'

'Some of them do sir, yes.'

'As the market inspector I assume that you have an interest in meeting people like Shahid Jalal?'

Al-Mursi stopped fiddling with his ring. 'As market inspector yes, I am interested in what goes on here in the suq. As you said General, that is my job.'

'Then as part of your job how long have you known that Nasim is involved in the illegal sale of ambergris?'

Al-Mursi's well-practised composure vanished. He looked at the floor and breathed heavily. 'General I give you my word,' he said slowly. 'This news only came to my attention yesterday.'

'How did you find out?'

'A trader from the perfume suq told me. He has the shop next door to Nasim and he asked to see me. When I met him at the Al Bisharah teahouse he told me that Nasim had been brought here, and that you and the Vizier were asking questions about ambergris. That is when I found out.'

'You realise that the Caliph could have Nasim's head for this?'

Al-Mursi nodded. 'Yes sir.'

General Ghalib opened the journal and flicked through the pages. 'Do you have any reason to suspect anyone else of being involved in the sale of ambergris, or any other prohibited goods?'

Some colour returned to al-Mursi's cheeks. 'No sir. I give you my word that...'

'I don't want your word al-Mursi. I want to know who else is involved in the illegal sale of ambergris from your suq. Now, as the city's teahouses are doing their usual job of keeping everybody informed I want you to do something. First I want you let it be known that the Caliph will seek the most severe of punishments for anyone involved in the supply, transportation, sale or purchase of any of the items on the prohibited list.'

Al-Mursi nodded. 'Sir...'

Ghalib slammed the table with the journal. 'Don't interrupt me! I also want you to make it clear that anyone with any information about the whereabouts of Shahid Jalal is to contact the Chamberlain's office here in the Alcazar. Is that clear?'

'Yes sir.'

General Ghalib stood up and placed both his hands on the desk. Towering over al-Mursi he said, 'Finally I want you to understand that if I suspect, even for a moment that any of the entries in this journal are because of your position as market inspector I will ask the Vizier to appoint a replacement immediately. Your position does not give you the right to extract money from visiting merchants, agents or local traders in exchange for them going about their business. Your job, as you seem so keen to point out, is to ensure the effective operation of the suq; not to make yourself rich. Is *that* clear?'

Al-Mursi nodded. 'Yes sir.'

Chapter 38

Hasdai was alone in his office in the Alcazar Palace. He had come back here to think and sat clicking his prayer beads as he looked out of the window at a pair of finches feeding at the bowl of sunflower seeds. On his desk next to the draft of the Caliph's address that still required his attention, lay the two jars of ambergris and the list of names that had been found in Admiral Suhail's room.

The Caliph was due back in Cordoba the following afternoon in advance of the ceremonial send-off for the new Admiral of the Fleet, Bandar bin Sadiq, and the remaining navigators. Both the Caliph and the Crown Prince would be expecting to learn who had murdered Admiral Suhail, and more importantly they would be expecting to see the culprit crucified between dogs. Hasdai wondered how he could tell them that the Admiral was murdered because he was mixed up in a plot to smuggle a large quantity of contraband ambergris out of Cordoba.

As he contemplated all this the door to his office opened and the corridor guard admitted General Ghalib.

'Ah, General,' said Hasdai, 'please!' he said gesturing to a stool. 'Did you speak with the market inspector?'

'Yes Excellency. He said he hadn't met Shahid Jalal until the evening of the Night Journey of Mohammed, but he said he got the impression that Jalal and Nasim were professional acquaintances.'

'I think he might be right about that. Did you check the rest of the journal?'

'I did sir. None of the other names from the list you found in the Admiral's room appear there.' Ghalib put the journal down on the desk and opened it to show Jalal's name. 'Here is the entry for Shahid Jalal, but there is no mention of any of the other names.'

Hasdai looked at the journal and then at the names on the list. 'There are a dozen names here General. I had one of the clerks look through the palace archive to see if we had any prior record of any of these names. Nothing so far.' He let his prayer beads fall to the desk.

'I did have one or two ideas sir,' said Ghalib.

'Tell me General, we need something.'

'Well sir, we know Jalal had a large quantity of ambergris in his storage area. We suspect the Admiral was trying...' the General stopped at a look from the Vizier then started again.

'Sorry sir, we suspect *someone* was trying to move a large quantity of ambergris using the supply chain being co-ordinated from Camp Maaqul. I was there this morning so I can see how it could be done. It is difficult, but possible if you have the right people involved. I will need Ali to confirm it though.'

'Go on,' said Hasdai. 'What about the names?'

'Well sir, getting the ambergris out of the funduq using the cover of the Night Journey is one thing. Getting a quantity that large together in the first place is an entirely different challenge.'

Hasdai nodded and retrieved his prayer beads from the desk.

'This man sir, this Shahid Jalal, he is clearly taking huge risks doing this.'

'Doing what?'

'Selling ambergris sir.'

'The rewards would be very high, though, General.'

'I'm not disputing that. But it struck me that he may not be doing this as a single deal.'

'What do you mean?'

'Sir, I don't think that either of us believes he was in Cordoba because he is a merchant. I think he might be a supplier of...well, prohibited goods.'

'Like ambergris?'

'Amongst other things maybe, yes sir. If that *is* the case what is the one thing he will try and do above everything else?'

'Apart from not getting caught?' said Hasdai with a sigh. 'I don't know General. I suppose he would want to keep his...' Hasdai broke off and let his hands fall to the table. He stared intently at the bathhouse journal and the list from the Admiral's room. As he did so his eyes widened.

General Ghalib picked up the list of names from the desk. 'That's what I thought sir. He would want to keep his identity secret. I think there are two possibilities. Firstly that these names are all the same person.'

Hasdai shook his head. 'I think that is unlikely. If he had been to Cordoba before using any of these names someone would have recognised him. Unless that is, al-Mursi was lying to you.'

'Well sir, al-Mursi said that whilst he had not met Jalal until the evening of the Night Journey it was possible that he has been using a series of agents to do his work for him. That would also explain why nobody knows him. The second possibility is that the other names on the list were his agents.'

Hasdai wiped his beard and swallowed. 'What does he look like?'

'Sir?'

'Shahid Jalal, what does he look like?' Hasdai rummaged around in a drawer. 'Where is the description that Omar Jaziri gave us? Ah, here it is.' Hasdai read the piece of paper quickly and handed it to Ghalib who also read it.

'He looks, well sir, he sounds...'

'Ordinary General. He sounds ordinary. Medium height and build, dark hair... he shaves his beard thanks to the style set by Ziryab the musician. He sounds like many people in this city. He could blend in and completely disappear. No wonder nobody seems to have noticed him.'

Hasdai picked up the prayer beads and clicked them together quickly as he thought. 'We need to get word to Zaffar at the funduq,' he said. 'I want to know how far back Jaziri's records go. If you are right General, and these names refer to Jalal's agents then we might find one of them in an earlier entry.'

As General Ghalib stood up the pain in his knee made him wince. 'No not now,' said Hasdai. 'We haven't finished here yet.'

Ghalib grimaced as he sat back down on the stool.

'Did you arrange for Ali to start work at the camp?' said Hasdai.

'Yes sir. He is on his way there now. He'll be responsible for checking records. It should give him the right access to which goods go with which animal. If the supply chain is being used to smuggle goods, he will be able to see exactly how it can be done.'

'Good. Make sure we keep in regular contact with him,' said Hasdai. 'We don't need any more bodies on our hands.'

'I think Ali can look after himself sir,' said Ghalib. 'Did you learn anything at the Yemeni bathhouse?'

'I honestly don't know general. Yousef confirmed Nasim's story in that he was there playing knucklebones with the Admiral and that the cloth merchant, Antonio, joined their game.'

'Sir, if al-Mursi is right and Nasim did already know Shahid Jalal, do you think…'

'…do I think Nasim introduced the Admiral to Jalal?' asked Hasdai.

General Ghalib nodded.

'Yes, that thought had occurred to me,' said Hasdai looking at the glass jars on the desk. 'As had the fact that these two jars we found in his room were proof that Nasim and Jalal could actually supply ambergris. But I can't believe that the Admiral did this deal, if indeed he did any deal at all, on the back of a chance meeting. Surely an enterprise like this takes a long time to organise?'

'Yes sir; but we have been preparing for war for almost two years. That is enough time to arrange something.'

Hasdai stood up and placed his hands in the small of his back as he stretched. 'I spoke with Ali earlier today in the captains' office. He thinks that the highest demand for Andalusi ambergris would be in Damascus. He also thinks that one of the ships from the main fleet could make land and unload the ambergris south of Saida on the Syrian coast. Using the astrolabe… that would be a simple diversion. From Saida it could easily be transported to Damascus.'

'It could sir, but what about all the…'

Hasdai held up his hand. 'You are correct General. There would be several hundred witnesses. I hadn't considered that at first. However, I also hadn't considered something which reached me from Malta earlier.'

'From the advance flotilla sir?' said Ghalib.

Hasdai nodded. 'At least what is left of it, yes.'

'Sir?'

'Do you remember the meeting with Ali on the evening you told me about the murder of the Admiral?'

'Yes sir. He told us about the anthrax they had found outside of Baghdad.'

Hasdai sat down again. 'Right. Well it seems that three of the four ships from the advance flotilla made land safely in Malta. One wasn't so lucky. When they found it, they knew instantly it had been infected by anthrax. All the men, at least three hundred of them in total, and the horses were all dead.'

'Anthrax?' said Ghalib.

Hasdai nodded.

'A very effective way to get rid of three hundred witnesses at sea and make it look like an accident, don't you think?'

Ghalib sighed deeply and wiped his moustache with the palm of his hand. 'Sir, I...'

'No, neither do I General. I don't know what I think at the moment.'

Both men sat in silence for several minutes. Eventually Hasdai said, 'Take that message to Zaffar at the funduq and then come back here. And bring Nasim bin Faraj with you. We need to find out just how well he knew Shahid Jalal.'

Chapter 39

Ali had arrived at Camp Maaqul dressed in anonymous work clothes.

The huge military camp was teeming with soldiers and porters and pack animals all jostling to make their way between piles of stores and equipment which stretched out in line after line to the distant boundary walls. Sergeants were barking orders and mule drivers goaded their animals. Camels blubbered and belched and groaned their complaints as they were coaxed into position at the loading bays by their drivers. Everywhere was movement and noise and the sweet, ripe smell of dung which was being gathered up by an army of sweepers busy with their baskets and short-bristled besoms.

It was just before the Asr prayer and Ali had reported to the sergeant quartermaster as instructed by General Ghalib and the Vizier. For now he was to follow the orders of this man who was in charge of the mule and camel trains setting out from Cordoba to the naval headquarters in Almeria.

'You'll start at the south of the camp by the feeding lines,' the quartermaster said.

Ali simply nodded in agreement.

'Down there,' said the quartermaster waving his arm towards the Wadi al-Khabir. 'The animals get fed and are inspected by the farriers before they are made up into trains.'

The quartermaster handed Ali a board on which was bound several sheets of heavy paper. A short reed pen dangled from a string attached to one corner. In a hole at the top of the board was a small ink-well half-full of glutinous, thick black ink.

'The ink is thick but you'll still have to be careful not to spill it all over your papers. I take it you can write well enough? I forgot to ask General Ghalib.'

Who does this man think he is? thought Ali, then he replied meekly, 'Yes sir, I can read and write.'

'Ah, good, that's fine! I had to make sure,' said the quartermaster. 'Right, the farriers make up the trains of animals. There are sixty in a camel train and eighty in a mule train. The two animals in the lead of the train and the two at the rear will be branded, each with two letters and three numbers. The others are unbranded and roped between them. After the trains are made up they are taken to the loading bays at the north gate to the camp by the Almeria road. I suppose you came in that gate.'

Ali nodded again.

'Good! That's where they are loaded up and sent on their way. There are three sets of loading bays, one set for weapons and other military supplies, one for food and provisions, and one for chandlery supplies for the navy. The camels are used for the heavy military stuff and navy stores while the mules carry the food and provisions. All you have to do is record the brand numbers for the leaders and the rear two animals in a train then make a note of what that train is loaded with. The foremen of the labourers loading the animals will tell you what's in the cases. Then you bring your docket back to me here so I can put it down in my ledgers. That way we have a complete record of what is leaving the camp and how many animals are on the road at any one time. Do you understand?'

Once again Ali's meek expression belied his feelings about the quartermaster. 'Yes sir, I understand sir, thank you.'

'The general said you should work on the food and provisions supplies. You'll meet another three clerks who are working between the farriers' lines and the loading bays. They all do the same thing but there is only one doing food at the moment. In fact here he comes now with his latest docket. He'll take you down to the farrier's lines. I'll tell him you have to work together on the food trains. His name is Nasr.'

The man who approached them didn't look much like he could live up to his name. He looked anything but a victor. He was a small, weedy character with bad eyes. His left eye was so far out of true that he held his head permanently twisted so he could focus his good eye on whatever he was trying to see. He looked like someone who was forever expecting a good slap on the ear. Ali couldn't help wondering why he hadn't tried to do something about his affliction. After all there were plenty of good eye surgeons in the hospitals of Cordoba.

'Nasr,' said the quartermaster as he took the docket the man offered him, 'this is Ali. He has just started today. Can you let him see how things are done? Then maybe tomorrow he can start to make up his own mule trains. He'll be working in food supplies.'

Nasr started to protest in a thin, warbling voice which Ali would have laughed at were he anywhere but in an army camp. 'Why do we need anyone else? Am I not doing…?'

The quartermaster turned on him immediately. 'Just you follow my orders, d'you hear? Another word out of you and you could find yourself back in your village. Now go! Get on with it!'

As Nasr walked off Ali followed him saying, 'What's the matter? Don't you want any help?'

'I don't need help. I do a good job,' Nasr squeaked.

'Yeah, fine, fine! Whatever you say,' said Ali. 'Just let's get on with it.' He didn't like this little man one bit but he would have to curb his feelings and not let them interfere with his judgement. He was here to do a job and for some reason he got the impression that this Nasr was a shifty character. He would have to keep an eye on him. Ali chuckled to himself at the thought of that. Nasr could do with all the eyes he could get!

Soon they were approaching the feeding and inspection lines. Here the noise was so loud that it was hard to speak over it especially with a voice like Nasr's and it stank as well. The animals were braying and snorting and pissing everywhere as they were pressed towards the mangers.

'What did you say?' Ali shouted.

'We pick up our mules down here,' Nasr trilled as he pointed to the end of the line of mangers. 'We always get them from this section of the lines. Look the farrier has the next lot ready for us. I'll show you the brands on the first two mules and then you can go to the back of the line to see the ones on the last two. Don't bother about the mules in between, they are not marked.'

Once they had inspected the two lead mules Ali started to go back down the line of animals to the end. It was then that his training for undercover work came to the fore. Ali was a man who counted things. In all of his service he had had to report back to his masters on some movements or other. Counting was second nature to him. He had already committed to memory the number of lines of stores in the camp. He knew the number of clerks working for the quartermaster. He had a clear mental image of the number of mangers and farriers there were. He could work out the proportion of mules to camels and the number of drivers each train required. Already he could give a reasonably good estimate of how many trains of animals a day would leave Camp Maaqul and how many would arrive. Now, as the animals trudged steadily towards the loading bay, he counted the mules in the line. There were eighty four. That's very strange, he thought. There should only be eighty.

When they reached the loading bay for foodstuffs there were labourers swarming everywhere and the mules were loaded in no time at all. Ali went to the front of the line to talk to Nasr who was deep in conversation with a heavily-bearded man wearing a black hooded burnus.

'What are they carrying?' Ali asked.

'Bitter orange jam and dried lemons,' piped Nasr turning from his companion. 'Why do you want to know?'

'I have to put it on my docket,' said Ali. 'And another thing, how many mules are there in a train?'

Nasr twisted his head to look at his companion. 'We told you, eighty.'

'But I counted the mules in this line,' said Ali. 'There are eighty-four.'

The man in the burnus turned on his heel and disappeared into the crowds of labourers and animal drivers.

'No,' said Nasr in his strained voice while staring at Ali with his good eye. 'You have made a mistake. There are only ever eighty mules in an army mule train. Why would the farrier give us four extra animals? You must have made a mistake.'

Chapter 40

Hasdai looked out of the window at the lengthening shadows. Behind him, on the other side of the room Nasim bin Faraj, the perfume trader, sat with his head in his hands. He had been alone in the Alcazar prison with only Ghalib's jailor for company and knew that his own execution was now imminent. As he lifted his face he tried to use the sleeve of his robe to wipe away the tears that filled his eyes.

'And there is no other solution?' he said, his voice cracking.

The Vizier shook his head.

'No. Unless you tell me what you know there is nothing else I can do to help you. The jars we found in the Admiral's room came from your shop. The knife we found at the bathhouse, which was used to kill the Lieutenant, belonged to you. The Crown Prince will insist you are executed. How that happens is up to you. If you help me I give you my word it will be swift and painless. If not you will be crucified between dogs.'

Nasim rocked backwards and forwards on his stool. As he glanced up he caught General Ghalib's eye.

Ghalib voice was laced with meaning as he spoke. 'What is your choice?'

As Nasim sat there gazing at Ghalib there was no sound but the steady click of Hasdai's prayer beads and then the keening call of the muezzin summoned the faithful to the Asr prayer.

Hasdai turned from the window and looked at Nasim. 'I will arrange for you to pray,' he said.

Nasim wiped his eyes and nodded. 'I will tell you what I know.'

*

After prayers and when the servant had cleared away the tray of hot tea and lemon, Hasdai nodded at the General.

'Look at this. Why is your name not listed here?' said Ghalib.

'It is,' said Nasim. 'Here, this is me,' he said pointing to the list. 'Jalal communicated with me using this name.'

'What do you know about the others?' said Hasdai.

'I haven't met any of them but I have seen the names before. I've sent

154

them packages.'

General Ghalib went to speak but was stopped by a look from the Vizier.

'Was that part of the arrangement?' asked Hasdai.

Nasim nodded. 'We never met. That was how Jalal wanted it. He didn't want us knowing the whole plan; just our own part of it. He said it was safer that way.'

'How long did it take to put the ambergris together?' said Hasdai.

'The ambergris at the funduq took half a year. My job was just to supply the glass jars. They had to look like a consignment of bitter orange jam, but inside each earthenware pot of jam there was a smaller jar filled with ambergris.'

'How did you move it around?' said Ghalib.

'Every time there was a festival or major celebration we moved a small quantity of pots. With the crowds on the streets and the city gates being open it was easy. Each time we did it the first dozen pots, the top layer in each crate, was simply made up of bitter orange jam. That way if anyone looked closely we had a chance of diverting their attention. Nobody cares about bitter oranges.'

'When did you first meet the Admiral?' asked Hasdai.

Nasim wiped his eyes and gave a dry laugh. 'I didn't *know* he was an Admiral until you told me yesterday. To be honest I didn't know who I was expecting to see in my shop.'

'I don't understand. How did you know who to talk to?' said Ghalib.

'Jalal told me that in the days leading up to the Night Journey of Mohammed a man would visit my shop several times. On the final occasion he would buy perfume for his wife and talk about knucklebones. That was how I was to know.'

'What happened then?' said Hasdai, scarcely able to believe what he was hearing.

'I was to give him three glass jars. Two of them you found in his room. I don't know where the third one is. Then I was to invite him to play knucklebones at the old Yemeni's bathhouse.'

'What about Jalal?'

'I was told that if the man turned up at the bathhouse I was to go and meet Jalal and confirm that the deal was to go ahead.'

'You met Jalal at the bathhouse owned by al-Mursi the suq inspector?'

Nasim nodded. 'Yes. On the evening of the Night Journey.'

'This all seems so elaborate,' said Ghalib.

'It is. The ambergris that Jalal has here in Cordoba was only a small part of the total consignment. The names on that list spent nearly two years sourcing it, disguising it as bitter orange and, when the time was right moving it.'

Hasdai's eyes widened as Nasim spoke. The clicking of his prayer beads got quicker. 'You are saying that the ambergris at the funduq is only part of what Jalal was putting together for the Admiral?'

'Yes. From the number of jars I supplied I would say that there is at least five times that amount.'

Ghalib and Hasdai looked at each other.

'Where is the rest?' said Hasdai.

Nasim shrugged. 'I honestly don't know. I only dispatched the jars. I was never told what happened to them after that.'

'What happened when you met Jalal at the bathhouse?' said Ghalib.

'I told him that the man had come to see me as planned. I said that I had given him the jars and met him to play knucklebones.'

'What did Jalal say?'

'Nothing. That was the whole point. I wasn't supposed to know what the plan was.'

'So how was the Admiral supposed to know what to do?' asked Ghalib.

Nasim looked at the floor and then at the Vizier. 'Isn't it obvious?' he said.

'Apparently not,' said General Ghalib. 'Perhaps you…'

'General, please,' said Hasdai. He clicked his beads as he looked Nasim directly in the eye. 'It was the other man wasn't it?' he said.

Nasim nodded. 'Yes. Jalal told me that during the knucklebones game a man would ask to join our game. I assumed that he was also working for Jalal and that he would inform the Admiral about what needed to happen next.'

'What was to happen next?'

'That's what I am trying to tell you sir,' said Nasim. 'I don't know.'

'The other man at the knucklebones game,' said Hasdai. 'He said he was a cloth merchant from Sevilla.'

Nasim nodded. 'That probably isn't true. He works for Jalal, but not as a cloth merchant.'

Hasdai nodded and stood up, gesturing to General Ghalib as he did so. 'You have been very helpful,' he said eventually. 'You will be taken back to your cell. I will arrange for you to be allowed to pray at the Maghrib prayer.'

General Ghalib opened the door and spoke briefly to the guards outside. As Nasim bin Faraj stood up he wiped his eyes once more. 'That man,' he said, 'the one who was killed at the bathhouse. You have to believe me sir. I didn't kill him.'

Hasdai looked at him for a moment and then waved his hand for the guards to take him away. As the door closed he sat back down and knuckled his eyes.

'General,' he said. 'I want you to let it be known that Nasim was killed by his guards when he tried to escape. Make sure that story gets talked about in the suq.'

Chapter 41

In the crystalline afternoon sunshine after the Asr prayer, a steady stream of men and boys made their way past the Great Mosque, through the Bab al-Qantara city gate and crowded across the Roman Bridge over the Wadi al-Khabir river. Some of them were carrying large, closed baskets of sturdy cane from which came scuffling and scratching and the occasional raucous crow of a fighting cock. As the throng crossed the river the flocks of white egrets which nested in the scrub on Mill Island rose and wheeled and settled and rose again. The crowd was headed towards the cock-pit south of the river not far from the wharf. The preparations for war meant that the wharf was full of boats and some sailors had joined the procession laughing and slapping each other on the back, happy to have some entertainment and respite from their labour.

Yazid al-Haddad was also in the crowd but he was far from happy. He had ordered his apprentice to come with him today. He might need a witness to swear he had been with him all afternoon so now they were walking together over the bridge.

Behind Yazid's cold, empty eyes his mind was racing. He hadn't planned to come to the cockfight at all today but he had no choice once he got the message. His thumbless right hand was clutching it in his pocket right now, the sweat of his palm reducing the paper to pulp and the inked symbol to an indecipherable smear.

He'd only been half listening when the symbol had been explained to him. They hadn't wanted to use writing. An obscure symbol could only be interpreted by those who had agreed to its meaning. He remembered it was some Berber thing, some kind of reworking of an old barbarian sign for a god. He seemed to remember the name 'tanit'. The fact was he couldn't care less what the symbol was, to him it meant only one thing, kill anyone who was in on the plot. He shuddered as he thought of what he had to do. At least if he got the chance to lay a few bets the gambling might shut out everything else for a few moments. He had managed to scrape together twenty dirhams by calling in some small debts and selling a couple of pairs of shears and now he had the familiar dry mouth and the knot in his stomach that any opportunity for betting gave him. Or maybe it was the thought of the killing which had tightened his guts. Whatever it was he would surely pick some winners today but there would be one loser.

As they got closer to the cock-pit Yazid could smell the food stalls. The sweet smell of roast goat mingled with wood smoke came to him along with the sound of the zajal singers and the guffaws of their audience. People had been singing zajals in Al Andalus for centuries. Comic songs accompanied by hand drums and tambourines where a song was made up for each new occasion with the singer singing a verse and the audience singing it back to him. Today's songs were all about men behaving like fighting cocks... strutting around and fighting each other only to be conquered by the hen when they got home. All fighting cocks ended up in the pot one way or another. It was obvious from the fun that the audience were having that the arak sellers had been doing good business too.

As they went past the singers towards the cock-pit Yazid spotted Bilal the barber just ahead of them. He seemed to be in some kind of argument with a suq trader who for some reason was taunting him.

'What are you doing here?' the man was saying. 'Do you think you can sell some perfume to this crowd? They don't look like the kind that would need your services. These are real men here.'

Bilal turned to face his tormentor and a gap opened up in the crowd with the two of them in the middle facing each other. The barber was shaking so much he could hardly control his voice but somehow he found the strength to speak. 'Who do you think you are, talking to me like that?' he cried at his tormentor.

Yazid gave a grim smile as he saw Bilal being humiliated.

'I can talk any way I like you perfumed leech,' shouted the trader, incensed by Bilal standing up to him, especially in front of a crowd. Now they were surrounded by a ring of onlookers as they circled one another like fighting cocks and the man screwed up his courage enough to prod Bilal in the chest.

Some of the crowd started to shout encouragement to the contestants:
'Go on!'
'Get on with it!'
'Have him, why don't you?'
'Get stuck in!'

Yazid couldn't help thinking that this was definitely not Bilal's lucky day.

The trader and Bilal were both panting now in anticipation of the fight. But it was not to be. A giant of a man stepped from the crowd and put himself between the combatants. He was a merchant ship's captain and was being egged on by his crew, who were laughing and cheering, much the worse for the arak they had drunk.

'Stop this now!' he bellowed and grabbed both men by the fronts of their robes. 'We are civilised people here in Cordoba! We don't want our afternoon at the cockfight spoiled by you two brawling in the road.'

To the delight of the crowd the giant shook Bilal and the trader like two naughty children then let them go one at a time to slink off into the crowd. Yazid held his apprentice back for a while then followed on behind them at which point a zajal singer shook his tambourine in the air and started to march the last fifty or so paces to the cock-pit singing a refrain about two small cocks being defeated by one great big one. The verse was eagerly taken up by the marchers amid peals of laughter. Meanwhile Yazid, with his apprentice right behind him, managed to elbow his way to the edge of the cock-pit.

'What was all that about?' said the apprentice.

'Shut up,' said Yazid. 'Just shut up. If you open your mouth again I'll shut it for you. Do you understand?'

The boy had enough sense to say nothing. He'd seen the smith fly into a rage in the past and still had the scars. It was better to concentrate on the afternoon's business.

The cock-pit was at the bottom of a natural hollow among some ruins not too far from the river bank. This had once been a thriving suburb of the city but a century before it had been levelled by the amir, al-Hakam I, after the population there had rioted. Seventy-two people had been crucified on this spot to quell the riot and from then on this part of Cordoba had had a strange, oppressive atmosphere which was somehow suited to the bloody business of cockfighting. The dense scrub by the river bank obliterated the view of the Great Mosque and the city beyond. The ring itself was a circular enclosure about twenty paces across formed of a smooth mud brick wall about waist height and the floor of albarro, shiny compacted red clay.

Looking across the ring, Yazid could see Bilal glowering at everyone around him but the business of the afternoon was about to start so he turned away. Two men had taken their fighting cocks from their baskets and, clasping the birds over their wings, they stepped into the ring. These were the best fighting birds in Al Andalus. They were bred from stock originally from the coastal city of Shareesh. Shareesh was of course famous for its fortified wine but also for the ferocity and power of its fighting birds. These were not tame farmyard cockerels bred to service hens but muscular, fast, fighting machines which would use their formidable spurs and beaks to tear each other to shreds in the ring. One of the men held his bird up and walked round the ring, showing it off to the crowd which murmured its appreciation. It was a silvery-white bird with huge arced tail plumes in blue-black. Its plumage glistened in the afternoon sun as the bird crowed and struggled to be released flexing its powerful thighs and clawing at the air. The second bird was just as impressive but this time a lustrous red-gold with a black chest and bright tan coloured tail feathers. It too crowed and struggled as its owner paraded it in the ring. Now the birds were held face to face, struggling to get at each other and it was at this point that the betting began. This was simple man to man betting. Wagers were made as to which bird would kill the other.

Everyone in the crowd fancied themselves as experts and there were heated exchanges about which bird would win. All you had to do to make a bet was to find someone who disagreed with your choice of winner. Once the bets were made the hubbub subsided and the only noise was that of the cocks braying at each other, still being held in the centre of the ring. Then they were released.

As they exploded towards each other their ruff feathers stood out like the capes of galloping horsemen and the cocks leapt into the air to bring their spurs into play. The birds fluttered and hacked and pecked at each other until the blood streamed from their wounds. Eventually the white turned the red cock on its back and crowed in triumph as it put a foot on its head and pecked furiously at its neck and eyes. In a matter of moments it was over. The white bird had won and the gamblers who had bet on the red cursed their luck. Yazid was pleased. He had doubled his money but he still had the knot in his stomach. He looked across the ring but the barber was nowhere to be seen. *I'll find him*, thought Yazid.

The smith's apprentice could hardly take his eyes off the ring. There were eight more fights that afternoon and at about the fourth or fifth the boy turned to Yazid to comment on the fact that one of the cocks, a huge, jet black bird was a sure winner, but his master was gone. The boy thought nothing of it and turned again to concentrate on the fight. Sure enough the black won and the lad cursed the fact that he had had no money with which to make a bet.

By the last fight Yazid was back. He had obviously taken a couple of araks to ease the knot in his stomach and he'd ended up with nearly eighty dirhams in his pocket. The apprentice noticed that his master's smile was fixed by the liquor as they started to make their way with the crowd back to Cordoba in time for the Maghrib prayer. The boy knew better than comment on it.

As they approached the river they saw a group of people in the centre of the bridge looking over the parapet and pointing to the water below.

'Something's going on in the water,' the boy said to Yazid. 'Let's see what it is.'

They pushed their way to the centre of the bridge then through the melee to the parapet and looked over. There was a body floating face down in the water. It was being forced by the current against the dam at Mill Island right under the squawking egrets. The man's robe, ripped to ribbons by the act of disembowelling, was streaming in the current along with his entrails. Two of the guards from the Bab al-Qantara were trying without much success to heave the corpse out of the water with body hooks on long poles. As they did so they turned the man over.

'Look!' said the apprentice pointing at the body, 'it's your friend the barber.'

He turned to Yazid but by now the smith was pushing his way through the gawping crowd in the direction of the Bab al-Qantara. In a moment he was gone.

Chapter 42

Day 1: The Night Journey of Mohammed

'I wish you would let me come with you,' said Lieutenant Haytham as the two men stood in the entrance to the Yemeni bathhouse.

'Haytham, listen to me,' said Admiral Suhail. 'Jalal is expecting to see someone on their own. I am to meet this cloth merchant as arranged, and then he will introduce me to Jalal. If you are there too it will make everyone suspicious.'

Haytham shrugged.

The Admiral smiled. 'You are so like your father,' he said.

As the Admiral opened the hatch to the bathhouse door the noise from the crowded streets grew louder and the smell of smoke from the hawkers' kebab grills filled the entrance. As he peered out into the crowded streets the Admiral shivered.

'Here,' said Haytham. 'Take my cloak.'

'Thank you.'

'And take this as well,' said Haytham. He took a short sword from his belt. It had a heavy, angled blade wider at the point than the hilt. He offered it to his uncle.

'What's this?' asked the Admiral 'A falcata? Why are you carrying a falcata?'

'It's my personal weapon. I had it made in the metalwork suq. Please, uncle, take it.'

The Admiral smiled and grasped his nephew by the shoulders. He took the weapon.

'Thank you Haytham. I promise you, I will be fine.'

'I'm just worried about you,' said the Lieutenant.

'Look,' said Admiral Suhail. 'I've been tracking this plan for a year, I can't stop now. I have to see the ambergris for myself. The rest of the consignment is being loaded onto the main fleet right now. This is the final shipment.'

Haytham nodded. 'Just be careful,' he said.

'I will. If am not back by dawn then do as we agreed. Look, don't worry. This will be over very soon. I just have to see the ambergris for myself and then this will all be over.'

Haytham nodded and the two men embraced. As the Admiral eased open the door to the bathhouse he stood in the entrance for a moment and then slipped into the thronging streets which were packed with revellers. Once he had turned the corner and disappeared into a side street a figure in the shadows grasped a knife tightly inside his cloak and carefully pushed open the door to the bathhouse.

PART 2

In the suq there are butchers
With knives kept keen on iron rods.
Goats squeal in terror of the executioner
But men go quietly about their business
As new blood congeals over old

Labrat ben Menachim, Hebrew poet
Cordoba, 917-984

Chapter 43

Day 4

General Ghalib stared out of the window of Hasdai's office as the Vizier spoke to the clerk.

'This is fine,' said Hasdai. 'You can post it on the wall of the Great Mosque after evening prayers. I assume that a copy has gone to the office of the Palace Guard so the necessary arrangements can be made?'

'Yes Excellency,' said the clerk. 'The city gates will be open all night.'

'Good. You may leave.'

'Thank you Excellency,' said the clerk who bowed and gathered the papers from the desk.

'Is there something else?' said Hasdai, as the clerk lingered a little too long.

Ghalib turned to look at the man.

'Please, excuse me sir,' he said. 'I am sorry, but the Chamberlain asked me to see if you had any comments on the draft of the Caliph's address.'

Hasdai closed his eyes for a moment. 'Tell the Chamberlain that the draft will be with him in good time.'

'Very good sir.' The clerk bowed once more and quickly took his leave.

Once the door had closed the sound of Hasdai's amber prayer beads started up again.

'Two celebrations in a week General,' said the Vizier. 'First, the Night Journey of Mohammed and now the Crown Prince has seen fit to arrange a feria in honour of the Royal Fleet's departure. The people will be disappointed when things return to normal.'

'Yes indeed,' said Ghalib. 'They're getting spoiled.' As he spoke he was examining the correspondence that the clerk had brought. 'Sir, look at this,' he said. 'It's from Colonel Zaffar.'

Hasdai took the piece of paper that Ghalib offered him and read it quickly.

'Well,' he said. 'We'd better get to the funduq and find out what is so important.'

He took a red leather folder from the desk and held it up. 'Once we've done that I really do need to find time to work on this speech.'

'What does the Caliph want to say?' said Ghalib.

'The usual stuff. He wants to tell the people that our cause against Baghdad is just, and that the brave officers of the Royal Fleet deserve our eternal thanks for risking their lives in combat. The Chamberlain's office has had to rewrite it to focus on Bandar rather than Admiral Suhail.'

He let the folder fall to the desk. 'What's the matter General?'

'I'm not sure sir,' said Ghalib. 'For some reason I suddenly thought of Lieutenant Haytham.'

'Yes,' said Hasdai. 'I really am sorry about that young man. Did you visit his mother?'

General Ghalib shook his head. 'Not yet sir; I will do as soon as I can though.'

'Make sure you find time for that.'

'Sir,' said Ghalib. 'I've also been thinking about what Nasim told us earlier.'

'So have I,' said Hasdai. 'What do you make of it?'

General Ghalib pursed his lips and thought for a moment. 'Sir, I didn't know the Admiral that well. I couldn't really vouch for his character.'

'I think I know what you mean,' said Hasdai. 'You couldn't vouch for Admiral Suhail but you could for Lieutenant Haytham.'

The General nodded. 'Exactly,' he said.

Hasdai rubbed the back of his neck. 'I must admit the same thought had occurred to me. Either the young Lieutenant was an accomplice to the whole thing…'

'Or he found out what was happening and the Admiral killed him,' said Ghalib.

The two men were silent for a while.

As the muezzin began the call to the evening prayer Hasdai stood up and gestured towards to the door.

'Don't let's think about that now general,' he said. 'We need to go and see Colonel Zaffar. Hopefully he will have some good news for us.'

Chapter 44

Yunus nodded to the guard at the door of the classroom and walked in to find his daughter Miryam packing her astrolabe and almanac into a soft leather shoulder-bag.

'Where have they all gone?' he asked. 'Have you finished with them?'

'I expect they'll have gone to the Al Bisharah Teahouse,' she said. 'We finished what we had to do earlier than I thought so it seemed pointless to keep them hanging on here until you came. They were very good you know.'

'Yes,' said Yunus, 'I suppose they were all competent enough.'

'Competent? Yes they were all that. You know the best one was Siraj bin Bahram but he is such an arrogant man.'

'Yes,' said Yunus. 'I would hate to have to serve under his command.'

As he spoke Miryam reached into her bag and pulled out a small folded paper packet which she held out to her father. 'Look what they gave me,' she said.

Yunus unfolded the paper to reveal a delicately wrought silver pendant about as big as a dirham coin but in the shape of a crescent moon with a five pointed star set between the points.

'Goodness,' said Yunus turning over the beautifully made jewel in his fingers. 'That's lovely. They must have thought a lot of you. They didn't have to do that.'

'No,' said Miryam, 'you're right they didn't. It's so appropriate though as a gift from navigators… the moon and a star. They told me they had it made in the jewellery suq. It was very kind of them. When you think about it these men are going to war and they still have time for kindness like this.'

'Yes,' said Yunus. 'These are strange times indeed. Cordoba is full of contradictions at the moment. On the one hand the celebrations of The Night Journey and on the other these brutal murders that are going on. Hasdai and General Ghalib have their hands full.'

'That's true,' said Miryam. 'Hasdai told me that really he has a lot to do at the moment especially now that the Caliph is due back. He said he has to prepare the Caliph's address to the people and on top of that

Prince Hakam has told him to work together with the Chamberlain on a feria to celebrate the occasion of the navigators leaving for Almeria.'

'That's a strange one, that is,' said Yunus. 'To make such a big occasion of the navigators' leaving the capital is a big declaration of intent as far as our enemies are concerned. Every Baghdadi spy in Cordoba will have their ears pricked up at the moment. Still, I suppose the Caliph knows what he is doing. After all he has been on the throne for thirty-eight years now and he hasn't let us down yet. And if Hakam wants a feria that's what he'll get. I wonder if there will be a corrida de toros.'

'There's bound to be,' said Miryam as she wrapped her pendant in the packet and put it into her bag. When she had done so her fingers automatically went to her throat and she felt the gold Star of David which hung round her neck. This had been a gift from Hasdai ben Shaprut on the occasion of his being appointed vizier. 'I think you'd better tell Hasdai that I got the pendant from my students,' she said.

'Oh Miryam,' said her father with a laugh, 'don't worry about Hasdai. He won't mind in the least if you've got a gift from a group sailors! Now let's go home. What are we going to eat tonight?'

'I have no idea,' said Miryam. 'I have not had time to prepare anything. We can stop off at the bakery next to al-Mursi's bathhouse and buy some fresh bread then pick up a roast chicken in the suq.'

'I don't know why you won't have servants,' said Yunus. 'You do too much.'

'You know quite well that it's not a good idea to have other people in the house if Hasdai is visiting. Anyway I like things the way we are with just the two of us. I like my peace and quiet when I get home. I don't want to be constantly cleaning up after servants and worrying about what they are going to gossip about in the suq!'

'Yes, I know what you mean,' said her father. 'Sometimes they are more trouble than they are worth. Let's go now. Don't forget your cloak. I'll carry that bag for you.'

*

As Yunus and his daughter walked past the end of the Spicesellers' Row towards the bakery in the clear night air they took pleasure in the bustle of the lamp-lit street. Most people were hurrying along intent on buying provisions for the evening meal or going to the bathhouse but some stood, wrapped in their woollen cloaks, gossiping under the oil-lamps.

There was a lot for the citizens of Cordoba to talk about... the goings on at Camp Maaqul and other preparations for war and the ban on the transport and sale of a whole variety of items and, of course, the murders. Some said it was an admiral that had been killed, others said a spy. Whoever it was, they were important enough for the General commanding the Palace Guard and the Vizier himself to be involved in the investigation! It was impossible to keep these things secret in a city where nearly every family knew someone who was in the palace guard or worked in the caliph's administration or had heard the latest rumour in the bathhouse.

'What are you thinking?' said Miryam to her father who hadn't spoken for a while. 'You look worried. Are you thinking about the murders?'

Yunus stopped so suddenly that some people walking behind him stumbled into him. 'Excuse me,' he said to them as he stood to one side to let them pass. Then he looked at his daughter and smiled. 'Not really,' he said. 'Not about the murders. In fact I was thinking that we could have some dates with honey and almond paste after the chicken and that roast chicken and fresh bread really need to be washed down with sherry wine. I am going to go up the Spicesellers' Row to the Christian's shop to buy a flask while you get the bread.'

'Ah,' said the Astronomer Royal's daughter with a smile. 'It is good to know that the tribulations of the Caliphate are weighing so heavily on your mind! I'll meet you in the bakery!'

Chapter 45

Hasdai held a lavender scented cloth over his mouth and nose while with his other hand he sought comfort from the polished surface of his prayer beads as he clicked them on their silver chain. He nodded to Colonel Zaffar.

Zaffar pulled the cotton sheet down so that Shahid Jalal's head and upper torso were exposed. The Vizier fought the urge to retch at the smell.

'Where did you say you found him?' said General Ghalib as he peered at the corpse which had been laid out on a large table in one of the storage areas of the funduq. Several pitch pine torches had been placed around the table and their flickering light picked out the bruises on the victim's neck.

'In an area of thick shrubbery behind the building,' said Zaffar, 'not far from a path which follows the city wall to the *Bab al-Jadid*. One of the soldiers found him in the bushes. It was a dog that alerted him. The animal was tearing at the body. At the … the lower parts sir.' He went to lift the cloth higher. 'Do you want to see?'

'Thank you! That won't be necessary,' said Hasdai quickly.

'Had it been summer,' said Zaffar, 'we would have found him a lot sooner from the smell. As it is the body is not too much affected by the weather.'

'I think the smell is bad enough,' said Hasdai through the cloth.

'How long do you think he's been there sir?' said Ghalib.

'It is difficult to know General,' said the Vizier. 'But looking at the colour of the lips I would assume he has been dead for perhaps as long as the Admiral.'

'You think he has been there in the bushes the whole time?' said General Ghalib.

'Possibly,' said Hasdai. 'Was he lying on his back colonel?'

'Yes sir.'

'You are right about the weather,' said Hasdai, 'but it is still disappointing we didn't find him sooner.'

Zaffar hung his head.

'Don't worry colonel,' said Hasdai. 'I am not blaming you. You and your men have done a good job. It was only because you did more than we asked that we found him at all. Are you certain there is nothing else?'

'I am quite certain sir,' said Zaffar. 'We have inspected the entire length of the path along the city wall. There is nothing else there.'

Hasdai stared at the body. The smell made him feel sick, but his curiosity won against the desire to get some fresh cold air into his lungs.

'I think it is interesting that there is no knife wound,' he said.

'Do you think they were killed by the same person?' said General Ghalib.

'I don't know,' said Hasdai. 'If they were then it is odd that the Lieutenant's falcata wasn't used to kill both men. If they were two separate murders then it supports your theory General.'

'You mean Jalal killing the Admiral?'

Hasdai nodded. 'That is possible,' he said. 'But I'm not sure. If the Admiral was planning to buy Jalal's ambergris, why would Jalal kill him? I could have more confidence in that theory if Jalal had disappeared and taken the ambergris, and presumably the Admiral's money with him. But to find him dead, only a short distance from where the Admiral was killed doesn't seem to make sense.'

'Colonel,' he said, 'bring a light closer. I want to see these marks on his neck properly.'

General Ghalib and Hasdai ben Shaprut both peered at the body as Colonel Zaffar held one of the pitch pine torches above Shahid Jalal's face.

'You said you thought he had been strangled?' said the Vizier.

'Yes sir,' said Zaffar. 'Look at these marks under his chin. But he was also clubbed on the back of the head. Look.'

Zaffar forced the corpse's head forward and sure enough there was bloody depression in the back of the skull which had obviously had the attention of insects and worms when the man was lying in the bushes.

'Put his head back down,' said Hasdai who was steeling himself for the next part of his examination. 'I can tell you if he was strangled or not.'

'How sir?' said Zaffar.

Hasdai put his beads and the scented cloth in his pocket and took the torch from Zaffar. He bent over the corpse and pointed at the top of the man's neck. 'Just under our chin, here, we all have a bone which is shaped like a horseshoe. It inevitably gets broken when anyone is strangled by someone using their hands. But before I examine him I want you both to look at these marks on his neck. They're obviously bruises. Do they look odd to either of you?'

Colonel Zaffar and General Ghalib both leant in to stare at the man's throat. As he did so Zaffar gently rubbed his forearm

'What do you mean by "odd" sir?' said Ghalib.

Hasdai continued to stare at the marks on Jalal's throat. 'I don't know general. I am not sure,' he said. 'But something looks strange about these marks. I don't know what it is.' He shook his head. 'Anyway, let's see if he *was* strangled.' He handed the torch back to Zaffar and put his fingers underneath the dead man's chin He looked at the ceiling as he felt for the horseshoe bone.

'Yes,' he said. 'Just as I thought. It's broken. He was strangled.'

As he spoke a soldier came through the door and approached the table.

'What is it?' said General Ghalib.

The man bowed quickly to the Vizier then spoke to Ghalib. 'Sir, the three girls are waiting in Omar Jaziri's office as you requested. Once you have spoken with them we will arrange for Antonio the cloth merchant to be brought to you.'

'Good,' said Ghalib. 'Sir, are we finished here? Shall we go?'

Hasdai nodded slowly then turned to Zaffar. 'Colonel,' he said. 'At first light you are to ride back to Madinat al-Zahra and prepare to accompany the Caliph back to Cordoba. You know that means you will be in the saddle for most of the day.'

Zaffar nodded. 'Yes Sir.'

'Is your arm sufficiently healed for the journey?' asked Hasdai.

Colonel Zaffar immediately dropped his arm to his side and drew himself to his full height. 'I'm fine excellency. I am honoured you asked, but I will be fine.'

Hasdai smiled. 'Good.' Turning to the general he said, 'Let's go and talk to the girls. But I must wash my hands first.'

*

'Now then, what happened to your arms?' said Hasdai gently.

The girl blushed and tried to hide the bruises and long scratches on her forearms.

'I promise I won't hurt you,' said Hasdai. 'Do this.' He held out his

173

hand and turned over his palm. 'I just want to see if you are all right. Maybe I can clean your wound up a bit, so it doesn't sting.'

Slowly the girl held out her hands and allowed the Vizier to inspect her injuries.

'How did this happen?' said Hasdai.

'It was him,' said the girl quietly.

'Who?' said Hasdai. 'The Admiral?'

The girl shook her head. 'Not at first,' she said.

'What do you mean?'

The girl went to pull her arm away and Hasdai released his grip. 'I promise you, I only want to look at it,' he said.

'The bruises are from the other man, the cloth merchant. He became quite violent and grabbed my arms really tightly. He wouldn't let go. The Admiral was shouting at him to let me go. When he refused the Admiral pulled him off me. That's when I got the scratches. The Admiral was very nice and kept saying how sorry he was for hurting me.' The girl held her arm out once more.

'Why was the Admiral sorry?' said Hasdai taking care not to touch the livid red weals.

'He gave me the scratches sir. He didn't mean to, it's just that the nails on one of his hands were very long. He played the lute you see so he had long nails on his right hand.'

'I see,' said Hasdai. 'The general here told me that you mentioned the Admiral playing the lute for you and the others.' He glanced up at the other two girls who nodded. 'Did he say anything to you?'

'Not really sir,' said one of the other girls.

'You must have talked about something?' said Hasdai. 'I assume that is all you did; talk.'

All three girls nodded. 'Yes sir,' said the girl with the scratches.

'What did you talk about?' said Hasdai.

The girls looked at each other and hung their heads.

Hasdai shot a look at Ghalib who nodded and walked over to the office door. He conferred briefly with one of the soldiers outside and then closed the door leaving Hasdai alone with the girls.

'I assume you know that Admiral was murdered?'

The girls nodded.

'And you know that you were possibly the very last people to see him alive. That is except for whoever killed him.'

The girls looked at each other.

'Alright,' said Hasdai. 'You may go back to your rooms now.'

As the girls made their way to the door the Vizier held out his hand to one of them. He touched her gently on the elbow and said, 'Make sure you keep that wound clean and dry.' She smiled and nodded.

General Ghalib held the door open for the girls and then closed it behind them.

'Something went wrong,' said Hasdai.

'Sir?'

'This deal,' said Hasdai. 'Something went wrong and whatever it was it cost the Admiral and Shahid Jalal their lives. According to Nasim, the Admiral spoke with Antonio the cloth merchant at the Yemeni bathhouse during the knucklebones game. If Nasim is correct then Antonio will have given the Admiral the final instructions about the ambergris and Shahid Jalal. The Admiral came here, to the funduq, on the evening of the Night Journey of Mohammed to meet Jalal and collect the ambergris.' He clicked his amber prayer beads together. 'His plan was to move the ambergris out of the funduq storage area and have it sent to Camp Maaqul. From there it would be split up in to small quantities and then sent to Almeria where it would be loaded on to the main fleet. Except, instead of any of that the Admiral and Shahid Jalal get murdered, and the ambergris is still here in the funduq.'

Ghalib sighed. 'What do want to do now sir?'

The Vizier clicked his beads again for a moment and then put them carefully back in his pocket.

'I want to speak to this cloth merchant. I am going to give him the same choice I gave Nasim.'

Chapter 46

After sunset and the Maghrib prayer the clientele of the Al Bisharah teahouse changed from porters and suq traders who drank tea and ate hearty snacks to keep them able to work through the day to those who were interested in another kind of drink, the drink of either recreation or inspiration or oblivion. As a Christian, Simon the proprietor paid the tax necessary to allow him to serve wine and arak and he and many of the citizens of Cordoba made very good use of this concession.

Anyone passing along the Spicesellers' Row in the dark would be aware immediately of the Al Bisharah by the pool of lamp-light and music and laughter which flooded into the street from the double doors of the teahouse. Most evenings there would be a group of zajal singers on a tiny platform at the back of the teahouse. They would sit there with their instruments. The two-stringed upright fiddle, the rabab, would hold a tune while the tambourine and the tablah would give the rhythm and that prince of instruments the lute, in the hands of the blind lutenist, would provide the flourishes which would bring the audience to their feet stamping and clapping in unison at the topical comic verses of the singers. Simon didn't have time in the evenings to provide tea and a sympathetic ear. He was too busy in his role as *khmmar* dispensing cups of the fine wines of Sharish and Malaga and bowls of arak distilled from grapes or sugar cane. With each drink he would serve pickled or roasted nuts or a few dates or olives on a tiny plate.

It was busy tonight. At one of the tables in the centre of the cramped room a group of suq merchants were discussing the murders which had recently become public knowledge. Another table nearby was taken up by five of the so called *mujun* poets of Cordoba. They were in the Al Bisharah most nights when they would gather to read their verses. These were risqué works of love and the praise of alcohol and having a good time. The poets were sometimes a bit of a handful for Simon and occasionally he had to use his considerable bulk to keep them in order. By the door was a small table with a single stool. A man wearing a black hooded burnus sat there carefully nursing a cup of sherry. He moved his head like a carrion crow looking at each table in turn. He seemed to be listening for something all the time.

There were tables on either side of the musician's platform. At one sat the navigators who had decided that because their course of instruction was over, tonight was the night for a bit of a *zambra*. They were going to get drunk, toast their recently dead commander and sing a few of the old songs. For a dirham or two the musicians would play along. On the other table by the musicians sat Ali. He had come from Camp Maaqul for a cup of wine to relax after his day. The sight of the black clad man at the door intrigued him. Was it a coincidence that he was here at this time too?

Ali hadn't been long in the place when he had been joined at the table by a blacksmith who said he was called Yazid. He had stumbled through the teahouse holding himself up at the counter and blundering into people before he sat down heavily on an empty stool at Ali's table. He'd already had more than enough arak for the day.

'Do you want an arak?' he slurred at Ali lifting a bowl from the table.

'No thanks,' said Ali. 'This Malaga wine is enough for me.'

'The Malaga's good enough,' said the blacksmith as he swayed in his seat. 'But you can't forget on it.'

'I don't like to forget,' said Ali wondering how long this idiot was going to sit with him.

'D'you see that?' said the blacksmith as he held up his right hand. 'D'you see that thumb?'

'No,' said Ali. 'I don't see it because it's not there. What happened? Did you forget?'

'Forget what?' said Yazid.

'To pull your hand away?' said Ali as he took a sip of his wine.

Yazid shook his head violently and gave Ali a wide-eyed confused stare.

'I don't know what you're talking about!' Yazid shouted. 'I'm going to have another drink.' He turned in his chair and called out, 'Simon! Simon, come here! Bring me some more arak!'

As Simon came to the table with the arak a couple of the merchants turned and glared at Yazid.

'What are you two looking at, eh?' he shouted. 'Are you talking about me?'

'Now, now!' said Simon, 'Quieten down. Nobody's talking about you.

No wonder they are looking at you though with all the noise you're making.'

Simon signalled to the musicians who struck up a dance tune featuring the blind lutenist. The navigators all started to stamp and clap in time with the music.

'They're talking about me though, aren't they?' Yazid persisted loudly.

Simon looked at Ali who shrugged his shoulders and raised his eyebrows.

'Actually,' said Simon, 'they're talking about a murder.'

At this Yazid seemed to sober up a bit. 'A murder? What murder?'

'A body was found near the funduq,' said Simon. 'They say it was one of the people staying there, someone called Shahid Jalal.'

'What did you say? I can't hear you for the music,' said Yazid.

'Shahid Jalal,' Simon said loud enough for everyone in the place to hear. 'He's been murdered.'

At this the merchants nodded in agreement and the beak of the man in the burnus swivelled to look at Simon.

'Ach,' said Yazid, 'that's nothing to do with me.' He downed the bowl of arak in a single gulp then drew some coins from the pocket of his robe with his left hand. 'Here! That's enough for what I've had,' he said as he clattered the money on the table. 'I'm going now.'

Ali looked at Simon and shrugged again as Yazid stood up and stumbled towards the door.

As he stood swaying in the entrance of the teahouse a beggar boy pushed past him in the doorway and went straight to the man in black. While all eyes were on the blacksmith lurching into the night only Ali noticed that the coin the man gave the child was wrapped in paper.

Chapter 47

Hasdai stared intently at Antonio, the cloth merchant from Sevilla, as he was shown into the office. General Ghalib pointed at a stool in the centre of the room. Antonio swallowed, glanced at the Vizier and sat down.

When he had first questioned the merchant two days earlier Ghalib thought that he looked like a terrified, timid man who had unfortunately become caught up in a terrible situation. The man who sat in front of him now was different. He looked harder, completely aware of what was going on.

The click of Hasdai's prayer beads could barely be heard above the rain lashing at the windows of Jaziri's office. He pulled a stool across the floor and sat down in front of Antonio. The cloth merchant met Hasdai's gaze for a moment before he broke off and looked at the floor.

'I'll be brief,' said the Vizier quietly. Antonio's fat cheeks wobbled as he breathed deeply.

'I know about Shahid Jalal, I know about the ambergris and I know you were involved in the plot to smuggle it out of Cordoba.'

Antonio bit his bottom lip and gripped the sides of the stool.

'What I don't know,' said Hasdai, 'is what went wrong. I know the Admiral came here, to the funduq, to meet you and complete the deal. Then for some reason he was brutally murdered in the courtyard. I also know that the man you were to introduce him to was killed too, and his body dumped in the bushes that run along the path by the city wall.'

Antonio said nothing.

Hasdai paused briefly before he continued. 'Your involvement in the plot will cost you your life,' he said. 'If you tell me what happened then I give you my word you will not suffer any pain. If you refuse, then I cannot help you.'

Antonio wiped his mouth with the back of his hand. He looked first at General Ghalib and then at the Vizier. After a long pause he said, 'I have no idea what you are talking about.'

General Ghalib went to speak but was silenced by a look from the Vizier.

Hasdai turned back to Antonio and for several moments clicked his prayers beads.

Antonio held his gaze as Hasdai looked into his eyes for any sign that he would change his mind. None was forthcoming.

'Very well,' Hasdai said. 'Tomorrow's sunrise will be your last.'

*

'I can try and make him talk sir,' said Ghalib when the two men were alone.

Hasdai sighed and shook his head. 'He has made his choice,' he said. 'His God will pass judgement on him now.' He placed his prayer beads on Omar Jaziri's desk.

'Make sure Zaffar's men keep the funduq guarded. I want the restrictions on the guests to remain until after Bandar and his men have left for Almeria.'

'Yes sir,' said Ghalib.

'And make sure nobody goes in or out of that storage area without your permission. I don't want anything to happen to the ambergris.'

General Ghalib nodded. 'What are you going to tell the Crown Prince?'

Hasdai sighed and rubbed the back of his neck.

'I'm not sure yet. First I want to talk to Bandar and the navigators. Have them come to my office tomorrow morning. Once I've briefed them, Bandar and I can tell the Crown Prince what happened.'

'What do you think did happen sir?' said Ghalib.

As Hasdai smoothed his sparse brown hair and put on his head cloth he said, 'General, I honestly have no idea.'

Chapter 48

Day 5

Hasdai, General Ghalib and the four navigators were in the Vizier's office in his private wing of the Alcazar Palace.

'I am sorry you had to find out like this,' said Hasdai before pausing to allow the navigators a chance to deal with the enormity of what he was saying. There was no sound save the click of his prayer beads.

After a while Bandar spoke. 'Your Excellency, forgive me, but are you absolutely sure?'

General Ghalib noticed the look that Siraj, the vice-Admiral, shot at both of the younger navigators.

'As sure I can be,' said the Vizier. 'We know Shahid Jalal was able to source a large quantity of ambergris from his network of agents around the coast of Al Andalus and it was his name we found on this piece of paper in the Admiral's room.'

Hasdai handed the note to Bandar. 'In addition we found these two glass jars filled with ambergris. We know these jars were given to him by one of Jalal's agents who works as a supplier to the perfume trade here in Cordoba. We questioned this man and he told us that the Admiral was to go to the funduq, on the evening of the Night Journey to collect the ambergris. The Admiral would move the ambergris to Camp Maaqul, using the Night Journey festivities to conceal this activity. At the camp it would be split up into smaller quantities and sent by animal train to the main fleet in Almeria. Once loaded on board, the main fleet would set sail. During the crossing to Latakia one of the ships was to break off from the fleet and make land just south of Saida on the Syrian coast. The demand for Andalusi ambergris is extremely high there.'

'So what went wrong?' said Siraj.

Hasdai shook his head. 'I don't know exactly, but I know enough to brief the Crown Prince on what happened.'

'This agent,' said Bandar, 'the one who works in the suq. Did he confess?'

Hasdai nodded. 'He did in as much as he told us how the ambergris was collected and how Shahid Jalal operated.'

'How did he operate?' said Bandar.

'He used a series of other people and tried, as far as possible, to make sure these men never met, or at least that when they did meet they only had part of the plan; the part that related to their role, and nothing more.'

'And you are saying that this man, Shahid Jalal, is the man that was found dead near the funduq?' said Siraj.

Hasdai nodded again. 'Yes. Whatever happened at the funduq ended with both the Admiral and Shahid Jalal being murdered. I have to assume that this cloth merchant, Antonio, had something to do with it. That is what I will be telling the Crown Prince tomorrow morning.'

Siraj stroked his beard. 'Vizier?' he said. Hasdai waved his hand for him to continue. 'Why are you telling us this?'

Hasdai pursed his lips. 'I think I understand your question,' he said. 'I know this is very difficult for you to hear. The last thing I want to do is destroy the Admiral's reputation. The impact of this news on the morale of the fleet could be enormous. As a diplomat I fully understand how important it is to protect the men and the reputations of their officers. But the reason I am telling you all this, is because there is something else I think you should know.'

'What is it Your Excellency?' said Bandar.

Hasdai turned to General Ghalib, who nodded and started to speak.

'A few days ago,' said the General, 'one of our men returned from Baghdad where he had been working for us in secret.'

All four of the navigators stared intently at Ghalib.

'He told us that he had been watching a farm about a day and half's march from Baghdad. He noticed that animals and prisoners were being taken there, but that none ever returned. The place was riddled with disease. He got close enough to see that the prisoners were shearing the carcasses of the dead animals and putting the wool into pots which were then sealed.'

Siraj's eyes widened. 'But that could...'

'Yes vice-Admiral,' said General Ghalib interrupting him. 'That could kill in a devastating manner if used to deliberately target men.'

'Are you saying the Baghdadis are planning to use these jars as a weapon?' said Bandar.

'At some stage, yes,' said Hasdai. 'And until yesterday I hadn't thought any further about it, until I spoke to the Chamberlain.'

'What did he say?' said Siraj.

'He reported that we had received word from the advance flotilla which had reached Malta.'

'But that's good news,' said Bandar. 'It means we can leave for Almeria now and get the main fleet under way.'

'Not exactly,' said Hasdai. 'The chamberlain told me that the crew and the animals on one of the boats had been all but wiped out by an outbreak of anthrax on board. All of the animals and nearly all of the men were dead.'

Siraj put his head in his hands.

'What do you think this means?' said Bandar, still unsure of why the Vizier was telling them this.

'This may be extremely difficult for you to hear,' said Hasdai, 'but I think that the Admiral was planning for one of the ships from the main fleet to break away and unload the ambergris near Saida.' Hasdai swallowed slowly. 'And I think he was planning to use anthrax to ensure that once this had happened, there would no witnesses left alive to report back to the main fleet.'

The navigators sat open mouthed in silence.

Hasdai put his prayer beads back on the table. 'I am telling you this because if I am right, there is a container of sealed pots on board one of the boats in Almeria. These pots contain anthrax. The ambergris that the Admiral was planning to move from the funduq was destined for that boat.'

'We need to get word to Almeria,' said General Ghalib. 'We need to order a full search of the main fleet to make sure that we find that container.'

'And you need my assistance for that to happen?' said Admiral Bandar.

Hasdai nodded. 'That's why I had to share this information with you.'

Chapter 49

Day 1: The Night Journey of Mohammed

Admiral Suhail pulled the Lieutenant's cloak tightly around his chest and worked his way through the crowd thronging the streets. As he walked he could hear the cries of the hawkers who were doing a steady trade in the sale of toys and paper birds on sticks. Smoke from the kebab grills that dotted the outskirts of the suq filled the air and at each one a line of eager customers waited to buy something hot to eat. The entire city was out to enjoy itself despite the bitter cold. Parents carried sleeping children in their arms while the older ones ran about, ducking in and out of doorways and shrieking with delight when they were chased off.

The Admiral adjusted his pace and settled into a slow-moving group walking along the road to the city gate by the funduq, the Bab al-Jadid. He tried to ignore the festive mood, and twice turned down offers of roasted meat from eager traders who stepped into the crowd to brandish their wares. Near the gate the Admiral broke off and turned towards Omar Jaziri's funduq. As he left the safety of the throng a man wearing a thick hooded burnus of black wool stepped into the shadow of a doorway and watched him go. When Suhail reached the main entrance to the funduq and stepped inside the courtyard the man pulled the hood over his eyes and re-joined the crowd as it passed through the city gate. As he did so he slipped a coin wrapped in paper to a passing beggar child.

'*A salaam u aleikum,*' said Antonio the cloth merchant from Sevilla as the Admiral walked across the courtyard towards him.

'*Wa aleikum a salaam,*' said Suhail. 'Is everything ready?'

Antonio nodded. 'Shahid Jalal will signal for you when it is safe.'

'Safe?' said the Admiral as he gestured towards the door.

Antonio said nothing and stepped inside the main building of the funduq. The two men went up the stairs to the first floor and walked along the corridor.

'I've arranged for us to wait in here,' said Antonio as they stopped outside one of the rooms.

'We're not waiting in your room?' asked the Admiral.

Antonio ignored him, opened the door and stepped aside to let the Admiral pass into the lamp-lit room. There was a small dull fire of charcoal in the grate which wasn't giving out much heat.

As the door closed behind them Admiral Suhail looked at the three girls who were sitting on stools arranged along the wall and then turned to the cloth merchant.

'Don't worry. Nobody will ask what we are doing in here,' said Antonio.

The Admiral pointed to the girls. 'If they see this they'll know exactly what we are doing,' he said.

'And if they do see then they won't ask any more questions,' said Antonio. 'Here,' he pulled over a stool. 'Take a seat.'

As the Admiral sat down Antonio handed a few coins to the girls. 'Sing for us,' he said then he went to the window and looked down into the courtyard.

Admiral Suhail stared at the three girls. They were very young and thin, dressed in flimsy, colourful clothes and they were shivering from the cold. 'Here,' said the Admiral. He took off Lieutenant Haytham's cloak. 'Take this.'

The girls bowed their heads and gratefully took the cloak. It was wide enough to go over the shoulders of all three of them.

'What happens now?' asked the Admiral.

Antonio turned away from the window and glared. 'We wait. Just as I explained last night,' he said. 'Look, have some wine. In fact let's all have some wine.' He walked over to the shelf in the corner of the room and poured several cups from the wineskin which hung from a hook under the shelf.

The Admiral handed cups to the girls who started to sing in between sips of wine. Then Suhail gestured to a lute on a side table near to the door. When one of the girls smiled he picked it up and started to play plucking the strings with the long nails of his right hand.

'Our very own zajal arrangement,' said Antonio with a scowl. He listened for a few seconds and then returned to his post by the window where he sat on the stool and stared out into the courtyard scouring the darkness for a signal from Shahid Jalal and trying to ignore the girls and their singing. He watched as a muleteer opened one of the doors to the stables and took out a shovel which he used to scoop up a pile of dung from the cobbles.

'What are you looking for?' said one of the girls who stood up and leant over Antonio and peered out into the darkness.

'Never you mind!' said Antonio grabbing the girl's hand and forcing her away from the window.

'Stop that,' said the Admiral as he put down the lute and moved to help. He grabbed the girl by the arm and forced the cloth merchant to let go. The girl shrieked in pain as the Admiral's long nails raked into her arm.

'I am sorry,' said the Admiral to the girl as she pulled away then he turned on Antonio. 'What do you think you are doing?' he said.

The cloth merchant ignored him and picked up his overturned stool. He smoothed his robes and pointed at the girl. 'You! Do not come near the window. Do you understand?' As the girl cowered from him the other two came to her and fussed over her arm.

'What are you doing?' said the Admiral again. 'You could have...'

'Don't tell me what to do,' Antonio hissed. He was furious. 'I am not one of your ignorant sailors that you can order around.'

Suhail had seen enough angry men to know that this was not a time to argue. So he stared at the cloth merchant until he regained his composure.

'Look! What's that?' said the Admiral as a light from the courtyard caught his attention. 'Look, there.'

Antonio put his nose up to the window. 'It's time,' he said. 'Shahid Jalal will see you now.' With that Antonio got up from the stool and walked over to the door. Without looking back he swung open the door and strode out into the corridor.

Once Antonio was gone the Admiral looked through the window and saw that the light was now moving towards a staircase in the far corner of the courtyard. He watched for a few moments before turning round to the girls. He gave a sad smile. 'I am so very sorry,' he said to the one who was dabbing at her bleeding forearm with the hem of her skirt. 'I didn't mean to hurt you.'

Admiral Suhail turned towards the door and made to leave. As he did so one of the girls came towards him. 'Take this,' she said handing him back Haytham's cloak. The Admiral smiled again and squeezed her hand gently.

Chapter 50

Day 5

'Sit down Admiral! Your pacing up and down won't get us in there any quicker.'

Hasdai found the nervous demeanour of Bandar bin Sadiq irritating almost beyond measure. He calmed this irritation by slowly manipulating his prayer beads.

'If you are in this state now how are you going to talk coherently to the Crown Prince when he does call us in? Just sit down and pull yourself together.'

The guard at the door of the prince's private audience room smirked. He'd heard some strange things in his time but this was the first time he'd heard an Admiral of the Fleet told off like a naughty schoolboy.

Bandar sprang to his feet as the gleaming brass-studded mahogany door swung open. It was as if he was expecting Prince Hakam himself to open it.

'His Highness will see you now Your Excellency,' said the strikingly beautiful young woman who had opened the door. She bowed from the waist to the Vizier and then to the Admiral. As she did so the gold threads in her dark green silk robe shimmered in the beam of clear morning light which came in at the window in the corridor and a long tress of glistening black hair escaped from the rose-pink headscarf which she had tucked into the neck of her robe.

Hasdai drew on all his diplomatic experience to conceal his surprise but Bandar was clearly astounded.

The vizier nodded. '*A salaam u aleikum*, Lubna bint Marwan.'

'*Wa aleikum a salaam*, Your Excellency.... Admiral. Please follow me.'

Having followed Lubna through the antechamber Bandar stood back to let Hasdai pass first into the Crown Prince's audience room. As he did so their eyes met and Hasdai's scowl brought the admiral to his senses.

Prince Hakam, dressed in riding clothes, sat on a cushioned divan next to a blazing fire. His dun-coloured woollen leggings were tucked into supple brown leather boots and the belt at the waist of his thigh-length robe supported an exquisitely worked Persian khanjar dagger. His small, tight turban of red and gold sparkled in the light of the flames.

A richly embroidered screen depicting scenes of stag hunting in the Alpujarras had been drawn across the balcony doors making the room seem small and intimate despite the light flowing in at the high broad windows. A second divan and a low, round camphor wood table had been placed in front of the screen as had a small writing desk and stool.

As the Vizier and the Admiral bowed with their right hands on their hearts, the Prince stood up. '*A salaam u aleikum* Vizier Hasdai... Admiral Bandar.'

'*Wa aleikum a salaam*, Your Highness,' said Hasdai, pleased that Bandar had the good sense to say nothing at all.

'Please be seated,' said Prince Hakam as he indicated the second divan. 'I think you know Lubna bint Marwan, Vizier? She has joined my personal staff and will be making a record of our meeting this morning. I understand you have matters of some importance to discuss.'

'This is indeed the case Your Highness,' said Hasdai. 'Matters which may affect the security of the Caliphate.'

'Then let us not stand on formality. Tell me.'

'Your Highness, we have discovered a plot against the fleet. Our enemies have attacked and destroyed one of the ships in our advance flotilla killing the entire crew and its complement of fighting men and animals.'

'How have they done this?'

'By bringing a pestilence to the ship Your Highness,' said Hasdai who then explained the pots of anthrax to the Crown Prince. 'We now have good reason to believe that there are such disease carrying pots on many if not all of the ships in the fleet.'

The Crown Prince turned to Bandar. 'What is you assessment of this situation admiral?'

'I think, Your Highness, we have to delay the departure of the fleet until each ship can be thoroughly searched. I have little doubt that we shall find these things on the ships. When we do find them they will have to be very carefully handled and their destruction by fire will have to be absolute or we risk setting off a plague which could wipe out the population of our naval base in Almeria.'

There was a moment of profound silence in the room punctuated only by the scratch of Lubna's pen as she wrote her notes. Then the prince spoke.

'You are right admiral. The entire fleet must be searched. We must postpone the departure of the fleet until we know that our men are safe from this disease. Vizier, you will send a message in my name immediately after this meeting to our naval command in Almeria. Admiral, I am making it your responsibility to see that the search is organised effectively and that these weapons are destroyed completely. Do you have a man in Almeria who you can trust take on this task?'

'Yes sir. There is an old and wise flotilla commander who I am sure will do the job. He is known to General Ghalib as he was in command of supplying the Northern Frontier when he was on secondment to the army.'

'Good. Now, the Caliph will not take kindly to this turn of events. This is clearly something of a victory for Baghdad before we have even managed to marshal our troops. I shall inform the Caliph myself of the situation and tell him what action is being taken. Admiral Bandar, as soon as your commander has assessed the situation we must decide on a new departure date for the fleet. This will be your responsibility. Do I make myself clear?'

'Perfectly clear, Your Highness.'

'Now, Vizier Hasdai, I understand you have another matter to discuss.'

'I do Your Highness. It concerns the late Admiral of the Fleet, Suhail bin Ahmad.'

'He was murdered. What of him?'

'Your Highness, we have come to believe that the Admiral was involved in a major smuggling ring which was directly flouting a decree of His Majesty the Caliph and it was this activity which led to his murder.'

'What were they smuggling?'

'Ambergris, Your Highness. They were going to use the pack caravans from Camp Maaqul to transport the ambergris to Almeria where it was to be put on a naval ship for export to the east.'

Again there was silence in the room save for the creak of Lubna's pen on paper then even that stopped.

After a long moment during which he stared at the screen behind

Hasdai and Bandar the Crown Prince Hakam sighed deeply then spoke in a voice which belied his obvious fury.

'The Surah An-Nisa of the Holy Quran tells us that "Allah does not love him who is a traitor". We trusted this Suhail bin Ahmad. He was appointed by His Majesty the Caliph. He was trusted by my father. There must indeed be truth in the proverb that trust makes way for treachery. But what is to be done? The man is dead. Do we have others who are involved in this treachery… this arrant disregard of the Caliph's decree?'

There was another moment of silence during which Hasdai was acutely aware that he was about to condemn a man to perhaps the most hideous of deaths. Lubna's pen started up again.

'Yes Your Highness,' said Hasdai.

'Explain,' said the Crown Prince.

'Your Highness we have, or rather had, two men in custody who were in league with Suhail bin Ahmad.'

'What do you mean you *had* them in custody? Who were they and where are they now?'

'One is, or rather was, a trader in perfume in the suq. He was called Nasim. He tried to escape from custody and was killed by his guards.'

As he said this to the prince Hasdai was careful not to look at Bandar who knew that what he was saying was not true. Again Hasdai was relieved by the fact that Bandar had enough sense not to speak. The young admiral was learning diplomacy fast.

'A pity,' said the prince. 'Two crucifixions tend to concentrate the minds of the population rather better than one. And the second traitor… or rather the third?'

'He is a Christian cloth merchant from Sevilla, Your Highness.'

'You have him still?'

'Yes Your Highness.'

'Then let him be crucified *now*! Immediately! Between dogs at the gates of Camp Maaqul. This Antonio was anxious to use the road to Almeria. Let him have his wish. Get it done! That will be all. You may go now.'

Chapter 51

Day 1: The Night Journey of Mohammed

As he closed the door and stepped into the courtyard of the funduq Admiral Suhail's breath hung in the cold air and was briefly illuminated by the moon which broke through the clouds. He paused for a moment to check inside his robe and his fingers brushed against the hilt of the Lieutenant's falcata before he set off towards the secure storage area. As he walked he could hear noise from the crowded streets which were still full of revellers enjoying the Night Journey celebrations. When he reached the storage area the door opened a crack. He could see the flicker of a pitch pine torch being held behind the door as a man beckoned him inside.

'I suppose you want to check the jars?' he said as he closed the door.

'Are you Shahid Jalal?' asked the Admiral.

'I am.'

'Good, then yes, I want to see the jars.'

The man nodded towards one of the locked storage units. 'They're over there,' he said. He gave his torch to the Admiral and bent down to open the door. As it creaked open he gestured for the Admiral to look inside. 'It is all there,' he said. 'See for yourself.'

For a moment or two Admiral Suhail tried to pull open the top of one of the crates. When it wouldn't budge he reached into his cloak for the falcata and used it to prise open the wooden lid. He reached inside and pulled out one of the earthenware pots. Using the long fingernails on his right hand he dug into the beeswax seal then stuck his finger into the jar and drew out some of the bitter orange paste which he put to his tongue. Satisfied that these were the pots he turned it upside down and shook its contents onto the lid of the crate with a squelch. Holding the pine torch to the paste on the lid he gazed for a moment at the smaller glass jar that had been positioned inside. Even in the poor light offered by the torch he could see that this was one of the jars of ambergris. He wiped the jar with his hand, opened it and sniffed the contents.

'It's all there,' said the man. 'You can count the jars if you like.'

'I don't think that is necessary,' said Suhail as he wiped his hands with some of the straw packing. 'If there is anything missing I'll know where to find you.'

The man nodded. 'Shall we go and finalise the arrangements? Here,' he said as he handed Suhail the falcata, 'you'd better not forget this.' The admiral tucked the heavy bladed weapon into his belt then, with the storage unit locked up, the two men stepped back out into the main courtyard.

'Are you going to move it tonight?' said the man as he led the way towards a set of stairs in the far corner.

'Yes,' said the Admiral. 'These celebrations are the only chance I'll have to move the crates without arousing suspicion.'

'Then we should be quick. The crowd will start to thin out soon.' He pointed towards the dark archway in the corner of the main courtyard by the foot of the stairs. 'Here, my room is this way.'

When the Admiral reached the foot of the stairs he had no time to react as a figure leapt out of the darkness and punched him hard in the stomach. Sinking to his knees in pain he felt the falcata being torn from his belt and the last thing he saw was the flash of moonlight on the heavy blade before it smashed into his skull.

Chapter 52

Day 5

'Ah, General Ghalib, Admiral Bandar, come in. I wasn't asleep. I was just resting my eyes.'

The two men at the door of the Vizier's office looked at each other as they came in. General Ghalib smiled. 'It's all right sir,' he said. 'I also need to rest my eyes more now than I did when I was younger. We are having too many late nights and it's too warm in here with that fire. Shall I open the window?'

'Yes, let's get some fresh air in here then you must both come with me to the chamberlain's office. General, have you had today's brief from him yet?'

'No not yet. I think there's too much going on at the moment. I'm not surprised he can't get all the reports done on time. Is that why you want to go and see him?'

'Well, among other things. I think what is most important though at the moment is that he gets the message from Admiral Bandar here to Almeria that the fleet must be searched for anthrax.'

Hasdai held up a red leather document case of the type the caliph used for direct communication with the vizier. 'I also have to see him about this.'

'Is that the Caliph's address to the people?'

'No. It's a message from His Majesty that he wants to meet me this afternoon as soon as he arrives from Madinat al-Zahra. I presume he wants to finalise his speech then.

'As far as the reports are concerned, I sympathise with the chamberlain to some extent but he needs to be told that we have to have them on time. Look at today for instance. I can't be meeting the caliph without having first read the daily briefing from the chamberlain.'

Both the general and the admiral nodded in agreement.

'Come on now,' said Hasdai. 'Let's go to his office. Close that window again, will you.'

*

As the three men entered the chamberlain's secretariat the clerks all stood up, greeted them and bowed. With a wave of his hand Hasdai acknowledged their greeting and they went back to work as he, the general and the admiral walked through the secretariat and into the chamberlain's office.

'Good morning chamberlain, how are you?'

Before answering the chamberlain looked at the admiral and wondered why he was here.

'I must say Your Excellency we are a bit stretched at the moment. There is much to do and as usual we don't have enough staff. I have only this minute finished the daily briefing papers for you and General Ghalib.' He held up two documents. 'Thankfully there is not much new to report. If there had been anything important I would have tried to get the papers to you sooner. Please accept my apologies for them being late.'

'I think you had better let us decide what's important,' said General Ghalib as he took the documents, 'and just get the papers to us on time.'

'Exactly,' said Hasdai who then lowered his voice. 'Now chamberlain, Admiral Bandar and I have some instructions for you which must be kept in the strictest of secrecy. Let us go in your soundproof room.'

As the three men filed into the small secure room and closed the door Ghalib sat down on a stool next to a table on which was a pile of grubby, damp clothes which stank of the river. As he massaged his knee the general couldn't help wondering why they were here in the chamberlain's office.

Moments later the door to the strong room opened and as the three men emerged the chamberlain, clearly shaken, said, 'The birds will be sent immediately this meeting is over.'

'Good,' said Admiral Bandar who turned to Hasdai. 'Now, with your permission Your Excellency, I would like to meet with my colleagues to plan our departure.'

'Of course,' said the Vizier. 'You may leave us now.'

With the Admiral gone the chamberlain spoke. 'General Ghalib, I have to ask your pardon.'

'What for?'

'I have received a petition which came too late for me to include in your briefing papers.'

'What is it?'

'The mother of Lieutenant Haytham came to the secretariat and asked if she could meet with you.'

The general sighed deeply. 'Yes of course I will meet her. I had intended to do so anyway. I'll get a message to her and arrange a meeting.'

The vizier turned to the chamberlain. 'Good, I think we have finished now unless there is anything else general?'

'I do have one thing sir.'

General Ghalib nodded towards the pile of clothing on the table.

'Why have you got these in your office?' he said to the chamberlain.

The chamberlain looked at Hasdai who simply raised his eyebrows to reinforce Ghalib's question.

'Oh those,' said the chamberlain. 'I don't suppose they're important.'

'There you go again,' said Ghalib. 'Deciding what is and isn't important. If they're not important why are they here stinking out your office?'

Hasdai couldn't help smiling at the chamberlain's discomfort and said, 'Look, just tell the general why these things are here.'

'They were brought in by the corporal of the guard at the Bab al-Qantara. They belonged to a body they fished out of the river yesterday.'

'Did he drown?' said Ghalib who stood up and drew his dagger to lift up the clothing with its point. He grunted as he put his weight on his leg. 'This robe is ripped to shreds at the front and these are obviously bloodstains.'

'Yes,' said the chamberlain. 'He was disembowelled before he was thrown in the river.'

'Where is the body now?' asked Hasdai.

'It has already been buried. The guard saw to that.'

'Was there anything in the pockets of the robe?'

'Just some knucklebones and a few dirhams and some copper coins.'

'Knucklebones you say?'

'That's right. Here they are.'

The chamberlain took a small bowl from his desk and passed it to Hasdai who examined the gambling pieces and the coins.

'Do we know who this man was?' asked Ghalib

'He was a barber, Bilal bin Safwan. He has a shop on the Clothsellers'

196

Row by the entrance to the perfume suq.'

'The perfume suq?' said Hasdai

'That's right. Can I ask if that's significant?'

General Ghalib caught the vizier's eye. 'You can ask,' he said, 'but we're not going to tell you; at least not yet. Is this corporal of the guard on duty today?'

'He should be, yes,' said the chamberlain.

Ghalib and the vizier looked at each other again and Hasdai nodded.

'I think I'll need to talk to him,' said the general.

'Indeed,' said Hasdai, 'but before you do get a message to Ali and have him meet us back here later. I want to know what, if anything, he has observed at Camp Maaqul.'

Ghalib nodded.

Hasdai held up the bowl with the knucklebones and the money and said to the chamberlain, 'I'll take these.'

Chapter 53

Day 1: The Night Journey of Mohammed

'Here, take these,' said Yazid al-Haddad, as he handed over the Lieutenant's cloak and the falcata which ran with blood.

'What I am supposed to do with them?' said the man. His hands shook as he looked at the body.

'I don't care, just hide them somewhere,' said Yazid.

'Is he dead?'

'Of course he's dead,' said Yazid. 'Now move, quickly.'

The man looked around frantically. The noise from the crowded streets was growing louder and he could hear voices on the other side of the courtyard. He tucked the cloak and the heavy blade into a bundle under his arm and hurried to the stables where he pushed it deep down to the bottom of a water trough. He waited a moment until the cloak was soaked and stayed down, weighted by the falcata. He threw some straw on top of the water and hurried back to the staircase where Admiral Suhail lay dead.

'Did you hide them?' said Yazid.

'Look I don't know what is going on here…'

'Good,' said Yazid interrupting. 'You are not supposed to know what is going on. That's the whole point. Now did you hide the cloak and the blade?'

'Yes, but they are bound to find the bundle if they look in the stables. The only place I could think of was the water trough.'

'Don't worry about that,' said Yazid. 'I hope they do find it.'

'Why?' said the man, his eyes wide with fear.

'Because the longer they spend trying to work out how a cloak that a dead man was wearing ended up in the water trough wrapped around the falcata that killed him, the longer it will be before they start looking for us.' Yazid looked around. 'Quickly,' he said. 'Follow me.'

The two men hurried to the main gate and slipped into the street. There they turned against the crowd which was streaming towards the city gate.

'Why are we going this way?' asked the man. 'The gate is back that way.'

'And so is the corporal of the guard,' said Yazid through gritted teeth. 'If he sees the blood on your face he might start asking questions. Here,' he said taking a cloth from his pocket. 'I'll wipe it off. You've caught the spray.' The man recoiled in horror as he looked at the smear of blood that Yazid wiped off his neck and face.

'Good, that's it, now let's keep moving,' said Yazid and the two men pushed against the crowd until they reached an alleyway that lead to the city wall. 'Stand here with me and keep quiet.'

The two men stood in the mouth of the alley until a group of people who had clearly been enjoying themselves staggered past and out of earshot.

'Now,' Yazid said with one hand on the man's arm. 'Tell me exactly what you know.'

'What I know?' said the man loudly.

'Quiet! You need to keep calm,' said Yazid as he clamped a hand over the man's mouth. As he nodded Yazid slowly released his hand. 'Good. Now tell me what you know about tonight. What were you told would happen?'

'I was told to meet a man at the funduq. I was told he would want to check the contents of the crates in one of the storage units and that he would come out of the door furthest away on the left hand side of the courtyard as I looked at the main gate.'

'Then what?'

'When he was finished I was told to lead him to my room. Which is where you were waiting at the bottom of the stairs.'

'Did you leave anything in your room?' asked Yazid.

The man shook his head. 'No. I haven't been back there since I went to the bathhouse to play chess earlier.'

'And did you speak to anyone at the bathhouse?'

'Yes of course I did. It's hard not to speak to anyone when you are trying to place a bet.'

'Alright, calm down,' said Yazid. 'I mean did you introduce yourself to people?'

'Yes. I did everything I was asked to do. I said my name was Shahid Jalal and that I was a merchant in town for business.'

'Good,' said Yazid. 'Look, go this way,' he said gesturing down the alley to a path that hugged the city wall. 'It leads directly to the city gate. We'll be safer this way.'

He nodded and set off down the path.

Yazid al-Haddad looked around quickly then followed him down the path towards the city gate.

Chapter 54

Day 5

'Did you actually see what happened to him?'

'No sir, I didn't,' said the young guardsman to General Ghalib. 'We were just about to step in to stop them from fighting when this huge sailor got hold of Bilal and the other one and shook some sense into them. It was quite funny really.'

'Who's "we"? asked Ghalib.

'I was on duty at the cockfight with another member of the guard, sir. Our sergeant sent us to make sure there was no trouble in the crowd.'

'Is there usually trouble?'

'No, not really. Occasionally there are arguments about bets but it's normally nothing serious. This is the first time there has been a killing connected with the cockfight for as long as I have been here.'

At this the sergeant of the guard leaned over the table and said, 'General, I have carried out my duties here in the Bab al Qantara gatehouse for nearly twenty years now and every time there is a cockfight all we do is send over a couple of men just to keep order if necessary. There has never been anything like this in all my time.'

'What have you done about this killing?' asked Ghalib.

'As soon as the body was found I organised a search for the merchant that Bilal was arguing with.'

'Did you find him?'

'Of course,' said the sergeant. 'It was no problem. We just went into the suq and the guardsman here recognised him.'

'How did you know where to find him?'

'We started at Bilal's barber shop and worked our way along the Clothsellers' Row. He has a cloth business about four shops down from Bilal.'

'So he didn't try to escape from Cordoba?'

'Apparently not.'

'Did he admit to the killing?'

The sergeant snorted a laugh. 'No, but they never do though, do they?

He swears blind that he didn't do it. He says he doesn't even carry a knife.'

'What do you think guardsman?'

'Well, he seems the obvious murderer,' said the young soldier. 'As far as I know no-one else would have done it. The trader seemed pretty angry with Bilal.'

'Do you know why he was angry?'

'No. Once the sailor let them go they both just slunk off into the crowd and the next time I saw Bilal was when we hooked his body out of the river.'

'Did you ask this cloth-seller why he was angry?'

The soldier shook his head. 'No sir we didn't.'

'Where is he now?' said General Ghalib.

'He is in the cells at the barracks,' said the sergeant. 'Can I ask why you are interested in him sir? Do you think this has something to do with the other murders you are investigating?'

'On the face of it, it doesn't look like it has,' said Ghalib. 'This just looks like an argument between two traders which has got out of hand. But, do nothing with this man until you hear from me. I may want to talk to him later. Is that clear?' He got up to leave the guardhouse.

'Yes sir,' said the sergeant. 'Let me see you out.'

Chapter 55

Hasdai stared at the light brown, leather-bound journal from al-Mursi's bathhouse that lay on his desk. He set his prayer beads to one side and placed his own fingers on the ink marks that had been left by General Ghalib's, then he turned the journal over and ran his fingertips over the general's thumbprint on the leather cover. He put the book on his desk, knuckled his eyes with both fists, stood up and walked over to the window.

Standing at the window he rolled up the left sleeve of his robe and held his forearm to the light. Slowly he pulled the fingernails of his right hand down the inside of his left forearm then stared intently at the white marks that his nails had created. Then he wrapped his right hand around his left forearm and squeezed tightly. Again he looked at the marks left by his fingers and thumb. He closed his eyes and rubbed the back of his neck as he walked back to his desk.

'Enter,' he said, as the guard in the corridor knocked on the door.

'Excellency, I know you're expecting General Ghalib, but one of the Admiral's navigators has asked to see you. He's been waiting for some time.'

'Send him in,' said the Vizier. The guard bowed, and stood to one side to let the navigator enter.

'Please,' said Hasdai gesturing to the stool in front of his desk. 'Sit down.'

The young navigator nodded and sat down opposite the Vizier.

'Now,' said Hasdai as he picked up his prayer beads. 'What is it you want to see me about?'

The navigator glanced around the office before answering. 'I wanted to talk to you about the Admiral,' he said eventually.

'I see,' said Hasdai. 'Do you mean Admiral Suhail?'

The man nodded. 'Yes Excellency.' He twisted his head cloth between his fingers and looked at the floor before continuing. 'I've been thinking about what you told us earlier.'

Hasdai manipulated his beads along their silver chain. 'I'm sorry you had to hear that,' he said. 'Was there something specific you wanted to discuss?'

The navigator took a deep breath before he spoke. 'I would have followed that man to my death,' he said. 'I cannot believe that he'd be involved in a plot to release anthrax in the fleet.'

'As I said during the briefing,' said Hasdai, 'I appreciate that this is a very difficult thing for you to be told.'

'Forgive me Excellency, but I am not sure you do,' said the man as his eyes filled with tears. He hung his head for a moment before continuing. 'The Admiral I knew is not a traitor and nor is he a thief. This thing about the ambergris, it doesn't make sense. It is so completely out of character.'

Hasdai placed his prayer beads back on the desk, reached inside a drawer and took out a small earthenware flask. He poured a cup of arak and handed it to the navigator.

'Thank you sir,' said the young man then he took a sip of the arak. 'The day before he was murdered I overheard him having an argument.'

'Who with?' said Hasdai.

The navigator shook his head. 'That's the problem. I'm not sure.'

'Are you certain it was the Admiral?'

The navigator sipped his arak and nodded. 'We had just finished classes for the day,' he said. 'I was on my way back to my room here at the Alcazar when I realised I had forgotten one of my books. We were coming to the end of our training and I wanted to do some more work on the charts we'd studied earlier that day.'

'So you went back to the University?'

'Yes sir. When I got to the classroom I heard the Admiral's voice. He was very angry.'

'What was he saying?'

'He was shouting. I'd never heard him in such a rage.'

'Who was he shouting at? Was it one of the other navigators?'

The navigator shrugged. 'I honestly don't know. I could only really hear the Admiral's voice.'

'What did you hear?'

The navigator drank down the rest of the arak. 'He kept going on about ambergris. He was saying how long he'd been piecing things together and that now he was ready.'

'Ready for what?'

'I don't know sir.'

The vizier stared at the navigator for a moment. 'What happened next?'

'I heard footsteps from inside the room coming towards the door. I didn't want the Admiral to know I was eavesdropping so I turned and left. I came back here to the Alcazar.'

'Did you go back to the university later?' said Hasdai.

The navigator shook his head. 'No sir, a short while later an officer from the Palace Guard came by and told me that I was to remain in my room until first light. He said that all of us were restricted to our quarters outside of classes. He said that this was an order from the Admiral.'

Hasdai glanced at the ink-stained journal on the desk then looked the young man in the eye. 'Why are you telling me this?' he said eventually.

The navigator wiped his mouth. 'I told Admiral Bandar and Vice Admiral Siraj what I had overheard.'

'When was this?' asked Hasdai.

'Yesterday, at the teahouse.'

'What was their reaction?'

'They said that I should say nothing. They wanted to protect the Admiral's reputation and they didn't want the rest of the men to know what I had heard. They were concerned it would damage the morale of the fleet.'

'So why are you telling me now? If your Admiral has given you an order why are not following it?'

The navigator looked down at his hands for a moment then raised his head. 'Sir, I can't be certain, but I think that the argument I overheard was between Admiral Suhail and Bandar. If I am right, and what you said earlier about the ambergris plot is true, I am worried that Bandar is involved as well.'

Hasdai stared at the navigator. As he did so he took up his prayer beads and clicked them together. As the two men sat in silence there was a knock at the door.

'Yes?' Hasdai shouted.

The door opened. 'Excellency,' said the guard. 'General Ghalib and Ali are here to see you.'

'Wait,' said Hasdai then he turned back to the young navigator. 'Thank you for coming to see me,' he said. 'I am very grateful. What you say may be important. Now, the best thing you can do is go back to your quarters and rest. You have a lot ahead of you.'

The navigator rose to his feet. 'Thank you Your Excellency.'

As Hasdai watched the young man leave he squeezed his prayer beads tightly in his hand. Resisting the urge to pour himself a cup of arak he called to the guard to admit General Ghalib and Ali then he got up and walked over to the window.

Chapter 56

The porter made steady progress through the crowded metalwork suq. 'Gangway! Mind your backs! Mind our backs! Gangway!' he called as he loped along. The yoke on his shoulders had a basket full of hammers, iron chains and sickles at each end and workers ducked out of the way of the swinging baskets as the porter threaded his way through the claustrophobic, charcoal-strewn alleyways. A smell of sulphur hung in the air and the bubbling hiss of red hot metal being plunged into water troughs could be heard between the incessant strokes of hammer against anvil.

'Shut up!' said the man in the black woollen burnus as the porter's calls passed down the alleyway on the other side of the sackcloth curtain. He grabbed Yazid al-Haddad's shoulder and pushed him to the back of the shop. 'Be quiet. Get into the yard! Nobody will hear us there.'

The two men went into the open space by the forge at the back of the shop. Now they could be certain that they would not be overheard by anyone in the alleyway.

'Do you have any idea how long we have been planning this?' asked the man as he pulled the hood of his burnus down.

As he spoke Yazid's apprentice pressed himself flat to the ground behind the water tub. They hadn't seen him when they came into the yard and he wasn't about to show himself now. He stayed as still as he could, struggling to control his breath as his heart hammered at his ribs. He heard Yazid reply slowly and deliberately. 'I think I've got some idea,' said his master. And I've done everything you've asked of me. Everything, do you hear? Every message you've sent to me with that beggar child I've dealt with. The Admiral... the man at the funduq who was pretending to be you... Bilal the barber who helped me move those crates to the funduq...I've dealt with all of them.'

'And now, after all that, when we are this close, you want to stop?'

Yazid nodded and picked up a hammer that was lying on the anvil. 'There's nothing more to be done. Both Nasim and Antonio are dead, or if not they are as good as dead. All the evidence will point to the fact that the deal went wrong and by the time the Caliph addresses the people tomorrow you'll be safely out of Cordoba. Everyone will think the Admiral was to blame.' He wiped his mouth with the back of his hand. 'So yes, I want to stop. I want my money and I don't want any further part in this business. I don't want to end up nailed to a plank on the road to Almeria like Antonio.'

The man in the burnus glared at Yazid long enough for the metalworker to break away from the gaze and look at the floor. Yazid put the hammer back on the anvil before he spoke.

'You said you'd look after me,' he said looking up again.

'And I meant it,' said the man in the burnus. 'We are family after all.'

Yazid rubbed the back of his neck with his thumbless right hand. 'Yes I suppose we are,' he said.

'Do you remember two years ago when that group of Baghdadis escaped from the Alcazar prison? There were soldiers crawling all over the countryside looking for them, but it was you, Yazid, who found me a safe route into Cordoba.'

Yazid nodded and looked up. 'Yes, I remember that.'

'And when the Caliph imposed the restrictions on the movement of goods, it was you who got me inside Camp Maaqul. I haven't forgotten any of that. You are my cousin, and we made a deal.'

Yazid gave a weak smile. 'Does that mean you'll look after me?'

'Oh yes, Yazid. I'll look after you all right.'

From his hiding place behind the water tub Yazid's apprentice heard the head of the hammer chink against the anvil as the man in the woollen burnus picked it up. Then he heard his master call out 'No!' and there were three sickening cracks like a watermelon being split with an axe as the man swung the hammer again and again into Yazid's head.

The apprentice held his breath for what seemed like an age then he heard a sighing grunt as Shahid Jalal swung the hammer high above his shoulder before with a final splintering crack he buried it deep in the skull of the blacksmith.

The boy froze in terror as he heard Shahid Jalal panting as he stooped over the body of the blacksmith.

'I said I would look after you,' Shahid muttered before pulling the hood of his burnus down over his eyes, walking across the yard, through the shop and out into the crowded alleyway.

Chapter 57

Hasdai stood by the window staring out into the courtyard. Ali and General Ghalib, sitting on stools in front of his desk, knew better than to interrupt the vizier when he was in this mood. Eventually Hasdai put his prayer beads in a pocket in his robe and turned to face the two men.

'So, general, did you find out who killed this Bilal? He was a barber wasn't he?'

'That's right, sir, he was. His shop is on Clothsellers' Row just at the entrance to the perfume suq.' As General Ghalib spoke he turned his knee towards the heat of the fire and tried to rub away the pain. Normally he loved sitting by the fireplace in Vizier Hasdai's private office. The curved fire-back threw the heat straight out into the room together with the perfume of pine resin which today mingled with that of the cardamom and mint tea they had been drinking. Usually the vizier and he would talk of more pleasant things than murder.

'The guards are sure they have the man who did it in the cells. It seems there was some argument at the cockfight and this person, a merchant, killed the barber.'

'Has he admitted as much?'

'No, he denies it completely but the guards are convinced that he did it.'

'Have they got any witnesses?'

'No sir, they haven't, but one of the guards saw him arguing pretty fiercely with Bilal before the cockfight.'

'There's something not right about this,' said Hasdai. 'Did you talk to this trader?'

'I didn't have time sir you wanted me here. Do you want me to go and talk to him? I have told the guards not to do anything with him until I tell them.'

'I think you may need to. There's something about this Bilal that I can't quite put my finger on.'

'Why are you suspicious?'

'Do you remember when we were at the Chamberlain's office and I took the contents of Bilal's pockets?'

'I do. I wondered why you wanted them.'

Hasdai sat down at his desk, reached towards a bowl and picked out two knucklebones. They were smooth with a deep brown patina of age. He passed one to Ghalib.

'Look at it carefully.'

'What am I looking for exactly?' said the general. 'It's just an old knucklebone.'

'That's right,' said Hasdai, 'but if you look at the edge here,' he held up the other bone and pointed, 'you'll see a nick cut into the bone with a file.'

'Oh yes,' said Ghalib. 'I can see it. What's the significance of that though?'

'The significance is that all of the bones at Yousef the Yemeni's bathhouse are marked with this nick.' Hasdai reached inside the desk drawer. 'Here,' he said handing over two more knucklebones. 'I took these from his bathhouse yesterday morning. They are identical they have the same nick cut into them. He only allows people to use his own bones for gambling in his premises. These bones are not weighted or tampered with. So Bilal the barber has been gambling at Yousef's bathhouse... that means there is a possible connection between his murder and that of the Admiral.'

'But where does that get us?' said Ghalib. 'You've already given the Crown Prince your explanation of what happened.'

'I know that General. But there's still something about all of this that I don't like. I don't know if it gets us anywhere, except perhaps to say that if the merchant in the cells did kill Bilal, then it might be the case that he also had something to do with the other murders.'

'But sir,' said Ghalib.

Hasdai held up his hand to cut Ghalib off. 'I know what you are going to say. But I want to show you something.' He picked up the ink-stained journal from al-Mursi's bathhouse which lay on his desk. Hasdai held up the book and pointed at Ghalib's hands with it. 'Your fingers are still stained with ink.' He smiled at the general. 'You look like a schoolboy just home from your lessons. What happened? Are these your finger-marks on the cover?'

Ghalib put down his cup and returned the vizier's smile as he rubbed his knee. 'They are, yes. I turned over the ink pot on al-Mursi's clerk's desk. It made a hell of a mess! I can't say that I'm sorry though. Cleaning it up would give that weasel something useful to do.'

Hasdai put the book back on the table, took his prayer beads out of his pocket and stared long at the general's thumbprints on the pale leather binding.

The fire cracked loudly as it settled in the grate.

'Shall I put some more wood on the fire?' said Ghalib.

Hasdai was deep in thought. 'Sorry?' he said. 'What did you say?'

'Wood... on the fire?' said Ghalib.

'I'm sorry! Yes do that. You know earlier when I was here on my own I realised something about these marks on this book.'

'Like I said, it's just ink,' said Ghalib as he took some logs from the basket by the grate and put them on the fire. Ali watched the Vizier intently.

'But these here are your thumb prints.'

'That's right and if you turn the book over you'll see a perfect set of marks from my fingers on the back,' said the general, who had no idea whatsoever why this conversation was happening or where it was leading. He gave a laugh. 'I really did make a mess.'

'Do you remember the girls we spoke to in the funduq... and one of them had bruises on her arms?'

'The one the admiral scratched with his nails?'

'Yes, that's the one. She had a perfect set of finger marks too, in the bruises on each of her arms. Just like yours on this book... a thumb on one side and four fingers on the other.'

'That's right she did. But you would expect that if a man with any strength grabbed her.'

'Exactly,' said Hasdai looking Ghalib in the eye. 'That's what was bothering me; and earlier this morning I think I worked it out.'

'What?' said the general.

'Shahid Jalal's body!'

'What about it?'

'He was strangled!'

'That's right,' said Ghalib.

'Think about it,' said Hasdai. 'If you were going to strangle me now with your bare hands how would you do it? Stand up and come at me.'

Ali looked at the general who grunted as he put his weight on his bad knee then approached the vizier with his hands outstretched as if to throttle him.

'That's it!' said Hasdai. 'Look! You would use both hands. And both thumbs would leave marks on the neck, one on either side. On Shahid Jalal's neck there was only one thumb mark on the left side. So the murderer only used one hand, his left hand, to strangle Shahid Jalal. I think we are looking for a murderer with no thumb on his right hand. And it will have to be someone with a good deal of strength to be able to hold on to his victim's neck with one hand and throttle the life out of him.'

'Well,' said Ghalib. 'What you say makes good sense.'

'And there's another thing,' said the vizier. 'There may be another link with gambling at Yousef's bathhouse.' Hasdai reached for the knucklebones on the desk. 'When I was there Yousef told me a story about a time before he took over the baths when people would gamble a thumb against a year's pay and he also said that these people would place large bets at the cockfight. So perhaps there is a link between the murders of your barber Bilal and Admiral Suhail.'

'Sir, are you suggesting we now look for a man with one thumb?' asked General Ghalib.

'That's not as strange as it sounds,' said Ali turning to face Ghalib. 'I saw a metalworker in the Al Bisharah teahouse last night with only one thumb. He certainly looked strong enough to do what the Vizier just described.'

General Ghalib sighed and smoothed his moustache. 'Would you like me to find this metalworker sir?' he said.

'Not yet,' said Hasdai. 'First I want to hear your report about Camp Maaqul, Ali.'

The vizier clicked his prayer beads as Ali spoke.

'Excellency, I am certain that the General's assumption is correct. If the Admiral was planning to move ambergris out of Cordoba to Almeria then Camp Maaqul is set up to allow this to happen. There are camel trains for heavy military equipment and mule trains for food and provisions. The ambergris would be sent on a mule train with the bitter orange jars being logged on the manifest.'

Hasdai and General Ghalib listened intently.

'Each mule train is made up of eighty animals, and only the two at the front and the two at the rear are branded. The others are unbranded and roped between them. Each train is prepared and taken to the loading bays at the north gate. That leads directly on to the Almeria road. All that happens is that the numbers and letters on the branding are recorded and their allocated cases are then loaded on to the animals. When I was there yesterday I was shown how the process worked. But I also saw something very interesting.'

'What was that?' said General Ghalib.

'Sir, the mule trains are made up of eighty animals. But I saw one which had four extra mules.'

'Perhaps they were surplus,' said Ghalib. 'Or they were to be used in the event that some of the other mules were lame or unfit to travel. It doesn't sound so unusual that the quartermaster would have additional animals available to him.'

'Yes sir, I appreciate that,' said Ali. 'But there is something very strange about this.'

'Which is?' said Hasdai.

'Well for one thing sir, if the animals were surplus to requirements then they would have been returned. Animal feed is in short supply and any extra animals are costing the quartermaster money.'

'So what?' said Ghalib.

Ali turned towards the General. 'Sir, the extra animals are not booked onto the manifest for tomorrow, and according to the schedule they are not surplus either. So I checked the stores with the whole manifest and there's something you need to know.'

Ghalib looked at the Vizier who waved at Ali to continue. He clicked his prayer beads as he listened.

Ali wiped his mouth with the back of his hand. 'There is a consignment of bitter orange jam in the stores that's not been allocated to any particular mule train.'

Ghalib looked at the vizier who put his prayer beads back on the desk.

'Go on,' said Hasdai

'Sir, it is not a secret that the Admiral was murdered. Nor, thanks to the city teahouses, is it a secret that we've found Jalal's body. Now *we* know that the Admiral and Jalal, who are both dead, were probably the principal two agents in the smuggling process. I saw Antonio's crucifixion between dogs by the gate to Camp Maaqul earlier so he's probably dead by this time too...'

'Let's hope so for his sake,' Ghalib muttered.

'Let Ali talk general,' said Hasdai.

'We seem to be assuming,' said Ali, 'that the Admiral, Shahid Jalal and the two agents are all of the people engaged in this smuggling operation... that no-one else is involved, at least here in Cordoba. But what if that's not the case? What if there are others? I know that we have the ambergris that they were planning to smuggle using the additional animals in the pack trains from the camp. What's strange however is that even with all these people dead...'

'Someone is still coordinating the smuggling operation!' said Hasdai.

Ali nodded. 'Exactly sir! And given that we have the ambergris, what are they expecting to smuggle?'

'Excellency,' said General Ghalib. 'Do you remember what Nasim told us about the ambergris?'

Hasdai nodded. 'Yes I do. He said that the ambergris at the stores was only one part of the consignment. I had assumed by that he meant the rest was already on the main fleet and that this was the last batch.' He reached once more for his prayer beads and sat for several moments as he tried to make sense of this assessment from Ali. 'General,' he said eventually.

'Yes sir?'

'I wonder if we've been looking at this from the wrong direction.'

'What do you mean sir?'

'I'm not one hundred per cent sure myself yet,' said the Vizier. 'I'll have to think this through. It's a good thing we still have time before the Caliph's feast tonight. Ali, do you know who this metalworker is?'

'No sir, but it won't take me long to find him. He made such a racket last night that somebody is bound to remember him. Simon from the Al Bisharah will probably know where he can be found.'

'Good,' said Hasdai. 'Now, General Ghalib, go and see this trader in the cells. Find out what you can from him about Bilal then come and meet Ali and me back here after prayers. But before you do that get another one of your men into the funduq, someone you can trust absolutely and who has never been there before so he won't be recognised by anyone watching the place. Get him dressed as a funduq worker and tell him to search the storage unit thoroughly.' He closed his eyes and, fingering his prayer beads, thought about what the young navigator had told him earlier. 'If Ali is right and there *are* other people still involved in this then they know more than we do. I want to know exactly what is in that storage unit.'

Hasdai looked for a moment into the fire before he spoke again. 'I want both of you back here as soon as you have done what you have to do. I sense that we have a lot more work to do tonight but I want to be absolutely sure before I say anything else.'

Chapter 58

'Ah,' said Miryam, 'so you managed to come home to eat after all.'

'Yes,' said Yunus as he hung his shawl on a peg and sat down on a low stool by the brick stove on which two clay pots bubbled. Escaping steam lifted the lid of one of them with a rhythmic click.

'I'm hungry. What have we got for our meal today?' He rubbed his hands in the heat of the stove then picked up a rough cloth, leaned forward and lifted the lid of a pot. Wafting the steam to his face he took a long sniff of the aroma of pepper, lavender and cinnamon scented meat juices which escaped from the pot. 'Mmmm! *Jimliyya...* I love this stew.'

'Well,' said Miryam, 'you'll just have to wait until it is done. Pass me the jar of *murri*.'

Yunus smiled to his daughter as he gave her the jar of tangy sauce. He remembered his wife's recipe item for item and had taught Miryam himself how to pound the dark-toasted breadcrumbs with the honey and quince and then to add the salted walnuts and dry roasted fennel, celery and onion seeds. She made it just like her mother.

'I am not putting any eggs in it,' said Miryam as she spooned the fragrant sauce into the stew.

'Why not?' said her father.

She stopped what she was doing and pointed at her father with the wooden spoon. 'Because you,' she said, 'forgot to buy them!'

'Ah!' said Yunus, 'I'm sorry. But can you blame me? There is so much going on at the moment.'

'Have you talked to Hasdai recently?'

'No. I haven't had a chance to speak to him. He is very busy trying to get everything finished before the Caliph gets back to Cordoba.'

'What about General Ghalib?'

'He spends most of his time with Hasdai. They have a lot on their minds at the moment with this spate of murders. You know Ghalib's leg seems to be getting worse. I am sure he is in constant pain.'

'The way the Crown Prince keeps them running around it's not surprising that it is getting worse. I think the general is getting too old to be doing what he does.'

'I wouldn't like to be the one to tell him that,' said Yunus. 'Prince Hakam will be the only one to tell him when it is time to retire from service.'

'He doesn't show much compassion, does he?'

'Who, the prince? No indeed he doesn't. I suppose you know that the crucifixion went ahead?'

Miryam shuddered. 'Horrible... horrible,' she said. 'I had heard. All that does is reinforce Hakam's reputation.'

'Well, he did break the law and I suppose as crown prince he has to keep order somehow.'

'It's his reputation that I am worried about.'

'Prince Hakam's?'

'Yes.'

'What do you mean?'

'He has got my pupil Lubna to start working in his secretariat.'

'That's no bad thing for you though is it?' said Yunus.

'I am not worried about myself,' said Miryam. 'It's her I am worried about.'

'She is more than capable of working there.'

'I know that but I hope he leaves her alone.'

Yunus gave her a half smile. 'I shouldn't worry, if she were a good looking eighteen year old man though she'd be in real danger.'

'I suppose so,' said Miryam. 'It's just that I find it hard to come to terms with the streak of cruelty that's in Prince Hakam.'

'You'd better not let anyone hear you talk like that,' said Yunus. 'You may be right but even Hasdai wouldn't be able to help you if your thoughts on that got out. When are you seeing Hasdai again anyway?'

'The last time I spoke to him he said he might be able to come here after the navigators leave for Almeria.'

'I do hope he manages to come. It is wonderful to see the two of you together.'

'Hmm,' said Miryam. 'I wonder where it will all end.'

Chapter 59

'May God destroy your house! You son of a whore!' Ghalib screamed again and again at the top of his voice.

The young soldier, clearly terrified, looked down at the General of the Guard writhing in agony on the cobbled floor of the guardroom. Ghalib's sword and dagger clashed on the stones adding to the din and as he lashed out with his foot he struck the leg of a table, sending cups and water jars crashing to the floor.

The door burst open and the Captain of the Guard rushed in with his hand on the hilt of his sword. 'What in hell's name is going on here?' he shouted before he recognised his commanding officer who was now curled up into a ball among the mess of pottery shards clutching his right knee and whimpering like a whipped dog.

'Sir... sir! It's the General sir.'

'*Y'Allah!*' said the captain 'I can see that! What in the name of God did you do?'

'Nothing sir. He was standing behind the door when I came in. I opened the door quickly and I think it must have struck his leg.'

'Get out of here... now! Go to the medical room and ask the physician for a flask of willow bark and poppy juice tincture and get a bottle of arak and some very cold water and some clean cloths.'

The captain knelt by Ghalib and gently took hold of his shoulders. 'General Ghalib sir,' he said quietly, 'it's me Captain Hussein. I know what's troubling you sir and I've sent for something for the pain. It won't be long now.'

*

'I think you can stop apologising now young man,' said Ghalib his eyes dark-ringed and heavy with the combination of the drugs and the arak. 'If I thought for a single moment that you had done it deliberately you would be dead by now. Come, share a drink with me.'

The general managed a half smile which did nothing to cheer up the wretched young soldier sitting opposite him but the boy took the cup of arak with a quivering hand and drank it down.

'Captain Hussein here was with me on the Northern Frontier when the sword shattered in my knee. Although you weren't a captain then were you Hussein?'

Ghalib peeled the wet cloths from his knee and put them on the bench beside him.

'No sir I wasn't,' said the captain. 'I wasn't much older than Suleiman here. That was a hard fought campaign.'

The three men sat in silence for a moment before Hussein spoke again. 'Now sir can I ask you why it is that you are here today. You don't often visit the cells.'

'No, thank God. I have come to talk to the man you have in here for the murder at the cockfight.'

'The trader?'

'That's right.'

The captain turned to Suleiman. 'You know which one it is, do you?'

'Yes sir.'

'Go and fetch him,' said Ghalib, 'then leave us here with him.'

*

When the trader had been taken back to his cell Ghalib turned to Captain Hussein. 'What do you think?' he said.

'I don't think he did it sir. You just need to take one look at him to see he hasn't got it in him to do what was done to Bilal.'

'I think you are right,' said the general. 'The quarrel he had with Bilal was something or nothing. It was enough to get angry about but not enough to kill a man over. I think he just got agitated when he saw Bilal out to have a good time with what he thought was his money. If the sailor hadn't separated them they would have traded a few slaps and that would have been it.'

'Do you believe him, sir, when he said that he saw someone else going into the bushes with Bilal?'

'Yes, I think I do believe him. And I also believe what he said about being too scared of the guards when he was arrested to mention it to them at the time. He is clearly a very timid person who was pushed into a confrontation when he saw Bilal going to the cockfight. I am almost certain he didn't kill Bilal. He has never been in any trouble before.'

'In that case, sir,' said Hussein, 'what do you want us to do with him now?'

'I think you had better keep him here for the time being. At least that way we'll know where he is. I have to go back to the Alcazar now to discuss this with the vizier.'

'How is your knee now sir? Will you be all right to walk back there? I could get a staff cut for you from a spear-shaft if it would help you.'

Hussein knew immediately from the glower he got from General Ghalib that he had said the wrong thing.

'Ha!' said Ghalib, 'it's not enough that the vizier wants to cut my knee open and dig about in it for the pieces of metal eh? Now you want me to walk about the streets with a stick like a cripple.'

'I'm sor…'

'Do *not* apologise. I've had enough apologies in here today from young Suleiman. Just pass me that poppy juice. I'll have another cup of that then I can get back to the Alcazar. *Without* a stick.'

Chapter 60

Simon, the proprietor of the Al Bisharah knew about people. He had seen and heard all kinds in his teahouse; Christians like himself and Jews and Muslims, soldiers and traders, local people and travellers from far-off lands.

People talked in a teahouse especially in the evenings when the arak flowed. Then they would tell all kinds of things better kept secret... whose marriage was failing, who had made a huge loss in business, how the defence of the northern frontier was being bungled, what the crown prince was up to with his male harem and his female one, how the Vizier was spending more and more time with the daughter of the Astronomer Royal.

Simon knew better than have an opinion on any of these matters and simply listened and nodded and brought more barad, tea or arak. Now, however, he was being questioned by this Ali character. He couldn't work Ali out, this smallish, compact man who also listened a lot but had a very quick eye. He had told Simon that he had been sent by the Vizier. Simon knew one sure thing about Ali though. He knew he was not someone to have as an enemy.

'There is a man who comes in here who has no thumb on his right hand,' said Ali. 'Do you know who he is and where I can find him?'

'I think I know who you mean,' said Simon. 'His name is Yazid. He's a blacksmith.'

'How can he be a blacksmith with no thumb on his right hand?' asked Ali.

'They say he has an apprentice who does the heavy work and anyway he only produces small, fine items like razors and lancets.'

'Do you know where his workshop is?'

'I do. It's in the metalworkers' suq just off the road that runs between the Bab al-Amir and the Bab al-Jabbar.'

Ali stood up and took a few coppers from his pocket and put them on the table. He drank down the remainder of his mint tea.

'*Shukran*,' he said. 'Thank you. *Ma as-salaamah*,' as he walked out of the teahouse.

Simon shook his head gently as he gathered up the money, the cup and a plate from the table.

*

It didn't take Ali long to locate Yazid's workshop. He knew he had to be right when he saw a giant razor hanging over the narrow street from a bracket above the sack-cloth curtain which served as a door to the shop.

As he stood before the curtain he put his hand in the pocket of his robe. Inside the pocket was a slit through which he could feel the pouch on a belt next to his body. He felt in the pouch for the short, heavy bar of iron with four finger-holes, slipped his fingers into the holes and gripped the bar. This close-quarter weapon, which added a fearful power to a punch, had saved Ali's life more than once in the past.

Ali pulled back the curtain and put his head carefully into the shade in order that his eyes could become accustomed to the gloom inside the shop before he stepped over the threshold. He looked around and saw the usual clutter of a small shop selling metal goods. He smelt the acrid tang of worked iron.

It was then that he heard the sobbing coming from the yard at the back of the shop. Holding his knuckle duster at the ready Ali tiptoed towards the entrance to the yard. There, next to the anvil, he saw Yazid's apprentice sitting on the ground next to his master's body. The boy was clutching his knees to his head and rocking backwards and forwards sobbing his heart out.

Yazid's corpse was stretched out by the anvil, his eyes wide open and his head smashed like a calabash. The head of the hammer was still embedded in his skull and the shaft pointed at the wailing apprentice whose feet were in the puddle of dark red blood which had spread from Yazid's horrific wounds.

Ali approached the boy and touched his shoulder. He put his hands in the pool of blood as he scrambled to his feet then stood in front of Ali with his fingers dripping gore. His eyes looked like they would start out of his head.

'Did you do this?' said Ali. He put his knuckle duster back in its pouch and pointed at the body.

The boy crumpled to his knees again.

'No, my guess is you didn't,' said Ali.

'Sir! Sir! He's dead! Dead!' said the apprentice then he took in a long

222

shuddering, quaking breath of air.

'I don't think there is much doubt about that,' said Ali.

'I heard it happening, sir!' the boy said. He stood up again. 'It was the hammer sir!'

'I think you are probably right there too,' said Ali. It was all he could do not to laugh. 'If it wasn't you then, who was it?'

'It was a Berber, sir. A man dressed like a Berber.'

'Was he wearing a black burnus?'

'Yes sir, he was.'

'You'd better come with me.'

The boy looked at Ali and drew back in fear.

'Who are you? Why do you want me?'

'I am working for the Vizier. He'll want to talk to you.'

'How do I know what you say is true?'

Ali reached into his pocket and when he withdrew his hand he brandished the knuckle duster in the boy's face.

'Trust me,' he said in a low, clear voice. 'The choice is yours. You can either walk with me to the Alcazar like a good boy or I can drag you there by the hair after I have hit you with this. Now which is it going to be?'

The apprentice fell to his knees again snuffling and nodding his head.

'That's good,' said Ali. 'Now, pull yourself together, give yourself a wash in the tub there and we can get to the Alcazar. The Vizier won't want to see you covered in blood.'

*

'There's not much point in sending a guard to watch Yazid al-Haddad's movements now your Excellency,' said Ali as he settled himself on a stool in the Vizier's office in the Alcazar.

'Why not?' said Hasdai.

'Because he is not going to move. He is lying next to his anvil with his head smashed to a pulp.'

'Ah!' said Hasdai. 'And do we know who is responsible for this?'

'I think we do Excellency. I have left Yazid's apprentice in the guard room downstairs. He saw the murderer briefly then heard his master's brains being bashed out.'

Chapter 61

'I can't wait to get out of this place. I've had enough of it. I'll be glad to get on the road back to Almeria tomorrow.'

As he spoke the young navigator from Qadiz was stuffing clothing into a sailcloth bag as hard as he could. His colleague from Abdera who was sitting on the bed nodded in agreement.

'Yes,' he said, 'I'm the same. I've done my packing already. I want to get back too. There's been a strange atmosphere about this place since we lost Admiral Suhail. I'll be glad to get back to a navy town. There's too much evidence of the army here for my liking.'

'What do you think of that General Ghalib?'

'He's a tough old bugger and no mistake,' said the man from Qadiz. 'But I don't trust anyone who is that close to the Vizier.'

'That Vizier is a strange one too, isn't he? How could a Jewish doctor work his way up to his position? He must be well in with the Caliph.'

'What I find strangest about him is the way he carries on with the Astronomer Royal's daughter. Everybody knows about it.'

'Oh her! The high and mighty Lady Miryam! She's something else though, isn't she?'

The man from Abdera gave a laugh. 'Well, I'll say this for the Jewish doctor he has good taste. She's got a great arse!'

His colleague laughed in agreement then said, 'You have to admit as well though, that she really knows her stuff when it comes to astronomy and mathematics. She taught us very well.'

'That's something else about Cordoba against Almeria. It is so different here. Women are doing all sorts of things that they don't do in the provinces. You'd never see a woman teaching men in a place like Qadiz. I'm not sure it's a good thing. In fact I'll be glad when we get to sea; back to a man's world.'

'I wonder if she'll be there tonight.'

'At the feast? She's bound to be there. I must say I am not looking forward to it at all.'

'Nor am I. I could perfectly well leave Cordoba without meeting the Caliph or the Crown Prince.'

'It is going to be some event though. Imagine them giving us all new clothes. These shawls and the cloaks they gave us must have cost a fortune. And the sandals are amazing. I've never seen leather like it,' said the man from Abdera.

'Some people here in the capital wear stuff like that every day. It must be great to be rich. Anyway, come on let's get changed now. Bandar wants us to meet in his room before we go. I think he has a flask of arak. He said he wanted us all to have a drink together before we go to the Caliph's chambers.'

'I hope he doesn't speak to me,' said the man from Abdera.

'Who? The Caliph? Why? He's just a man like us. And,' said the man from Qadiz, 'he needs people like us. Without us his campaign in the east will fail. He needs navigators to get his fleet across there otherwise he is never going to get the better of Baghdad.'

'I suppose you're right. Come on let's get washed and into our fine new clothes,' he said with a laugh. 'I'll see you in Bandar's room.'

The man from Qadiz laughed too. '*Admiral* Bandar, please! It's *Admiral* Bandar now! Don't forget!'

*

Bandar had poured cups of arak for himself and his three colleagues.

'I wanted to speak to you all together before we go in to the feast. There are a couple of things which the Vizier told me that you all need to know. The first thing is that we are all going to be presented to the Caliph. Vizier Hasdai has asked that you don't start any conversation with the Caliph. If he wants to talk he will ask you specific questions. However most of the talking will be done by the Crown Prince. You need to remember that he is completely aware of all of the military and naval preparations that are going on. Don't talk to the prince about anything tactical or say anything about the new astrolabes or almanacs and do not *under any circumstances* talk to him about Miryam bint Yunus, the Astronomer Royal's daughter.'

Bandar turned on the navigator from Abdera who had snorted with laughter when he said this.

'What's the matter with you? Did I say something funny? No! So you'd better behave yourself in there. Remember that Prince Hakam had someone crucified earlier today. He can do the same for you if you step out of line.'

'I'm sorry sir,' said the young man, 'it's just…'

'It's just nothing!' snapped the Vice Admiral Siraj bin Bahram. 'So just shut up and let Admiral Bandar speak!'

'Yes sir, sorry sir,' said the chastened young man as he looked into his cup of arak.

'There will be at least one other woman present at the feast,' said Bandar. 'Her name is Lubna and she works in the Crown Prince's secretariat as a scribe. She will be making a record of the proceedings and none of you are to engage with her in any way. Is that clear?'

The three men murmured their understanding of the situation.

'Good,' said Bandar. 'Now before we go in I just wanted to say thank you to you all. We have been through a lot in the last days what with losing Admiral Suhail and learning about the new instruments and the almanac but you have all done well.' He looked hard at the young man from Abdera. 'This is a serious business that we are about.' Here he paused to pick up his copy of the almanac which he waved above his shoulder. 'But with the information we have here we can become the best navigators in the Dar al Islam and do our duty by the Caliph.'

As Bandar thumped the book back down on the table a piece of paper fluttered from it and landed at the feet of the vice admiral Siraj who picked it up.

With the speed of a striking snake Bandar's hand lashed out and grabbed the paper but in the instant before he did so Siraj managed to see that the tiny handwriting on the paper was headed by a curious symbol.

One that he had seen before when he had journeyed to the Berber lands of Ifriquiya.

Chapter 62

'All of them?' said General Ghalib.

'Yes sir,' said the officer. 'All except the jars on the top. It's only the top layer of jars that have ambergris in smaller jars inside. The others only contain bitter orange jam.'

The General nodded. 'Thank you,' he said and closed the door.

'Let me ask you this General,' said Hasdai as he looked out of the window. 'Before he died did you ever meet Shahid Jalal?'

The General shook his head. 'Never Sir.'

Hasdai turned round to face Ghalib and Ali. 'So when you saw the body how did you know it was him? In fact how did Zaffar and his men know it was him?'

'We had his description from Omar Jaziri, and, come to think of it, from Hamid al-Mursi the market inspector too.'

'Good,' said Hasdai. 'How did *they* come to know who Jalal was?'

'He was staying at the funduq, and he also visited al-Mursi's bathhouse. He placed several bets which we have in the journal.' Ghalib pointed to the ink-stained journal on the Vizier's desk.

Hasdai nodded. 'That's right General,' he said then turned to Ali. 'Don't you find that strange?'

'Yes sir, I do,' said Ali nodding.

'In what way is it strange?' said Ghalib.

'From what we've discovered, this entire smuggling operation has taken nearly two years to put together,' said Ali. 'It has involved a network of agents, an intricate way of disguising the ambergris and a complex method of transporting it to the main fleet.'

Ghalib nodded.

'And yet on the very night the ambergris is due to be moved,' said Hasdai. 'Shahid Jalal, the mastermind behind the entire operation, is betting on chess and knucklebones in a bathhouse. Not only that he is introducing himself to strangers and allowing his name to be written down.'

'But sir, Nasim told us that it was part of the plan. He went on to confirm that the deal was set. That's why Jalal was at the bathhouse.'

Hasdai shook his head. 'I suspect General, that this is what we are supposed to think.'

'I don't understand sir,' said Ghalib.

'What is it that Omar Jaziri and al-Mursi have in common when it comes to Shahid Jalal?' said Hasdai.

Ghalib looked at the floor and thought for a moment, before shaking his head.

'Well for one thing General,' said Hasdai as he picked up his prayer beads from his desk, 'neither of them had met Jalal until he arrived in Cordoba.'

Ghalib nodded as the Vizier looked at Ali once more.

'Which could mean General,' said Ali, 'that neither of them had any reason to suspect that he wasn't Shahid Jalal.'

Ghalib's eyes widened.

'Exactly,' said Hasdai. 'I am beginning to believe that whoever it was that Zaffar's men found lying in the shrubbery, we are *supposed* to think that it was Shahid Jalal. That would mean that our conclusion would be that the Admiral was killed when the deal went wrong. Perhaps even that he and Jalal fought. But at the very least I think we are supposed to conclude is that Shahid Jalal is dead.'

'And you think that the real Shahid Jalal is still alive?'

'Well it seems interesting that the people, on whom we are relying for a description of Jalal, had never actually met him prior to him arriving in Cordoba.'

The three men sat in silence for several moments.

'Also, we assumed,' said Hasdai, 'that the jars in the storage unit at the funduq all contained ambergris. We now know that only the top row did so. The rest was just bitter orange jam. Nasim told us that when they moved the ambergris only the top row contained the jam and the rest had a smaller jar of ambergris hidden inside. That way if anyone paid any attention a quick check by a guard would not reveal anything suspicious. I can't be certain what happened, but I think that Admiral Suhail walked into a trap.'

Ghalib frowned and bent down to rub his knee.

'Earlier today,' said Hasdai, 'one of the other navigators came to see me. He said something which makes me suspect we've got this all wrong.'

Ghalib and Ali looked at each other.

'I appreciate that the Caliph is on his way back to Cordoba and that we have a feast here at the Alcazar tonight; but I think we have more work to do before then.'

Hasdai picked up the draft of the Caliph's address and handed it to Ali. 'Read the section about the navigators,' he said.

Ali took the document and scanned the page quickly. His eyes widened then he looked up at the Vizier who nodded slowly.

'What is it?' said Ghalib.

'It says here,' said Ali, 'that Admiral Bandar's first mission was to Saida, and that he has been back there many times during his career.'

'Now several days ago,' said Hasdai, 'Bandar told me his first posting had been to Malta, and that he was slightly envious of the advance flotilla and the fact they would soon make land there.'

'Why is Saida relevant?' said General Ghalib.

Hasdai looked at Ali.

'It is the perfect place to land goods destined for Damascus,' said Ali. 'Assuming that whatever you wanted to land had come from Al Andalus.'

General Ghalib looked at the Vizier.

'Damascus is the largest market for ambergris outside of Al Andalus,' said Hasdai as he held out his hand. 'Thank you Ali. This document has been on my desk for over two days,' he said. 'I should have got to it sooner.'

'Sir you've had a lot to deal with,' said Ghalib. 'I don't think...'

'I didn't even think to search the rest of the jars at the funduq,' said Hasdai. 'I just didn't have the time to think properly.'

Ghalib shot a look at Ali. 'Sir,' he said. 'Are you sure that both Admiral Suhail and Bandar were involved in this?'

Hasdai sighed deeply.

'Involved, but in different ways. Do you remember the scratches on the girl's arm at the funduq?'

'Yes sir, she said the Admiral made them trying to free her.'

'Correct. It didn't occur to me until earlier that I have seen the same scratches before, but on someone else.'

'Who?' said Ghalib.

'Bandar,' said Hasdai. 'On the morning after the Night Journey he and

Vice-Admiral Siraj were here at the Alcazar. We went to brief the Crown Prince. Before we did so I gave Bandar some treatment for several scratches on his arm. He told me he had been scratched by a cat. I didn't think anything of it at first, but now I am quite sure those scratches came from Admiral Suhail. The markings were the same size as the ones on the girl's arm. That was no cat.'

'Do you think Bandar murdered Suhail?' said Ghalib.

Hasdai shook his head. 'No. Not directly anyway. When the Admiral and the Lieutenant were killed the navigators were all confined to their rooms. The order came directly from Admiral Suhail. One of the navigators came to see me earlier. He said he had overheard Suhail arguing with someone at the University. He thought it was Bandar. Then he said that shortly after he got back to his room here at the Alcazar a guard arrived and said he couldn't leave until first light. That was the day before the murder. I think the scratches could have come from that argument.'

'What were they arguing about?' said Ali.

'Ambergris,' said Hasdai. 'The young man told me he thought that Suhail spoke about having spent a long time working on something.'

'You mean the plot to smuggle the ambergris?' said Ghalib.

Hasdai nodded. 'Except I think that Admiral Suhail was trying to *stop* the smuggling plot. I think he found out about it and spent a long time building enough evidence to confront Bandar. I think that what he discovered got him, and Lieutenant Haytham, killed.'

Ghalib frowned. 'I don't understand,' he said eventually.

Hasdai handed him a sheet of paper. 'This is the report from Zaffar's men at the funduq. Do you recall we asked them to check whether any of the other names from the list we found in the Admiral's room appeared in the funduq records? We only know Jalal, or whoever he really was, was on the list of current guests.'

Ghalib scanned the words on the page.

'The names I have marked appear on both lists. Now, they might be the same person, or for that matter *people*, but they stayed at the funduq at various times over the last years.'

Ghalib looked at the vizier who handed him yet another sheet of paper.

'This was in the briefing notes for the draft of the Caliph's address,' said Hasdai. 'If you look at the dates when those names were guests at the funduq and the dates when Bandar was here in Cordoba to attend to naval matters you'll see they overlap.'

'So when the navigator overheard Suhail arguing,' said Ali, 'you think he was telling Bandar that he knew about his smuggling plans?'

Hasdai nodded. 'Yes.' He sighed and said, 'I should have read this briefing sooner.'

'But what about the anthrax plot sir?' said Ghalib. 'Surely Suhail would have eventually found out about that?'

'Eventually, yes general,' said Hasdai. 'Had he still been alive he would have been party to the same briefing that Ali gave us several days ago when he first arrived back in Cordoba, and later, when we received word from Malta, Suhail would also have known about the advance flotilla. He may even have come to the same decision about ordering a search of the main fleet in Almeria.'

'But then the anthrax would have been discovered,' said Ghalib.

'Correct General,' said Hasdai. 'Except that Bandar would not have known that Ali was here with us in Cordoba. He would also not have known that Ali had brought us news of how Baghdad has worked out how to harness anthrax, from its natural form, into a deadly weapon. As such he would have been relying on the fact that Suhail would assume it was an ordinary, but tragic, outbreak of anthrax, and do nothing. If that is true, and we are right about the plot to destroy one of the boats then somewhere on one of the boats in the main fleet is a supply of anthrax sufficient to kill everything on board.' Hasdai picked up his beads and clicked them together for a moment.

'However,' he said, 'let's assume for a moment that he *had* planned for Admiral Suhail and the Crown Prince ordering a search of the main fleet. How would he hope to disguise the anthrax then?'

'What if the anthrax isn't on the fleet yet?' said Ali. 'What if it is on its way to Almeria by the trains being sent from Camp Maaqul? It could be in that consignment of bitter orange jam I found there. That is due to leave tomorrow morning.'

Hasdai nodded. 'That could work. Had Suhail not found out about the plot and the main fleet had set sail, then, if we are right, Bandar would have been the one commanding the boat destined for Saida. Once there he would simply disappear.'

'But wouldn't the Admiral and the others have known?' said Ghalib.

'They'd have found the dead bodies on the boat.'

Hasdai shook his head. 'After the boat from the advance flotilla was discovered, and it was confirmed that an outbreak of anthrax had occurred, they burnt the boat and let it sink. The same would happen with the boat from the main fleet, assuming they ever found it. Bandar could easily find a way to slip off the boat at Saida, unload the ambergris, and just not get back on again. The anthrax would take care of the rest and everyone would assume that his body was amongst those that were burnt. He'd have been a hero.'

Ghalib wiped his moustache and sat in silence trying to make sense of what he was being told. 'Could he have done the same thing having been made Admiral of the Fleet?' he said.

'As Admiral,' said Ali, 'he could have done whatever he wanted. In fact, being Admiral makes his job a lot easier. He can give orders without anyone questioning him. Having said that, nobody would question him anyway. From what you said a day or so ago Vizier, Bandar is the most skilled of the navigators with the astrolabe. If he were the only navigator on his boat trained in how to use it then nobody would know where they were once they were in open water and out of the sight of land. He could have landed at Saida and he'd be the only one who knew where he was.'

Ghalib frowned. 'But if the anthrax is not yet on board the boat, then surely the ambergris is there?'

'Yes general,' said Hasdai. 'But the thing is that Bandar knew all along that Suhail would know about the anthrax, or the ambergris but not both. Not without being dead that is.'

The General stared blankly at the Vizier.

'It took me a while to work a few things out,' said Hasdai. 'Firstly, this business of the Admiral confining the navigators to their rooms. It didn't make sense.'

'What do you mean?' said Ali.

'Well, I assumed that the Admiral did it so that he could investigate the ambergris plot without being disturbed by Bandar. That would also mean that Bandar couldn't get word to Shahid Jalal to warn him that the Admiral has discovered their plan.'

'Maybe he didn't need to,' said Ali. 'Maybe Jalal had set up the ambergris deal at the funduq to keep the Admiral away from what was really going on.'

Hasdai nodded. 'Precisely. According to Nasim he was told that a man would visit his shop several times before buying some perfume for his wife. Once that happened he was to invite the man to the Yemeni's bathhouse to play knucklebones. My guess is that this barber, the one who got murdered at the cockfight, was there at the bathhouse.

'I'm also guessing that this Yazid character was there too and that he is the one who is being told to get rid of anyone that has been involved in the plot. Yazid didn't need to go after Antonio or Nasim as the General had them arrested immediately. Now, once at the Yemeni bathhouse the Admiral knew he would be introduced to Antonio who would in turn take him meet Shahid Jalal... or someone pretending to be Jalal.

'But Nasim never said *who* he was expecting to come to his shop. He said he didn't even know who it was. Now we know that the Admiral gave the order for the navigators to be confined to their rooms outside of their astrolabe lessons the day *before* he died. That means that until then Bandar would have been free to walk about the city and he would therefore have known, or been told, that the Admiral was visiting Nasim at his shop.

'At first I wondered why Bandar didn't try to stop that from happening. That's when it struck me that he didn't need to. The Admiral confined the navigators to their rooms so he could meet Jalal at the funduq without Bandar following him. But I don't think Bandar ever intended to follow him. If this was a trap, and certainly a very clever one, then Bandar would have known the Admiral was going to be killed.'

'Which is why no-one would then be searching the main fleet for ambergris,' said Ghalib nodding.

'Correct general,' said Hasdai.

'This means we've been looking in the wrong place the whole time,' said Ali.

Hasdai nodded slowly. 'Somehow he must have suspected that the Admiral was suspicious of him. It would have been easy for him to let the Admiral find out about the perfume shop, and about Shahid Jalal at the funduq. He must have had this plan all along. Once he knew that the Admiral had visited Nasim all he had to do was wait for the murder. He's even got the perfect alibi. He had a guard outside his room the whole time.'

Hasdai paused for a moment. 'General,' he said. 'I want to talk to Nasim again.'

Ali shot a look at Ghalib. 'I thought he was dead sir. I heard he tried to escape and was killed by his guards.'

'You shouldn't believe everything you hear in the suq,' said Hasdai.

'What do you mean?' said Ali looking puzzled.

'I told the Crown Prince that story this morning and I made sure that enough of the suq traders got to hear about it. But he is very much alive. He's still in the prison downstairs.'

Ghalib looked at Hasdai and smiled slowly. 'Would you like me to fetch him sir?'

'Bring him here at once,' said Hasdai. 'I need to be absolutely sure that Nasim didn't know the identity of the man who was going to come to his shop. And when you have done that I want you to go and see Lieutenant Haytham's mother. If Suhail was not involved in this, and he was trying to expose Bandar, then he must have known what danger he was putting himself in. The only person, other than his nephew, Haytham, that he would have trusted with what he was doing would have been Haytham's mother. Go and see her, and find out if he told her anything. We shall meet at the feast later tonight.'

Ghalib stood up, nodded and walked over to the door.

When the door was closed Hasdai clicked his prayers beads together quickly. 'It will do us no harm if the suq is full of stories about how Nasim has been killed. In fact it might even help us. Now, tell me more about the metalworker's apprentice,' he said to Ali.

'There's not that much to tell,' said Ali. 'He's not making a lot of sense. He is still hysterical.'

'What did he see?' said Hasdai.

'He said he caught a glimpse of a man in a black woollen burnus. He heard him and Yazid talking about something they had been planning for years and how everyone would think the Admiral was to blame. Yazid said he wanted to stop, he wanted out and he wanted money. Then he heard him kill Yazid with a hammer. Apparently the man in the burnus and Yazid were cousins.'

'Do we know anything about this man?'

'I think I saw him at the camp yesterday; or at least I saw someone wearing a black burnus. I've also seen him in the Al Bisharah teahouse.

234

He was there last night when Yazid was extremely drunk.'

'Who was he with?' asked Hasdai

'He wasn't with anyone,' said Ali. 'He was on his own. But I did see him give a message to a beggar child. It was wrapped around a coin.'

'Who was the message for?'

'I don't know. It might have been for Yazid. His apprentice told me that from time to time a child would arrive at the forge with a message for Yazid. He said that his master would take the message, read it and then give the coin it was wrapped around to the child.'

'If he was in the same teahouse as Yazid last night why didn't he give him the message himself?'

'I don't know sir,' said Ali. 'Perhaps the note was for someone else.'

Hasdai nodded. 'Do you know what the messages said?'

'Not entirely sir,' said Ali. 'The apprentice said they were drawings. At least the ones he saw were. He said he thought they were Berber symbols or something like that.'

'Who do you think the man in the burnus is?' asked Hasdai.

Ali swallowed. 'If you are right about all of this, he could well be the real Shahid Jalal.'

'I want you to find this man with the burnus,' said Hasdai, clicking his beads together. 'He won't leave Cordoba without being sure the deal with Bandar is safe. If your assumption is correct then the bitter orange jam at the camp could well contain the anthrax. Find out what you can about him, but do not approach him directly.'

Ali nodded. 'What are you going to do about Bandar?'

Hasdai thought for a moment. 'For now, I am not going to do anything. I don't want to make him suspicious. But, if this man in the burnus really is the mastermind behind this whole thing, then he was using his cousin Yazid to silence anyone who got in his way.'

'By that you mean he might have killed the Admiral?' said Ali.

Hasdai nodded. 'The problem is I can't actually prove any of this, not without finding who the man in the burnus is. I've already presented the Crown Prince with my theory and on the back of that he ordered Antonio's crucifixion.'

Hasdai fingered his prayer beads and glanced at the lengthening shadows at the window as the muezzin started to call the faithful to prayer.

Chapter 63

General Ghalib hated this kind of thing but he knew that it had to be done so the sooner he got it over with the better.

Despite the promise of spring in the clear afternoon sunshine his mood was low as he walked up the street to the Bab al-Yahud past the modest dwellings which were crowded into this part of the city. These were the houses of the ordinary folk of Cordoba. Small, proudly-kept homes clustered round courtyards hidden from the street by high walls and heavy iron studded doors. As he walked he could hear the everyday sounds of family life from behind the walls, here the pounding of grain, there the screech of a windlass on a well, the song of a caged bird, an irate mother berating a child.

Following the directions of the Chamberlain's man towards the aqueduct, he eventually stood before the door to the family home of Lieutenant Haytham. The general was tugging down his leather jerkin as the door opened in answer to his knock.

Ghalib bowed slightly and said very gently, '*A salaam u aleikum*. Are you the mother of Lieutenant Haytham of the Royal Guard?'

'*Wa aleikum a salaam*,' she said in a low, strained voice. 'Yes sir... I am. I am Hadija bint Qays, Haytham's mother. You must be General Ghalib.'

As she lifted her grief ravaged face Ghalib saw that she had the same piercing green eyes as her son.

'Your messenger said you were coming. *Marhaba*, welcome to my home. Please come in.'

The general took off his fur cap and held it under his arm as he went past the slight figure. She was dressed entirely in black with a head scarf covering her hair.

Looking at the floor as she spoke she said, 'Come sir. Come to my sitting room where we can drink tea.'

'Please good lady,' said General Ghalib, 'Please do not put yourself to any trouble on my behalf.'

She looked straight at him. 'You are a guest in my house,' she said, 'I shall bring tea.'

'Thank you,' said Ghalib and he was shown into the cosy sitting room where he sat down beside a small black-wood table.

As they drank the mint tea Ghalib spoke. 'Are you alone Hadija?'

'No,' she said. '*Alhamdulillah*, I have a daughter with two children of her own.'

'Ah,' said Ghalib, 'daughters are indeed a blessing. *Insha'Allah* the children will be a great comfort to you.'

There was a pause before Hadija looked up at the general and spoke again.

'General Ghalib,' she said, 'I do not think you came here to speak of my daughter or my grandchildren. I have lost my only son and my step-brother. Should we not talk of them?'

The general slowly stretched his right leg and gave a deep sigh. 'Yes,' he said. 'We must talk of them. Haytham was a brave and loyal soldier. Both he and Admiral Suhail are a great loss to the Caliphate. The Vizier himself has told me to give you his condolences.'

'Please thank the Vizier for me but do you know why they were killed, general?'

'We have nothing more than suspicions at present Hadija. It would be wrong of me to tell you that we knew precisely why they were killed or who was behind it.'

'I have heard that someone was crucified on the Almeria road,' said Hadija. 'Was that anything to do with their killing?'

'No,' said Ghalib, perhaps rather too quickly.

'I see. And will you ask me if I know anything about who might have done it?'

Ghalib rubbed his aching knee and nodded.

'I have no idea,' said Hadija. 'All the menfolk in my family have been in the service of the Caliph but until now none have been murdered by their own people. My husband fell at the Battle of Simancas but at least he was fighting for His Majesty and the protection of Cordoba.'

General Ghalib started up, wide-eyed, at the mention of Simancas. It was at this battle to establish the Northern Frontier of the Caliphate eleven years before in 939 that he had been wounded. The battle was an awful event which had started with a total eclipse of the sun which struck terror into the hearts of both armies.

'I too served at Simancas,' he said. 'It was a dreadful, hard-fought business. If you lost your husband there you have every right to be proud of him. And you must also be proud of Haytham and your kinsman Admiral Suhail. They too have given good service to His Majesty. I must ask you though, is there anything you can tell me that might throw some light on who did these terrible deeds?'

'As I have said, I know nothing about their murder or who might have done it. I do know though that Suhail must have had some idea that he was in danger.'

'How so?' asked Ghalib.

'When he was here shortly before he was killed he gave me something and he said that if anything happened to him I must make sure that it was given to you. And that it should be given to you personally. The admiral said that you were a man to be trusted. That is why I went to the Chamberlain's office with my petition to see you.'

'What is it? Is it a letter or a message?'

'No,' said Hadija. 'Let me get it.'

She got up and went to a cloth covered wooden chest in the corner of her small sitting room. She carefully folded the cloth then took from the chest an earthenware jar which was sealed with beeswax.

'Here you are,' she said and handed it to Ghalib. 'I have no idea of the significance of this jar. From its looks and weight it seems to me to be an ordinary jar of jam but Admiral Suhail insisted to me that it was very important and that if anything happened to him I had to make sure you got the jar.'

General Ghalib managed not to show his surprise at this 'message' from the admiral but took the jar in both hands and thanked Hadija.

'I cannot explain the matter to you,' he said, 'but I can assure you that this *is* very important and may well result in us finding out who killed your son and the Admiral. Now good lady I must leave you and return to the Alcazar. But before I go is there anything I can do to help you.'

Hadija looked at the floor, sighed then shook her head gently as she plucked an imaginary thread from her skirt. 'No General. Thank you. There is nothing you can do for me. My daughter is coming to fetch me before the sunset prayer. I shall stay with her and her family and grieve over the loss of her brother and her uncle.'

Chapter 64

'You said that you were told that someone would visit your shop,' said Hasdai, 'and that they would engage with you in a particular way. They would talk about knucklebones and buy perfume saying it was for their wife but you weren't given a name. That's right isn't it?'

Nasim looked at the floor. 'Yes,' he said, 'that's right.'

'Didn't you have any thoughts about who it could be?' asked Hasdai.

'Do you mean their name?'

'Or what they would look like?'

Nasim shook his head. 'No,' he said. 'Why should I? I was just told that someone would come and what he would say to show me that he was the right person.'

Hasdai clicked his prayer beads along their chain and then put them down on his desk.

'The man who told you this,' he said. 'The man named Shahid Jalal that you told me about, when did he tell you what would happen in your shop?'

'About a month ago,' said Nasim.

'And did he tell you himself?'

'No. He sent me a message.'

'Do you still have it?' said Hasdai.

'No,' said Nasim. He looked up at the Vizier. 'Why are you asking me these questions?'

Hasdai stared at the perfume trader who lowered his eyes.

'The last time we spoke you told me you had never met Shahid Jalal until a few days ago.'

'That's right,' said Nasim. 'I met him for the first time at the bathhouse by the Bab al-Jadid on the evening of the Night Journey of Mohammed.'

Hasdai rubbed his neck and then smoothed back his hair.

'This may surprise you, but the man you met at the market inspector's bathhouse, is dead.'

Nasim stared at the vizier.

'Also, I don't think his name was Shahid Jalal and nor do I think it was him who set up this plot to smuggle ambergris. I think he was paid, on

239

behalf of whoever *is* in control of this operation, to impersonate Jalal. Once that was done he was killed and I suspect he was killed by the same person who killed the Admiral and his bodyguard.'

Nasim shook his head and gave a mirthless laugh. 'You accused me of killing the Admiral a day or so…'

A look from the vizier cut him off.

'If you know all of this,' said Nasim quietly, 'what do you want with me?'

'I still think you can help me,' said Hasdai.

Nasim stared fiercely at the vizier. 'You told me you would make my death quick and painless. This is anything but.'

Hasdai took his prayer beads from the desk. 'I told I would spare you a painful death and I will keep my promise. But first I have more questions.'

Nasim shrugged.

'The jars at the funduq contained bitter orange jam,' said Hasdai.

'I know sir,' said Nasim. 'I've already told you that.'

'Quite,' said Hasdai. 'But what you also told me is that inside those jars were smaller ones containing ambergris. Just like the ones you gave to the Admiral. The two I found in his room.'

Nasim nodded.

'You said that when the ambergris was being transported the top layer of jars contained bitter orange jam and nothing else.'

'Yes,' said Nasim.

'It seems that the consignment at the funduq was the reverse of that. Only the top layer had the ambergris inside, the rest was just bitter orange.'

Nasim lifted his head in surprise. 'Really?'

Hasdai nodded. 'I think the Admiral walked into a trap. I think that the real Shahid Jalal, if that is even his name, planned the whole thing as a decoy. Somehow Jalal found out that the Admiral knew about the ambergris plot and he devised a way of keeping him away from what was actually going on. A very clever way as it turns out and you were part of it.'

'Are you sure?' asked Nasim.

'As sure as I can be,' said Hasdai.

'But then who is Jalal's buyer if not the Admiral?'

'That's not important,' said Hasdai. He thought for a moment. 'What can you tell me about Shahid Jalal? Not the man you met, but the real Jalal, the person behind this plot.'

Nasim put his head in his hands and groaned. 'Please,' he said. 'I don't know what else to tell you. I honestly believed the man I met at the bathhouse was Shahid Jalal. I had no reason to suspect he wasn't.'

Hasdai got up and moved round to the other side of his desk. He placed a hand on Nasim's arm. 'I know you are frightened,' he said. 'I just need to know everything, no matter how hard this is for you. Had you ever heard anything about Jalal? Did you speak to any of the other agents about him?'

Nasim wiped his eyes. 'Not really,' he said. 'Someone once told me he was from Tripoli, but I can't remember who that was.'

Hasdai moved back round to his stool and sat down. 'Don't you find that odd?' he said.

'What?' said Nasim.

'If he was from Tripoli that would make him a Berber. For what it is worth I happen to think you are right about that.'

'Why is that odd?'

'The man you met at the bathhouse, the one we found murdered in shrubbery by the city wall was not a Berber. At least not from the colour of his skin or the way he dressed.'

Nasim raised his head and thought for a moment. 'That never even occurred to me,' he said.

Hasdai looked at him for a moment and then smiled. 'I think that is the point,' he said. 'Whoever the real Shahid Jalal is, he is very clever.'

Chapter 65

'You're going to have to be careful sitting down when you're wearing that,' Miryam laughed.

Hasdai couldn't help laughing too. 'I know,' he said, reaching down below his waist and hitching up the exquisitely jewelled, jade-hilted dagger which had slipped down to his crotch. It was a gift from the Caliph. 'No matter how often I wear it I can never get used to the weight of the thing. Here, tighten this belt for me, will you?'

He turned his back to Miryam and as she bent to adjust the buckle of his scarlet leather belt he could feel the hair on the back of his neck stir in her breath and he smelt the musk of her perfume.

They were in the Vizier's private chambers in the Alcazar waiting to be called to the royal audience hall for the banquet. They would have to go in separately of course but Miryam had sent a message to Hasdai to say that she wanted to speak to him beforehand.

She had left her father in one of the antechambers and, as she'd walked along the corridors of the Alcazar to Hasdai's rooms, the guards couldn't help but wonder at her beauty and the splendour of her dress. She wore a raw silk salwar khameez, the tunic of which was dark orange and gold and worn over tight fitting trousers of the deepest crimson with cuffs of gold embroidery. Her bright auburn hair was covered with a silk stole, also crimson and heavily embroidered in gold. She held the shawl in place with hands intricately hennaed with patterns of stars and the crescent moon. Perhaps the thing, apart from her ferocious intellect, that Hasdai most admired about Miryam was the fact that she seemed almost indifferent to the effect her beauty had on the men around her.

Hasdai put his thumbs in his belt and gave it a final adjustment, settling it on the top of his hips, the dagger now at his waist.

'Thank you,' he said and reached up to adjust his silk turban. 'What was it you wanted to talk to me about? Would you like a drink? We probably have time for a cup of Sharish wine. I have a flask here.'

'I won't have any wine thank you. We'll probably have enough later. I wanted to talk to you about a couple of things. The first one was my pupil Lubna.'

'Lubna? What about her?'

'You know she has been asked by Prince Hakam to attend tonight's banquet.'

'I did know that, yes. But why do you think that's important?'

'I was worried that the Crown Prince might have some plans for her other than keeping her just as a member of his secretariat.'

'To be frank,' said Hasdai, 'there is no way of me knowing precisely what his plans are for her but as far as I am aware all he wants is for her to act as a scribe and keep a record of court events. The woman is very intelligent and you have trained her very well indeed. She is competent, hardworking and above all very discreet. These are attributes which Prince Hakam values highly. No-one has given me any reason to believe that the prince has any other duties lined up for her. She won't take any part in the proceedings tonight. She'll be working.'

'That's a relief,' said Miryam.

'What else did you want to talk about?'

'Two things really.'

'We'd better be quick now!'

'Yes! The first thing is that I wanted to ask you how the investigation into the death of Admiral Suhail is going. I was thinking it over last night and there is something I need to tell you. It didn't seem significant when it happened but the last time the admiral was in the university I overheard him arguing with someone. I think it might have been Bandar but I am not sure.'

'That's interesting,' said Hasdai. 'You're the second person to have told me that... at least that Suhail was arguing. We need to talk about this when we have more time. What was the other thing?'

'Well, although the death of Admiral Suhail is important this may be more important still. It could probably affect the whole fleet.'

'Oh!' said Hasdai. 'In that case you'd better tell me what it is.'

'You know the almanac that we use with the new astrolabe?'

'Yes, I know about it but I don't understand it.'

Miryam gave a smile. 'No, but Bandar does. In fact he spotted what he thought was an error in the tables.'

'How did he do that?'

'For some reason he was particularly interested in finding the coordinates for a number of different places on the coast of Syria and not just the planned arrival point for the fleet at Latakia. Just to keep him quiet I gave him some extra exercises to do and sure enough he discovered that the tables were not quite accurate for that region.'

'What does that mean exactly?' the Vizier asked.

'It means that the readings on the astrolabe cannot be accurately transferred to the sea-chart south of Latakia. This is obviously important if any ships need to make land-fall in that area in an emergency. Their positions could be out by quite some distance.'

'Do you have a solution for this?'

'Yes, together with my father we identified which tables are not accurate and worked out an algorithm which can be used to bring them back into line.'

'Well, that seems quite simple then. Can you write that out for the navigators?'

'I could but it would be much easier for Yunus and me to have one more session with them before they left for Almeria. That way we would be sure they all understand the adjustments.'

Hasdai looked at Miryam for a long moment. 'One more session, you say?'

'Yes.'

'That can be easily arranged. And, it might be much more useful than you can imagine.'

'What do you mean?'

'I can't explain now,' said Hasdai. 'We have to get to the banquet. By the way have I told you that tonight you look utterly, stunningly beautiful?'

'No,' said Miryam quietly, 'you haven't.' She blushed and smiled as her hennaed hand went to her neck to grasp the gold Star of David which hung there. Her present from the Vizier. 'Thank you,' she said clutching the star.

Chapter 66

'Do you believe him?' General Ghalib asked the vizier.

Hasdai nodded. 'I do, yes. He seemed genuinely surprised when I told him that the rest of the jars were full of nothing but bitter orange jam.'

Ghalib grunted.

'If he is right about Jalal being from Tripoli then that would also help to explain how he came by the anthrax,' said Ali. 'It would have been delivered when the Baghdadi Emissary's fleet landed there two years ago on the way to Al Andalus. They say that disease can live for years and years.'

'That's right,' said Hasdai, 'it can.' He fiddled with his belt adjusting his dagger. 'Did you speak with the Lieutenant's mother?'

'Yes sir,' said Ghalib. 'I gave her your condolences and she asked me to thank you. She also gave me this.' Ghalib reached inside his cloak and placed a jar on the table. 'I think this is the missing jar from the three that Nasim gave to the Admiral. Apparently he gave it to her and said that if anything happened to him she was to give it me personally. That is why she came to the Alcazar looking for me. I wish he'd told us what he was doing, instead of it all ending up like this.'

'Don't think about now General,' said Hasdai. 'We can't change it.' Turning to Ali he said 'Did you find anything out about Jalal?'

'I'm not sure,' said Ali. 'I haven't seen him, but I did go back to the Camp and check on the mule trains for tomorrow.'

'And?' said Hasdai.

'Well sir, it struck me that if Jalal was trying to get out of Cordoba he wouldn't do it on his own. Everyone is out looking for him and he'd be foolish to attempt to leave whilst that is the case.'

'Which means he is probably still here,' said Ghalib.

'Correct,' said Ali. 'It also struck me that the mule train would be an ideal cover for him. Each train has a gang of muleteers who ride with it. Jalal knows this and I wondered if he would try and use the supply chain as a way of leaving. Each train gets automatic passage through any gate or check point on account of it being part of the war effort. Once they leave the Camp they never get checked again until they arrive in

Almeria. He could ride with it as far as he needed and nobody would know.'

'We can't search every train though,' said Ghalib.

'I don't see why not General but we wouldn't need to anyway,' said Hasdai. 'Just the one with the bitter orange jam that Ali told us about earlier.'

The three men looked at each other. Hasdai walked over to his desk and reached for a pen and some paper.

'All right,' said Hasdai. 'Ali, whilst the General and I are in the banquet I want you to search the navigators' rooms. Start with Bandar's. If you find anything, anything at all then get a message to me via one of the court messengers.'

'Yes sir,' said Ali.

'And give this note to Colonel Zaffar,' said Hasdai as he wrote. 'You'll find him in the officers' room downstairs. Here,' he said handing over the paper.

Ali took the note and read the message. 'Are you sure this will work, sir?' he said.

'If it doesn't Ali, then in less than a day Admiral Bandar will ride out of Cordoba with the Caliph's praise and the cheers of the people ringing in his ears. Now then General, are we ready to go to the banquet?'

Chapter 67

The young navigator from Qadiz could hardly believe what he was looking at was real.

Surely, he thought, this was a room like no other in the Dar al-Islam; a room of riches beyond counting, beyond wealth or status. This was perhaps the most opulent room on earth. The pillars supporting the ceiling were of the finest pink marble with horse-shoe arches banded with crimson jasper. The multi-faceted, vaulted ceiling was covered in red gold leaf which shimmered like fire in the light of the wall-mounted oil lamps. Between the pillars, panels of white marble were set with intricate mosaics of flowers and foliage picked out in jade, agate and turquoise and in the centre of the room on the low banqueting table there was a gold tray of bright silver liquid metal which quivered and trembled when the table was touched by a servant, sending shafts of light dancing through the room. At the far end of the table was the *sitr*, the undulating curtain of thick *tiraz* silk sumptuously embroidered in flowing script with the Caliph's name and titles all in a frame of gorgeous representations of all of the blossoms of Al Andalus. This was the veil behind which the Caliph would sit and which would be drawn open by the *Sahib al-Sitr*, the Master of the Curtain, when His Majesty wished to speak to those present.

Then a thought struck the young man like a blow from a swinging spar at sea. This room was small, intimate; just the right size for the company assembled here and assigned their places by the *mutawali al-majlis*, the Master of the Audience Hall. In this palace, the Alcazar, there must be other rooms just as opulent as this but *bigger*! Audience halls for perhaps dozens or even hundreds of people and then of course there was Madinat al-Zahra. He'd never been there but if half the rumours were true then the opulence in the new city was even greater than here. The idea of such riches was almost too much to comprehend.

The guests at the banquet, well briefed by the *mutawali al-majlis*, stood on either side of the table in order of precedence back from the *sitr*. Crown Prince Hakam was closest to the curtain on the right hand side of the table. Opposite him was Hasdai ben Shaprut the Vizier then came the

Chamberlain and General Ghalib, Yunus ibn Firnas the Astronomer Royal and Admiral Bandar, Vice Admiral Siraj and Miryam Bint Yunus then the two youngest navigators. The young man noted that apart from the guards standing discretely in alcoves along the walls the only people with weapons were the Crown Prince who wore a gold-hilted *khanjar* dagger the scabbard of which was studded with rubies and the Vizier who had a magnificent dagger with a jade handle. Although he had been told not to by the *mutawali al-majlis* he had a quick look round. On either side of the door there were two small daises. On one, lit by an intricate bronze oil lamp suspended from the ceiling, was a small writing desk at which sat an attractive young woman with the paraphernalia of a scribe while on the other sat a lutenist softly playing classical Andalusi music.

The young man stood to attention with the other guests as a silver bell sounded and the lute fell silent. As the *sitr* was slowly drawn aside by the Master of the Curtain they all put their right hands on their hearts and everyone save the Crown Prince bowed deeply.

Abd al-Rahman III sat on a raised divan which was covered with an Andalusi carpet of blue and gold silk. He wore a simple white robe with a small closely bound white turban from the back of which cascaded his long black hair. His beard, close trimmed on his well-defined jaw, jutted from his chin. Apart from his bearing the only sign of his power was a gold wired leather belt in which was a short dagger with a gold scabbard and an ivory hilt. On a cushion by his right hand lay a matching long, curved damascene sword.

Protocol had it that it fell to the Vizier Hasdai ben Shaprut to greet the Caliph. He did so saying, '*A salaam u aleikum al-Nasir li-Din Allah, Amir al-Mu'minin Wa Rahmatullahi Wa Barakatuh.*'

'Greetings, O Defender of God's Faith, Commander of the faithful. Peace be unto you and also the mercy of Allah and His blessings.'

The Caliph returned the formal greetings in a clear, low voice then mentioned each of those present by name. The younger navigators were terrified to hear their names uttered by this most powerful of kings but he put them at their ease by mentioning where they were from and how long they had served in their posts. He had obviously been very well briefed by the Chamberlain.

He was especially warm in his greeting of General Ghalib and even spoke to him of his wounded knee saying that he hoped the general would soon find relief from his constant pain.

To Yunus ibn Firnas the Caliph was most cordial. He mentioned that he had recently had dealings with Yunus and Miryam in the construction of a new observatory in Madinat al-Zahra. The Caliph was obviously a great admirer of all things scientific and was knowledgeable and demanding in his quest to have the most modern scientific facilities in both Cordoba and Madinat al-Zahra.

Once finished with the welcoming of his guests the Caliph spoke to Bandar and his navigators of their coming task.

'Admiral Bandar, we are fortunate that we have officers of your experience to lead our navy. The Crown Price Hakam acted wisely in appointing you Admiral of the Fleet following the unfortunate demise of Admiral Suhail and we are sure that you will rise to the challenges before you and that you will lead our fleet wisely to the East and play your part well in the coming campaign.

'As to you other navigators, the Caliphate of Cordoba stands at a point in its history at which it depends for its future on you. The success of our alliance in the East will depend on your succeeding in your endeavours. With your skills, with your dedication to duty and with the learning you have gained from our Astronomer Royal and his assistant you will, *Insha'Allah*, safely deliver our armies to the battleground. This is a vital task and we are grateful for the part you will play in it.

'It is our pleasure now to ask you to eat and drink with us so we may personally mark the occasion of your departure.'

As the Caliph stopped speaking he raised his right hand in a sign for the banquet to begin and the lutenist started to play.

*

In years to come the navigator from Qadiz would relate his tale of the banquet to his children and then his grandchildren. He would tell them of the jewelled bronze incense burners in the shape of falcons which were passed round the guests that they might perfume themselves and their clothes before eating. He would describe the fact that the Caliph was served his food on a silver platter on his divan. And what food it was! The *Tabahajah* of lamb flavoured with dark brown *al murri* sauce and served with green mustard, rue and ciltrano, the delicate saffron and coriander chicken stuffed with a mixture of toasted and peppered breadcrumbs and quails eggs, the *Badinjan Muhassa* of eggplant, walnuts and green onions, the *A'Muzawwara* prepared with blanched lentils and crisp green vegetables stewed in cinnamon-spiced wine vinegar all served on ceramic dishes of startling blue and white.

There were strong wines and arak of sugar cane from Sharish with sweet wines from Malaga and exquisite, molasses-black, wines from the valley of the Wadi Shawsh, the salty river which the Christians call the Rio Guadajoz. But the highlight of the banquet came at the time of the desserts. Here were *sukkariyya*, a heavenly confection of sugar and rosewater sprinkled with chopped roast almonds, *hulwas* of all varieties and flavours and above all the final course of delicious *sharbas* of pomegranate, lemon and bitter orange iced with snow which had been carried by teams of runners from the high sierras. This was a truly magnificent banquet.

*

Throughout the meal the Caliph conversed only with the Vizier, Hasdai ben Shaprut, and Crown Prince Hakam. He did not appear to eat much himself and often he would sit back on the cushions on his divan and simply observe his guests as they wondered at the magnificent foodstuffs and drinks that they were being served. They all knew of course not to either look the Caliph directly in the eye or to engage him in conversation and Abd al-Rahman seemed content to be the beneficent provider of this wonderful repast.

As the *sharba* was being eaten the Caliph raised his right hand to shoulder level and once again the sounding of the silver bell silenced the lutenist. The assembled company rose silently and with hand on heart faced Abd al-Rahman. Again with the exception of Crown Prince Hakam they bowed low to their Caliph who took his leave with the simple formula, '*Allah ma'aakum. Fee aman illah*. Goodbye and May God be with you.'

As the Caliph finished speaking the *Sahib al-Sitr* drew the heavy veil then Crown Prince Hakam turned to the company and addressed them.

'*Bismillah ir-Rahman ir-Rahim*. Admiral, navigators, His Majesty the Caliph has asked me to reiterate that his best wishes go with you in your enterprise. He has also asked me to thank The Astronomer Royal and his assistant for their work on the new navigation aids which will help you on your voyage. Now please continue.'

As the prince took his seat the servants came round with more *sharba* and sweet wine. As they did so the man from Qadiz saw a court messenger enter the room, approach Hasdai and give him a folded piece of paper. The Vizier read the paper and immediately took his amber prayer beads from his pocket. He sat back from the table and manipulated the beads for a while before he leant forward and said something to the Crown Prince who immediately stood up nodded in a perfunctory manner to the company and left the room.

At this the Chamberlain spoke quietly with the Vizier and the Master of the Audience Hall then turned and said, 'Gentlemen,' he nodded to Miryam, 'Miryam bint Yunus, we must ask you now to leave the Audience Chamber.'

Chapter 68

Crown Prince Hakam sat perfectly still on the stool with his hands in his lap, finger tips to finger tips, whilst Hasdai spoke. General Ghalib stood next to the Vizier, listening intently.

When Hasdai finished there was complete silence in the ante-room where the three of them had gone from the banqueting chamber. Eventually the Prince Hakam spoke. 'Two days ago you woke me before dawn to tell me that Suhail, the Admiral of our Royal Fleet, had been murdered. This morning you told me that he was involved in a plot to smuggle ambergris out of Al Andalus knowing that the movement and sale of such commodities has been expressly forbidden. Do you recall we crucified someone that you accused of also being involved in this plot? And now, Vizier Hasdai, you tell me that Admiral Suhail was in fact trying to *stop* the plot, which, you now claim, was actually the work of Bandar, the man you recommended I appoint as his successor as Admiral. The man we have all just heard being lauded by my father in front of his officers and our guests.' The crown prince rose slowly to his feet. 'And *now*, you are advising me that Bandar must be arrested just because your spy has found some Berber scrawl in his room?'

Hasdai bowed his head. 'Your highness, forgive me. I know that I may have misled you as to what happened, but I am certain that Bandar is the one behind all of this. I just needed more time to assess the evidence. The plan to kill the Admiral once he had found out about the ambergris plot was a very clever one. It had me convinced. Your Highness, I am positive Bandar is going to use anthrax to wipe out the crew and the complement of soldiers on one of our boats once he unloads the ambergris in Saida. Anthrax which has come as a weapon from Baghdad. It is also worth considering what else the Baghdadis might have waiting for our troops when they arrive in Latakia if they have gone to the effort of harnessing the destructive properties of anthrax.'

'But you are not certain as to whether there is anthrax on board the main fleet, or in the supply chain making its way to Almeria?'

'No your highness,' said Hasdai. 'Not at this time.'

The crown prince breathed deeply for several moments. 'The Caliph has just bestowed the thanks of the Caliphate on Bandar and his men. Tomorrow, after prayers he will address the assembled people of Cordoba and give them the same message. What you propose will make the Caliph look like a fool and for that reason alone I cannot agree to your request.'

Crown Prince Hakam walked over to the door where he paused then turned to face Hasdai ben Shaprut.

'We expect better from you Vizier.'

Chapter 69

Day 6

It was a ghastly, hellish vision illuminated by the sickly-red flicker of pitch-pine flares.

On the verge of the road to Almeria, directly opposite the gate to Camp Maaqul, was the gibbet with the naked, crucified body of the cloth merchant nailed up for all to see. On either side of the stake bearing Antonio's remains, which sagged like some obscene display in a suq butcher's stall, there were two smaller posts each of which bore the bloody, nailed up corpse of a dog. In the grey, pre-dawn light a raucous flock of carrion crows had overcome their fear of the flares to peck at the eyes and tear at the open wounds of both man and dogs.

Shahid Jalal dragged his eyes away from the horrible sight but he couldn't throw off the thoughts of the cloth merchant's last moments. Antonio, probably with his eyes closed in prayer, would have heard the screaming yelps of the dogs as the nails rent their flesh and splintered their bones. He would have heard the laughter of the executioners above the cries of the crowd and the dull clanking thud of hammer on nail knowing that it would soon be his turn to bear the unimaginable pain of crucifixion. Shahid shuddered and pulled his woollen burnus closer about his chest. He put his hand gently on the flank of the mule plodding along beside him, glad to feel the warmth of life through the animal's rippling hide.

If everything went well it wouldn't be long now before the mule train was well on its way to Almeria. They were heading towards Al-Kulai'a east of Cordoba where they would turn south towards the coast.

Shahid Jalal had laid his plans well. He had added his own private cargo with the extra mules to this train as it was being assembled in the yard of Camp Maaqul. As far as he could see nobody had taken any notice of him. He was just another mule handler getting on with the job. At one point the lead muleteer had asked him his name and checked the animals he was roping into the line of mules but he seemed satisfied that Shahid's were just part of the train and were carrying bitter orange jam like all the rest.

'God knows why they need so much of this stuff,' the man had said.

'Well,' said Shahid, 'I suppose it's not just for the navy. They'll need it for the army on the other side. Who knows how long this war is going to last.'

'Yes, but why bitter orange jam?'

'They say it helps against disease on long campaigns and especially at sea when there are no fresh vegetables.'

'I suppose it's all right in porridge for breakfast,' said the lead muleteer, 'but I couldn't face eating it every day. Anyway! Let's get going. We need to get on our way before daybreak or we'll have to stop for prayers and that'll put us further behind.'

*

As the mule train plodded its way along the road to Al-Kulai'a Shahid Jalal couldn't help feeling relieved that at last he was quitting Cordoba. So many things had happened in the past week. He thought to himself that his was no way to live. Everything he touched was to do with death and destruction. How had he got into this? How often had he rued that day so many years ago when he had been approached in the baths of his home city of Tripoli by the spy from Baghdad. How stupid he had been to speak out against the Caliphate in Al Andalus. It was just young man's bluster really but it had got him involved in years of crime and terror. The Baghdadi had been so persuasive. He had radicalised Shahid over a period of months. He'd taken a simple young man from the Tripoli suq and made him into a killer. And for what Shahid wondered now? For what? For a few dinars and a promise of an easy life once the Caliphate of Abd al-Rahman III had been overthrown.

Hah! He thought. What hope is there of the Caliphate of Cordoba, of Al Andalus ever being overthrown by the Berbers? He'd seen it up close now. Their army was second to none in the Dar al Islam and now their navy was huge. They could defeat the Berbers at sea before they even set foot on Al Andalus. And now they were allied with the Khazars and if their naval plans were to come to fruition they would sweep through the Baghdadi Caliphate and crush it against the Persians. It was a standing joke in the teahouses in Cordoba that the Andalusi forces would crush the Baghdadis like a bitter orange. Shahid Jalal snorted a laugh at this thought. He here was risking crucifixion to smuggle anthrax weapons on to the Andalusi fleet in exactly that... bitter orange jam. If only they knew.

It was clear day now and from his position near the back of the train Shahid Jalal could see the long line of mules snaking into the distance with the lead muleteer holding the halter rope of the first animal. He could see the three other mule drivers walking along with their sticks keeping pace with their animals. And it was then that he heard hoof beats of the riders coming from Cordoba.

The four men galloped straight past him making the mules rear and kick in their traces then pulled up at the head of the train. Shahid Jalal saw one of the group bend down to speak to the lead muleteer and his heart froze as he saw the man turn and point back down the line. As the horsemen wheeled round, one of them hoisted the lead muleteer up behind him. Moments later he was pinned against a mule by four horses.

'That's him, Colonel Zaffar,' said the muleteer. He slipped down from the horse. 'And these four animals here are the ones he put in the train.'

'Cut the traces and get them out of the line,' said Zaffar as he dismounted. He grasped Shahid Jalal's arm and turned to one of the soldiers. 'Bind this man's feet and hands. He's coming back to Cordoba with us. Now,' he said, 'what you have got in here?'

Zaffar took his dagger and cut through the burlap cloth that was protecting the load on the pack-saddle. He reached in and pulled out an earthenware jar which was sealed with beeswax. He held the jar under Shahid Jalal's nose and went to plunge the dagger into the wax. 'Let's see what you have in the jar. Let's open it up shall we?'

Shahid's eyes started in his head as he held his bound wrists up to protect his face. He stumbled and fell against the mule which shuddered and stamped as Shahid slid to the ground.

'No,' he shouted. 'Don't open it! Don't open it up! It's...'

Zaffar held the dagger poised above the wax. 'It's what?' he said. Then he knelt and put the jar up close to Shahid's face as he started to slowly bore through the wax.

'No! Don't! It's full of poison! It's... It's anthrax! It's full of anthrax.'

'Is it now?' said Zaffar and he continued to gouge out the wax as Shahid tried to curl up into a ball. As the wax seal came away from top the distinctive odour of bitter oranges wafted from the jar. 'I think you'll find,' said Zaffar as he tipped the glutinous contents of the jar onto the ground in front of Shahid's face, 'that what we have here, thanks to this muleteer who has been helping us since yesterday, is four mule loads of bitter orange jam which the vizier himself asked us to substitute for your cargo of anthrax. Although, I must say that with what is waiting for you back Cordoba it might have been better for you if it had been anthrax.'

Shahid Jalal whimpered like a dog as Zaffar stood up and said to his men, 'Let's get him back to Cordoba.'

Chapter 70

'That was relatively easy, wasn't it?' said Miryam as she closed the almanac and handed it back to Admiral Bandar together with two sheets of paper with columns of figures in red and black ink. 'You have a talent for mathematics.'

'Thank you,' said Bandar, 'but if it hadn't been for you and Sheikh Yunus here, working out the algorithm to adjust the tables we could have been a long way out in our navigation on the coast of Syria.'

'Well,' said Yunus, 'it was simple enough to do once you had pointed out the need for it. But we won't have time now before you go to bring the other almanacs up to date. Are you absolutely sure that you can get a copyist you can trust in Almeria to do this?'

'Yes. There are a couple of people in naval headquarters that I can think of. They already work on secret communications so they can be trusted with this.'

'Good,' said Yunus. 'Now, I must leave you. I have to go and see the instrument maker in the metalwork suq. We need to make adjustments to one of the sun-dials for the observatory in Madinat al-Zahra. Will you walk back to the Alcazar with Miryam?'

Bandar smiled at the Astronomer Royal then turned to his daughter. 'I would be very happy indeed to do that. In fact I have something in my room for you.'

'But you and your colleagues have already given me a gift,' said Miryam.

'Ah yes, but this is personal, from me.'

'How intriguing,' said Miryam, 'a surprise!' She looked at her father who simply shrugged his shoulders then left the room in the university where they had been working.

*

Miryam found it difficult to talk to the Admiral but as they walked past the Great Mosque towards the Alcazar, Bandar was full of questions. He wanted to know how long she had been working as an astronomer, what her relationship was with Lubna the scribe, whether she had ever spoken to the Caliph. He was careful though not to mention Hasdai ben Shaprut.

Because of her relationship with the Vizier Miryam knew how to handle questions like these and her answers were oblique in the extreme. She was more amused by the questions than she was annoyed.

'Don't you want to know what it is that I have got for you?' Bandar asked as they walked between the Alcazar and the Great Mosque.

Miryam pulled her shawl close to her chest and put on a winning smile. 'No,' she said quietly. 'Surprises are best not given away before they happen. I am sure it's something very special.'

'I hope you think so,' said Bandar who was getting more and more sure of himself the closer he got to his quarters in the Alcazar.

He was a man who liked female company and it did his self-esteem no end of good to be seen walking with this beautiful woman. He thought he was doing well with Miryam. Who knows what might happen once they got back to his quarters. He shivered in anticipation.

'Look,' he said, pointing to the wall of the Mosque. Among the royal proclamations and exhortations which covered the wall was a large newly-whitewashed square on which was written in bold red and blue letters the announcement that on that evening there was to be a running of bulls in the Maidan Ziryab in the north of the city.

'Do you like the corrida?' Bandar asked Miryam.

'I neither like it nor dislike it,' said Miryam, 'but my father likes it very much.'

'Then perhaps the three of us could go together,' said Bandar.

Although Miryam could hardly believe how forward this man was being she merely nodded and said, 'Yes, perhaps we could.' At this Bandar's chest swelled like a strutting pigeon as they turned into the main gate of the Alcazar.

Most of the guards, both at the gate and in the corridors knew Miryam by sight. She was often to be seen in the palace either with her father or the Vizier. They nodded to her as she walked along the passageway of the guest wing in which Bandar was being accommodated. It wasn't unusual to see guards here but for a moment Bandar thought it strange that there were two directly across from the door to his rooms however his mind was put at ease when on seeing him approach with Miryam the guards sauntered off along the corridor.

With his hand on the door handle Admiral Bandar turned and gave Miryam the kind of smile which made her shudder inwardly then he opened the door and walked into his room.

His immediate reaction on seeing Shahid Jalal sitting hunched forward on a low stool in the centre of the room was to slam the door in Miryam's face. 'What in God's name are *you* doing here?' he rasped. 'I told you never to come here asking for me. You should be on your way to Almeria with the anthrax. We need to get the anthrax to Almeria! How did you get in here?'

By way of reply Shahid Jalal shrugged his burnus off his shoulders then lifted his arms to hold his bound wrists up to Bandar's face.

'Ah *Ya Allah*,' Bandar cried in despair, 'you've been caught with the anthrax!'

It was then that the door to his sleeping chamber opened and General Ghalib came in with Colonel Zaffar.

'*A salaam u aleikum* Admiral Bandar,' said Ghalib in a voice as cold as steel. 'I think you had better come with us. The vizier would like to speak to you.'

Bandar only had time to crumple to his knees with his face in his hands before the two guards he had seen at the door came in, hoisted him back to his feet and led him away.

Ghalib and Colonel Zaffar watched him go.

'What happens now?' said Zaffar.

General Ghalib shook his head. 'I'm not sure. The vizier has been talking with the Crown Prince all day. He is trying to convince him to change his mind. There must be a way of settling this without making the Caliph look like a fool. I hope he can find it before it is too late. If not Bandar will be on his way to Almeria.'

'And him?' said Zaffar pointing to Shahid Jalal.

'Oh him!' said Ghalib. 'He hasn't got long to go. Get him to a cell until we are told what to do with him.'

Chapter 71

For more than a century and a half the Great Mosque of Cordoba had been the centre of religious, academic and social life in the Andalusi capital. It was founded by the present Umayyad Caliph's forebear, Abd al-Rahman the first, who fled to Al Andalus from Syria after his family was massacred by the Abbasids, the head of which clan was now the Caliph of Baghdad. Today, in the Great Mosque after the Asr prayer, Abd al-Rahman III, Caliph of Cordoba, *Amir al-Mu'umin*, Commander of the Faithful, would address his people.

The Caliph spoke from a divan which had been set up by the *qibla*. On a lower platform to his right was the Crown Prince Hakam and to his left his vizier Hasdai ben Shaprut. Admiral of the Fleet Bandar bin Sadiq, Vice Admiral Siraj bin Bahram and the two younger officers sat between the prince and the vizier heavily protected by palace guards under the command of General Ghalib and Colonel Zaffar. The vast prayer hall of the mosque with its forest of columns and soaring red and white arches was heavy with incense and packed to capacity.

'*Bismillah ir-Rahman ir-Rahim,*' the Caliph began. 'People of Al Andalus, today we are embarking on a new path. Our fleet is about to set sail to Syria to establish once and for all that we are the true Caliphate and to avenge the slaughter of the Umayyads in the year 750.

'Our enemy, he who calls himself the Caliph of Baghdad, will soon join combat with the forces of our allies the Khazars. We have sworn to assist the Khazars in this mother of all battles and you will be aware of the strictures which we have had to impose on our people in preparation for this mighty campaign. We thought it fitting that we should present to you the officers who will command our fleet and ensure its safe passage to the coast of Syria.'

As the Caliph paused in his speech there was a low murmur of '*Allahu Akbar*. God is great' which gradually grew and grew in intensity as, one by one, he introduced the admirals and their officers and urged them to do their duty in the knowledge that the people of Cordoba were supporting their efforts in every possible way.

As Abd al-Rahman finished his speech and left the mosque surrounded by his guards the very pillars seemed to tremble under the onslaught of the unified voices of ten thousand people shouting again and again '*Labbaik*! We are ready! *Allahu Akbar*! *Allahu Akbar*! God is great!'

The men who were in the mosque would remember this speech for the rest of their lives. Especially those closest to the navigators who could see that the Admiral of the Fleet Bandar bin Sadiq was so overwhelmed by the occasion that all he could do was stare blankly at the floor in front of his feet.

*

Following the Caliph's address to the people their spirits were to be kept high by the spectacle of the running of bulls put on as a tribute to the admirals. This would take place in the Maidan al-Ziryab where a temporary arena had been constructed.

The rough plank terraces of the plaza were filling up now with families shouting greetings, drinking from wine skins and eating nuts while taking care not to let the smaller children fall down the gaps between the rows. Arena attendants were smoothing the sand in the plaza by dragging heavy wooden rakes over the surface.

One man with a hammer was walking round the edge reaching up to check that the barrier was solid and that the gates were secure. He banged in the occasional nail and paid particular attention to the stout strip of wood that ran along all four sides of the plaza at just below waist height. This was the emergency way out. It would enable the bull fighters to vault the barrier to escape from danger.

From below the stands at the northern end of the plaza and directly opposite the silk-draped royal box came the bellows and crashes of four pent-up bulls splintering the walls of their pinewood cells causing the whole structure to shudder. The smell of resin mingled with the acrid scent of the animals rose to heighten the excitement of the crowd who shrieked at every crash.

As Yunus and Miryam took their places in the south stand just to the right of the royal box they too could hear the roar of the bulls. Miryam wanted to be near enough to Hasdai, who would be in the royal box, to catch his eye. They had greeted their neighbours and settled into their places when Miryam turned to speak to her father.

'Not now,' said Yunus raising his hand. 'See, the musicians, it's starting.'

Three trumpeters took up positions at the front of the royal box and cut the afternoon air with a fanfare. The clear tones of the war trumpets quietened the crowd to a murmur but still the bulls continued to bellow and clash, as the Caliph, the Crown Prince and the Vizier entered the royal box and the two admirals and the navigators together with their military escort including General Ghalib and Colonel Zaffar, took their places one terrace below.

Yunus leant close in to Miryam. 'Admiral Bandar looks like he's enjoying himself,' he said.

'Yes, he looks ...'

She was cut off by the roars of the crowd as the gate at the opposite end of the plaza swung open and the *alguacil* rode in. This was the chamberlain's official in charge of the events in the plaza. He galloped his huge black horse to the centre of the arena, stopped dead in a cloud of sand and raised his right hand in salute to the Caliph then bade the crowd welcome in the name of their Caliph, Abd al-Rahman III. Then to cheers from the spectators he high-stepped his horse sideways around the whole arena pulling the shortened reins with his left hand before spurring the horse and charging back through the gate.

At that moment a flaming Chinese fire arrow rocketed into the sky with a thunderclap trailing a towering column of dense, white smoke. High above the applauding crowd the firework exploded in a great flash showering the plaza with a rain of golden sparkles. This signalled the entrance of the first mounted bullfighter, Elias ibn Mardanish, a Mozarab Christian horse breeder who supplied the Caliph's guard with the finest Andalusi stallions. He was mounted on a magnificent grey horse with red leather trappings. Behind him walked his cape-bearers dressed in short, quilted red silk tunics with leggings bound with thongs and soft leather shoes. Each was wrapped in a magenta cape of heavy cotton which they would use to position the bull for the mounted bullfighter. Elias had in his right hand an oak-wood lance with a long flat blade of steel which he would eventually use to kill the bull.

A trumpet brayed and an Andalusi fighting bull exploded into the sunlight to the gasps of the crowd. It must have weighed about 20 *aqfizah* which was more than Elias and his horse put together. The bull's curved needle sharp horns glinted in the sunlight.

The bull galloped to the centre of the plaza where it stopped, pawed the ground, shook its magnificent horns and gave a mighty roar of defiance, the hump of its tossing muscle rippling like black silk in the sun.

Elias handed his lance to an attendant at the barrier then walked his horse slowly with its left flank facing the bull, his cape-bearers in an arc behind. He held the reins short in his left hand and a hooked rosette of red paper aloft in his right. His men were holding their capes spread open in front of them feeling the sand through their soft leather shoes.

As Elias approached the pawing bull he waved his right arm up and down tantalizing the bull with the movement of the rosette. And then it charged; its head low; the horns directly aimed at the belly of the horse. Elias took the horse two steps back and caused it to rear high and as the bull passed below the belly of the horse he leant to his right and planted the rosette firmly between the horns of the charging beast. The crowd rose as one. '*Ya Allah*!' they cried. '*Olé!*' as the bull tossed its horns into the empty space where the horse and rider had been.

Now the cape-bearers stepped in front of the horseman and waved their capes to attract the attention of the bull which was plunging its head from side to side to rid itself of the rosette. '*Hey ta'ur… ta'ur,*' the men cried as the bull turned to face them. Once more the animal pawed the ground before attacking one of the capes which was deftly turned to leave the bull hooking at the air with its terrifying horns and again it was brought round sharply but this time to see Elias approach with a short lance bearing a flag. The bull charged the flag to be left once again attacking the air when the horse jinked away. Now the chase was on and the crowd was on its feet. The flag was held in front of the bull's nose and Elias spurred his horse the length of the plaza with the bull hooking and stabbing right and left at the flag which was always tantalizingly out of its reach. Elias arched backwards to hold the flag as close to his horse as possible. As the rider wheeled away at the south end of the plaza the bull stopped to think. Its tongue lolled out of its mouth and it was panting heavily but still it would lift its head to bellow its defiance. It was learning fast, too fast, to attack the capes or the flag again. Now it would go for the men. Now was the time for the kill.

As Elias rode to collect the steel-bladed lance the cape-bearers brought the bull to charge again and again each time bringing its head lower and lower until on one pass it ploughed into the sand with its horns and somersaulted onto its back only to scramble up again with the agility of a wrestler and try and hook the man with the cape. This manoeuver did not please the crowd and they whistled and booed the cape-bearer who had tipped up the bull. Nevertheless he had done his job well. The bull would now hold its head low enough for Elias to be able to kill it with the lance.

With more cries of '*ta'ur, ta'ur*,' in a series of passes with the cape the bull was brought to the north end of the plaza and lured into a corner. There two of the bullfighters used their capes to hold its attention and its head low while Elias slowly approached on his still prancing grey with the third cape-bearer walking behind the rider ready to attract the bull if the horse was gored. Two horse lengths from the bull Elias gave the command for his men to back away. As they did so the bull concentrated its gaze on the approaching horse, lowered its head, pawed the ground, charged and crumpled, dead, as the long-bladed lance was rammed in the space between its shoulder blades to sever its aorta.

The crowd was delirious and they cheered and waved their head-cloths in the air in a petition to the Caliph to award the Christian his trophies for the fight. After some deliberation the Caliph placed a white kerchief over the front of the royal box and nodded to the *alguacil* who strode over to the stricken bull, took his dagger from his belt, severed both of the animal's ears and passed them to Elias ibn Mardanish who held them aloft to the cheering crowd as the grey danced and wheeled in the centre of the plaza while the bull was dragged away by a team of mules. Now the Christian horse breeder rode sedately round the entire arena accepting the hurrahs of the crowd before finally throwing the ears to the crowd in the south stand.

While all this excitement was going on Miryam who had seen many such spectacles in her life hadn't been able to take her eyes off the Admiral of the Fleet. She grasped her father's arm and leaned close to him.

'Take a look at Bandar,' she said. 'He's about to go to war but he looks like he hasn't got a care in the world. But General Ghalib and his colonel...'

'Zaffar, you mean?' said Yunus.

'Yes that's right,' said Miryam, 'Zaffar. They look like a couple of whipped dogs. Do you know what's going on?'

'I really have no idea,' said Yunus. 'Hasdai has been acting strangely too. It must be something to do with the murders that have been happening.' He came very close to his daughter's ear as he whispered, 'It's always the same when the Caliph gets together with Hakam in the Alcazar. You can sense the tension between them.'

'Well,' said Miryam, 'it'll all be over soon. Bandar and the navigators are leaving the city right after the bullfight.'

'Yes,' said Yunus. 'In the meantime let's enjoy the next three bulls. The other bullfighter today is a captain in the royal cavalry. He should be pretty good. He's probably riding one of Elias ibn Mardanish's horses!'

*

General Ghalib bent to speak to Colonel Zaffar so he wouldn't be overheard. 'What do you make of all this?'

'What? The bullfight?'

'Ya Allah!' Ghalib whispered. 'No you idiot! I mean what's happening with Bandar.'

'Sorry sir, of course,' said Zaffar. 'I don't know really. It looks like they are planning to let him get away with it. Why else would he be here? They must need him to lead the fleet to Latakia.'

Chapter 72

After the running of the bulls Miryam and Yunus walked together in the gathering dusk towards their home by the Bab al-Amir, the north-western gate to the city. As they did so Yunus pointed to the sky.

'Look,' he said, 'the moon is in the first quarter. You know what the ancients used to say about that don't you?'

'I do,' said Miryam. 'They said it's a time of confrontation. A time when problems should be faced up to and plans put on firm foundations. Do you believe that stuff though?'

'Well,' said Yunus, 'we have certainly had enough confrontation recently.'

'That's true,' said Miryam, 'but when you consider what Hasdai has had to put up with we've had an easy time of it.'

'Indeed we have. Who knows what he has to deal with now?'

As they reached the gate to their house the muezzin called the Maghrib Prayer.

'*Insha'Allah* we shall see him later tonight,' said Miryam and her fingers went to the Star of David at her throat.

'*Insha'Allah*,' said her father with a gentle smile and he put his hand on her shoulder.

*

Hasdai was in a small secure room in the Alcazar together with Crown Prince Hakam, General Ghalib, Colonel Zaffar and Bandar bin Sadiq.

The Caliph Abd al-Rahman III had already taken leave of his son and was on his way back to Madinat al-Zahra with his escort. Vice Admiral Siraj and the two younger officers had been sent to Camp Maaqul to prepare for their departure to Almeria.

Prince Hakam dismissed the guards and as the door closed behind them Colonel Zaffar caught Ghalib's eye. Almost imperceptibly the General shook his head while Hasdai, unable to take comfort in his beads, stood with his back to the window, his hands firmly clenched by his sides.

One of the lamps started to gutter and smoke, filling the room with an acrid stench.

The prince turned to Bandar bin Sadiq who stood in the centre of the room. Hakam leant forward from the waist and put his face a hand span from Bandar's. 'Listen to me you treacherous son of a whore. What I am about to do gives me no pleasure,' he said in a voice as menacing as it was quiet.

Bandar stared blankly at the prince.

'You will be escorted through the Bab al-Jadid as far as the gates of Camp Maaqul where you will see what is left of your accomplice who was crucified between dogs. At the camp you will join up with the rest of your party and ride under escort towards Al-Kulai'a on the road to Almeria where *they* will spend the night.'

General Ghalib bit his lip and looked first at the Vizier and then at the floor.

Colonel Zaffar stared intently at Bandar and breathed deeply to calm himself.

The Crown Prince Hakam turned to Hasdai. 'Is everything ready?' he asked.

Hasdai nodded. 'Yes Your Highness.' The vizier shot a look at General Ghalib and gave a slight nod before turning to address Bandar. 'Once out of the sight of the crowds you will be shackled and brought back here to the Alcazar by Colonel Zaffar. Vice-Admiral Siraj and the others will continue to Almeria and wait for further instructions.'

Ghalib stared, astonished, at Colonel Zaffar who snapped to attention at this declaration from Hasdai.

The Crown Prince faced Bandar again. 'The people will be told you died an honourable death in battle,' he said. 'A luxury not accorded to your predecessor. Only those in this room will know the truth.'

Bandar started to tremble and looked with empty eyes at the Crown Prince who then whispered in his ear, 'You will beg for death.'

The prince turned to General Ghalib and Colonel Zaffar and said, 'Take him away.'

*

'It is a pity you didn't uncover the truth sooner,' said Hakam when he was alone with the vizier.

Hasdai bowed. 'Forgive me Your Highness.'

The crown prince waved his hand. 'No matter,' he said. 'This way the caliph will not look a fool. Now, tell me, what is your assessment of the situation with the Berbers?'

'Your Highness, I believe we need to investigate the extent of the threat that they pose to Al Andalus. If the man Shahid Jalal is acting alone then we can proceed with the operation to land the main fleet at Latakia. If he is being helped, or his contacts back in Tripoli are well organised then the threat to the Caliphate may be great.'

'You think this is more than smuggling?' asked the crown prince.

'It could well be sir,' said Hasdai. 'I suspect that Baghdad has had an outpost on the Barbary Coast for years. Until the invention of the astrolabe our fleet has always had to follow the coastline of Ifriquiya on voyages to the east. A fleet as large as ours would have been easily seen from land which means the Berbers would have knowledge of our movements. The astrolabe is so advanced that the Berbers', and so Baghdad's, ability to track our course is eliminated. Now, I think it is true that Baghdad knows we are about to depart from Almeria, the war effort is too great, and involves too many people for them *not* to know. But they can't know where we intend to make landfall, or which course we shall steer to get there.'

Crown Prince Hakam nodded. 'Do you think this Bandar was working for them?'

Hasdai shook his head. 'I honestly don't know Your Highness. If Shahid Jalal was radicalised by Baghdadi agents in Tripoli then he may have been working for them here in Al Andalus for years. What we don't yet know is whether Bandar was simply looking to become rich through the sale of ambergris to merchants in Damascus, or whether he was working directly for Baghdad with Shahid Jalal.'

'How rich would he have become?' said Crown Prince Hakam.

'Rich enough to disappear forever and never be found,' said Hasdai.

The prince thought for a moment. 'What do you suggest we do?'

Hasdai paused for a moment. 'Your Highness I think we should have Ghalib's men find out what they can from both Bandar and Shahid Jalal. If there is a Berber network here in Al Andalus then it poses a great threat to the Caliphate. We need to find out what we can.'

'Very well,' said the crown prince. He smoothed his silk brocade robes and walked towards the door. He paused briefly in the doorway then turned to Hasdai. 'Once Ghalib's men have finished I want you to grant whatever is left of Bandar what it is he begs for. Let him disappear and never be found.'

The Historical Context

In the year 950 most of the Iberian Peninsula was an Islamic Caliphate known as Al Andalus ruled over by the Umayyad Caliph Abd al-Rahman III from his palatine city Madinat al-Zahra.

While the rest of Europe languished in what has become known as 'The Dark Ages', Madinat al-Zahra was a magnificent, purpose-built city of palaces, mosques and fountain-filled pleasure gardens. The former ancient capital of the Caliphate, Cordoba, continued to play a vital role in the administration of Abd al-Rahman's realm.

Cordoba was a place of both light and enlightenment. The streets in the centre of the city around the Great Mosque and the Alcazar, the administrative hub of Al Andalus, were lit throughout the night as was the bridge over the Guadalquivir River. Aqueducts provided clean water from the mountains for public fountains and bathhouses and there was running water in many of the houses in the city. Cordoba was a sophisticated, cosmopolitan centre; a city with well-established universities, libraries, schools and hospitals. It was an important river port and commercial centre with well-regulated markets and exchanges under the control of a government appointed Market Inspector.

The population of the city was a mix of Muslims, Jews and Christians (the Mozarabs) who lived together more or less in harmony. It was possible for non-Muslims to achieve high rank in the Caliphate and our chief protagonist Hasdai ben Shaprut, a Jew, while never actually being entitled 'Vizier' to the Caliph Abd al-Rahman III, was in his time the highest ranking civil servant in the Caliph's court. He worked closely with the Crown Prince Hakam who was to take over the throne in 961. Hasdai was not only the highest ranking civil servant in Al Andalus; he was a polymath, a physician, a translator and a specialist in both Jewish and Islamic law. He was a skilled diplomat responsible for dealing with delegations from Otto I, the Holy Roman Emperor, and for setting up diplomatic relations with the Khazars, a Jewish nation with a not inconsiderable empire bordering the Black Sea to the north of Constantinople.

In Al Andalus women enjoyed a level of freedom, strength of purpose and independence unknown in the rest of Europe at the time. They worked as administrators in the civil service of the Caliphate. They found vocations as medical staff in the hospitals. They worked in the libraries and archives of the universities where some of them were active in scholarship. Women were scribes and copyists and played an important part in the culture of the Caliphate. Perhaps the most prominent of these women was the poet Walladah bint Mustakfi who died in 1091. She was renowned for her salon in Cordoba which welcomed scholars, musicians and poets and had a considerable influence on the cultural life of the capital.

The character Miryam bint Yunus, the daughter of Yunus ibn Firnas who was the Astronomer Royal, is a representative of the strong, scholarly and determined working women of Al Andalus while her father Yunus is a composite character based largely on a real astronomer and engineer, Abbas ibn Firnas, who died in Cordoba in 887. Abbas invented a water clock and developed astronomical instruments but is perhaps most famous for his attempts at flight from the minaret of the Great Mosque in Cordoba wearing a pair of artificial wings.

Astronomy and man's relationship with the heavens for the purposes of navigation and casting astrological charts were important sciences in Al Andalus and closely allied with mathematics. Significant advances were made in the construction of star almanacs and navigational instruments during the reign of the Caliph, Abd al-Rahman III. These advances in navigational science form an important aspect of the plot in this book.

In 950 Al Andalus was not only a world centre for the arts and sciences it was also a world power and as such it required considerable military resources. The Caliph Abd al-Rahman III was an extremely able military strategist and was responsible for building up the army and navy to the extent that they became the most powerful fighting forces in the Mediterranean and Medieval Europe. The Caliph's officers were skilled in warfare both on land and at sea. His Admirals were experts in sea navigation and both the army and the navy had sophisticated signalling capacity based on the use of homing pigeons. Officers in the army held important positions in court and it is entirely likely that Hasdai ben Shaprut as the senior court official in charge of external affairs would be in close contact with these military men. He would have had a particularly close association with the general commanding the royal guard, Ghalib al-Nasiri in this novel.

The real Ghalib al-Nasiri was the military commander of Medinaceli (Madinat Salim) a garrison town some one hundred and sixty kilometres north east of Madrid in the so called Middle Frontier region of Al Andalus. He served Abd al-Rahman III as a garrison commander but was most renowned for his service to the Crown Prince Hakam after he became Caliph in 961. In 963 the real General Ghalib secured the Northern Frontier of the Caliphate by capturing and holding the fortress at Calahorra.

Apart from Al Andalus there were three other major powers in or near the Mediterranean in the period in which the novel is set. One of these, Constantinople, does not concern us in this novel. The other two were the Abbasid Caliphate of Baghdad and the Emirate of Fars in Persia.

The Umayyad Caliphs of Al Andalus were descended from Abd al-Rahman I, the only member of the Umayyad family to escape a massacre by the Abbasids in Damascus in 750. Shortly after this massacre the Abbasids set up their new Caliphate capital in Baghdad while Abd al-Rahman I journeyed to Al Andalus where he established a powerful Emirate with its capital in Cordoba. This Emirate was later to become the bitter rival of the Caliphate of Baghdad when in 929 Abd al-Rahman III proclaimed a new Caliphate with himself as Caliph in opposition to the Abbasid Al Muti Lillah who held that position in what is now Iraq.

At the time of our novel the northern borders of the Caliphate of Baghdad were under pressure from the Khazars while the Persian Emir of Fars, Adud ad Dawlah whose capital was Shiraz, was a force to be reckoned with on the southern frontier. Ad Dawlah eventually captured Baghdad and dominated Al Muti Lillah.

Many of the historic buildings in Cordoba in this novel still exist. The city walls with the Seville Gate, the Alcazar, the great bridge over the Guadalquivir River, the aqueducts and bathhouses can all be visited today and of course the Great Mosque, the Mezquita, now a Christian cathedral, still stands in the centre of Cordoba as a testament to the Caliphate during which it was built. Even the zoo in present day Cordoba is in the same place by the river as Abd al-Rahman III had his menagerie and pleasure garden behind his Alcazar.

By 950 the royal court had moved to the palatine city of Madinat al-

Zahra which is some five kilometres west of Cordoba. This was at that time the largest and most sumptuous palace in the Islamic world; a magnificent marble city modelled on the Umayyad palace in Damascus from which Abd al-Rahman III's ancestors had to flee in 750. From its position at the foot of the Jabal al-Arus, the Bride's Mountain, Madinat al-Zahra had a commanding view of the administrative capital, Cordoba, and the main artery of the Caliphate the Guadalquivir River. It was in Madinat al-Zahra that our Caliph, Abd al-Rahman III, was to die in 961 and pass his kingdom to his son the Crown Prince Hakam.

Shortly before he died, Abd al-Rahman III is said to have written the following words in Madinat al-Zahra:

"I have now reigned above fifty years in victory or peace; beloved by my subjects, dreaded by my enemies, and respected by my allies. Riches and honours, power and pleasure, have waited on my call, nor does any earthly blessing appear to have been wanting to my felicity. In this situation, I have diligently numbered the days of pure and genuine happiness which have fallen to my lot: they amount to Fourteen: - O man! Place not thy confidence in this present world!" (Gibbon, E. 'The History of the Decline and Fall of the Roman Empire' Volume 9, p.354)

The Caliph was right not to place his confidence in this present world for in the year 1010 Madinat al-Zahra was sacked, plundered and left in ruins by a Berber rebellion. The eventual consequence of this rebellion was the total collapse of the Caliphate of Cordoba in 1031 when this once great power was split up into a plethora of small, independent and often mutually antagonistic *taifa* principalities.

In 1031, the sun set on what poets called The Ninth gate to Paradise in the West, Al Andalus.

Map

Bab al-Yahud

Aqueduct

Munyat abd-Allah

House of Yunus ibn Firuas

Maidan al-Zaryab

Bab al-Amir

Bab al-Jabbar

Yazid Al-Haddad's Workshop

Metalworkers' Suq

Bilal's Barber Shop

Perfume Suq

Funduq

Clothsellers' Row

Bab al-Jadid

Al-Murri's Bathhouse

Jayen and Almeria

Bakery

Camp Maaqul

Al Busharah Tea House

Spicesellers' Row

Old Yemeni's Bathhouse

Bab al-Jawz

Wadi al-Khabir River

Nuestra Señora de la Paz

University Hall

Great Mosque

Cockpit

Alcazar

Bab al-Ishbillya

Madinat al-Zahra

Botanical Garden

Bab al-Qantara

Scrub

River Gate

Bridge

Mill Island

Dam

N

Wharf

Cordoba
950 C.E.
338 A.H.

Printed in Great Britain
by Amazon